IMPERFECTLY INNOCENT

CW01496251

TONY AUFFRET

CRANTHORPE
—MILLNER—
PUBLISHERS

First published by Cranthorpe Millner Publishers (2025)

ISBN 978-1-80378-321-5 (Paperback)

www.cranthorpemillner.com

Cranthorpe Millner Publishers

Printed and bound by CPI Group (UK) Ltd
Croydon, CR0 4YY

MIX
Paper | Supporting
responsible forestry
FSC
www.fsc.org   FSC® C013604

...and here's to the few who forgive what you do.

Leonard Cohen
Night Comes On

PROLOGUE
Six months earlier

'I put it to you, members of the jury, that my client has been subject to unlawful harassment ever since he stumbled across a perfidious MI5 operation in Cambridge in 1991. An operation which, I should remind you, involved communicating directly with a Soviet germ warfare site and co-operating with an unfriendly power in the stabilisation of a germ warfare agent. All concealed by creating an elaborate deception involving the apparent arrests of complicit MI5 officers and the planting of false evidence to divert attention away from the group's true purpose.

'Such was the concern that Mr Bickley-Morris had for his life and liberty that, when accosted by a rogue MI5 agent as he was leaving a Cambridge hotel, he felt it necessary to flee. He regrets the injuries that the officer sustained as a consequence of her own reckless behaviour, but bear in mind, members of the jury, that the same rogue agent claimed an officer of Special Branch, an alleged accomplice of my client, was also present. Yet that officer was able to produce a cast-iron alibi that he was elsewhere.

'The prosecution brought forward supposed intelligence, of dubious provenance, from an unidentified Stasi officer – an enemy of this country, a person dedicated to causing disruption. Yet the officer concerned was neither brought forward themselves nor identified. "In the interests of

1

security", we were told. Or was that in the interests of the Security Service's obsession with justifying its own, somewhat questionable, behaviour?

'As for these latest allegations – what are they? A set of bogus accounts, downloaded by this same deceitful MI5 unit to my client's computer, which had already been, in common parlance, "hacked" by these rogue agents. Examination of my client's hard drive will show that these files were downloaded at a time when, as these duplicitous operatives themselves have stated, Mr Bickley-Morris was attending his bank on a nearby island. Given the choice of languishing in Athens' most notorious and unsafe jail or being detained at one of Her Majesty's military bases on the island of Cyprus, whilst he proved his innocence, what other choice would my client make?'

CHAPTER 1
One week earlier

'Hamilton? Sir Robert Hamilton? A Stasi agent?'

Huxley couldn't believe what Veronica was telling him. After his return to the UK, following the detention of Quinton Bickley-Morris, Huxley had written to her confirming that, as promised, he had posted her computer disk to Harry Nevile.

Until she had fled to the island of Aegina, Veronica Blakeridge, whose affectionate nickname was Ron, had worked directly for Harry, a senior officer in MI5's Bioweapons Counter-Espionage Unit. Huxley also reported to Harry, who, in turn, reported directly to Sir Robert Hamilton. Veronica's sudden and inexplicable disappearance had raised concern for her safety, but it had soon become clear that her actions had been premeditated, albeit at rather short notice. The contents of the disk had revealed the full story of why she had disappeared.

Although he had not read the contents of the disk, Huxley knew the story it told, having met with Veronica on the afternoon of Bickley-Morris' arrest, without telling Harry. He also knew that the disk contents would raise suspicions about her involvement in the death on the island of a corrupt former Special Branch officer, Roderick Graham. The Greek police had taken the view that he had stolen a motor scooter, whilst drunk, and crashed.

Despite her behaviour and the suspicions about her

involvement in the death, Harry had let it be known that he would take a lenient view should she wish to return work. His exact words: "Someone should tell her that. Someone really should tell her" had been directed at Huxley. The uncomfortable feeling that somehow Harry knew of his clandestine meeting with Veronica had stayed with Huxley ever since.

'I can't explain over the phone, Huxley – these calls aren't cheap, but I've found some things in Graham's house, some files and photographs, things like that. I'm coming back to London next week. I'll bring them with me, and you can take a look.'

Huxley's mood had dipped. He knew the main reason why Veronica was coming back to London was to put her affairs in order and her house on the market. In the months since Huxley had sought her out in the village of Perdika, he had written to her frequently and felt that they were growing close. He had even returned to the island twice to spend some time with her, although he had never told Harry.

Despite what Huxley had believed to be a flourishing affection, Veronica had told him that she was making her move to Aegina permanent. It was no easy decision, she'd explained, but she knew she couldn't return to work. Despite Harry's clear intent to forgive and forget, she could not forgive herself. She had passed on information about Harry's small MI5 group to former Detective Sergeant Roderick Graham. She didn't like the word traitor, but given her actions, it would be a difficult label to avoid.

Rod Graham's colleagues had, for good reason, given him the nickname "Black Rod". His true relationship with his so-called "sources" in the IRA had been a cause for concern with his superiors in the force, and he certainly had enjoyed a lifestyle that would be difficult to support on his police force income alone. There was no hard evidence, just guesswork. He had blackmailed Veronica's mother, his own cousin, into doing some of his dirty work for him. In due course, he had turned his attention to Veronica. Graham didn't stop at threats of violence; he made sure his targets knew exactly what he was capable of doing.

CHAPTER 2
Five days earlier

'Mr Kilsdale, if this grievance is not put right – and that's down to you now – my associates will be displeased. And when they're displeased, unpleasant things happen.' With that, the man who identified himself as Hector Alexander ended the phone call.

Matthew Kilsdale knew that Hector Alexander was an alias used by Quinton Bickley-Morris to evade detection. The fact that Bickley-Morris was connected to people who did not make empty threats caused Matthew significant anxiety. Only a year ago, he had been breathing a sigh of relief. MI5 had discovered that the company he had been working for, DCM Diagnostics Ltd, a small scientific instruments company in Essex, had allowed an outbuilding on their premises to be used to breed mice. Mice whose virus-infected droppings were intended for use in a bioterrorism attack on the government. There had been little doubt in the minds of Matthew and his fellow directors that there could be no innocent reason why the mice were being kept there, but the connection to terrorism had been an unwelcome and disturbing revelation.

It wasn't the only thing that the Security Service had discovered. They were aware that Matthew had started a fire as part of a cover-up, but more worryingly, they had made it clear they knew that bogus sales to a Greek company were part of a money-laundering scheme operated by Bickley-Morris masquerading as Hector Alexander. The Security Service agents, whom he had believed were two police officers, Superintendent Hamilton and Detective Sergeant Neville, had asked him to identify the men in two photographs. One had been Rod Graham and the other, Quinton Bickley-Morris.

Faced with the threat of prosecutions for money laundering, facilitating a planned terrorist attack and arson, Matthew had needed to think on his feet. It had been at that point that he had realised that if Hamilton and Neville, as they called themselves, were genuine police officers, they would have arrested both him and his managing director, Jack Poulter. They would not have revealed the details they knew and asked him to identify the two photographs. He'd taken a chance and called their bluff. As he'd begun to suspect, they were spooks, though that knowledge did little to ease his anxiety. Just how much they knew was uncertain, but what had been clear to Matthew was that lying was a risky option. The only chance he had to save his own skin was to tell the truth and nothing but the truth, though he had no intention of telling the whole truth.

Hamilton had made it clear that he would not disclose his sources, and Matthew had not hesitated to identify Graham. Matthew had become more closely, and increasingly more unwillingly, involved with Graham than he wished known.

It had started as a business scam: services provided by Rod Graham at premium prices, from which Matthew received what he liked to call "a commission". Graham had then started to ask for favours and made it clear that if they were not granted, Matthew would suffer. One of the favours that most worried Matthew was DCM Diagnostics Ltd acting as a parcel depot for the company notionally renting the shed: Usher Ltd. Hamilton's disclosure of the terrorist link to the mice had only confirmed Matthew's suspicions that Graham was using the company as a covert postbox for illegal goods. There had been one delivery that Graham had forewarned needed handling with extreme care. When Matthew had asked why, Graham had tried to make a joke of it: "Let's just say, if you like parties, it'll give you a real blast." Hamilton had just confirmed his suspicions.

The photograph of Bickley-Morris he then identified as being that of Hector Alexander; an investor turned extortionist in Matthew's opinion. That hadn't been at all difficult because it was true. The fact that he knew Hector Alexander's true identity, he had kept secret. More importantly, MI5 had believed his story that the company had been a victim of extortion, acting under threats of financial ruin and physical violence.

Matthew's own crooked accounting, which involved creaming off the legitimate income of the company, had also been known to the Security Service, and they had used it against him as a form of blackmail, though no further action had been taken. Nor had they exposed him to his colleagues. The next few weeks had been an anxious time for him. Would the Security Service unearth the extent of his complicity? At the time, he had been more closely involved with Rod Graham and, in many respects, only peripheral to Bickley-Morris' operations. He had only known the true identity of Bickley-Morris because Graham had told him. Matthew sensed that Graham's trust of Bickley-Morris had waned over the years, disclosing his true identity had been a kind of perverted insurance policy. Rod Graham had made it clear to Matthew that, if ever he exposed Graham or "Mr Hector Alexander", Bickley-Morris had the resources to exact what was bound to be a gruesome revenge.

That had been a great part of the reason why Matthew had not disclosed Hector Alexander's true identity. The other part was that there seemed little point. From what he had been told by Graham, Matthew was confident that Alexander's true identity was known to the Security Service. He knew he had taken a risk in identifying Graham, but it had been a calculated risk. His trust in Graham had never been high, and Graham's behaviour had been growing increasingly threatening. Matthew had felt trapped, and Graham's arrest offered the best, in fact, the only way out that he could see. And he had suspected that the relationship between Graham and Hector Alexander, or rather Quinton Bickley-Morris, had also grown strained. Graham had alluded to files he was keeping on people he either mistrusted or disliked, and it seemed reasonable to assume Graham was compiling a dossier on Bickley-Morris.

Matthew had chosen not to warn either Graham or Hector Alexander that the Security Service was investigating them. What he had not foreseen was that Graham would be tipped off about his imminent arrest. Even more surprising was Graham's claim that it had been a member of Hamilton's own team who had done so. Quite what Graham had meant by "it's time to get out", Matthew wasn't sure, though the promise to be in touch "even if it takes a little time" suggested Graham's disappearance would be only temporary. As the weeks had turned into months with no contact, Matthew had begun to hope that Graham had been arrested or that something more unpleasant had happened to him. Whichever it was, it was a matter of little concern to him; it was looking as though he was going to get away with his deceptive ploy.

A few weeks before this latest telephone call, much to Matthew's horror, Hector Alexander had made contact. Matthew's growing sense of security had been shattered. Rod Graham, he learned, was dead, but it was quite clear that Alexander knew quite a lot about his association with Graham. That information could only have come from Graham himself. What game Graham had been playing, he had no idea, but Matthew was now all too aware that he was still firmly on the hook.

Surprise hadn't overwhelmed him entirely, and he'd had the presence of mind to remark that he was no longer working for DCM.

'Forget DCM – it's you and Rod Graham I'm interested in,' Alexander had responded sharply.

Matthew had protested that it had been some time since he had last heard from Graham and had no idea of his whereabouts. Alexander had stifled a laugh.

'You won't hear from him unless you know a medium. He's dead. In hell, more than likely.'

It had taken a moment or two for him to register what he'd just been told.

'Then I don't see how I can—'

'Matthew, my boy – I *can* call you Matthew, can't I? After all, we shall be working together.' The far from convincing friendly tone had in no way masked the malice of Bickley-Morris' intent.

'Look, I really don't—'

Once caught in Bickley-Morris' web, there was no escape, nor was there any chance of a discussion.

'Graham stole from me. Money, documents. That needs to be paid back, one way or another. Graham can't do it, so that leaves one option, Matthew – his business partner. That's you.'

Matthew had tried hard to control a rising sense of panic. A sense that had begun to grow when he had sought to find out more about Graham's death. All that Bickley-Morris had said was, "They say it was an accident", but the way he had said it had left a great deal of doubt. Had Graham fallen foul of Bickley-Morris? There was no way of knowing, but that had only added to Matthew's distress.

With the latest phone call over, he was trying to make sense of what he had been told and how it connected with what he already knew. The effort came with a growing sense of despair. Bickley-Morris had told him Graham had some files that belonged to him. Files that could cause serious problems to him and his associates if they came to light. Files he wanted back. Matthew had protested that he knew nothing about any files, but that didn't seem to bother his persecutor.

'Oh, I doubt he trusted you with anything of value, Matthew.'

He had learned something else too. The person who had tipped off Rod Graham about his imminent arrest had been a relative: the daughter of his cousin. It hadn't been difficult to put two and two together. A relative who had tipped him off. A member of Hamilton's team who had tipped him off. The same person. Graham had somebody on the inside. Or rather, had in the past. A person who may very well be aware of Matthew's own involvement. A threat – *another* threat – to his future.

What else had Bickley-Morris said? "Well, if you *are* telling the truth, Matthew, and you haven't got the files, then she must have them. Graham stashed them somewhere before he fled."

It was only later that he realised the significance of "she". Bickley-Morris had used the pronoun "she", which meant that he must know who "she" was, and it could only be that one person. It would explain why Bickley-Morris was not chasing her for the files. "She" worked for MI5, and he must consider it too much of a risk to contact her directly.

Bickley-Morris had not given him a name, but he had given him an address. An address in Blackheath, South London. "If the files are there, I want them found." Bickley-Morris had been quite clear. There would be someone there to help, Matthew had been told, or as Bickley-Morris had put it: "Look Matthew, I know it's a fair-sized house and one you've never been to. But I'm not an unreasonable man – I don't expect you to do it on your own. I'll send someone along to help. Save you sending me the files too."

Matthew had been set up to do Bickley-Morris' dirty work. *Find the files. If you don't, something unpleasant is going to happen to you.* The risk was that he might be walking straight into the unwelcoming arms of MI5. Either way, neither party was likely to show him any mercy.

CHAPTER 3
Day one: Monday

Harry Nevile had been anticipating a reasonably relaxed day when he had set off for work that morning. Huxley had booked a day's holiday. At least it would be quiet in the office.

Now, on his way home to Montpelier Walk, he was in a sombre mood. His meeting with Sir Robert Hamilton had been as worrying as it had been unexpected. The fact that the proposed venue for the meeting was Victoria Square had been enough to set alarm bells ringing. Back in 1991, when Sir Robert had been stationed, temporarily, at the Ministry of Defence, the pair had often met there, sitting on adjacent benches as though they were two strangers engaged in polite but distant conversation. Victoria Square was a small, secluded garden square, close to Buckingham Palace Mews, and despite the garden being private, somehow the gate was always unlocked whenever a meeting had been requested. Since then, after Sir Robert had moved to Curzon Street House and subsequently to Thames House, they had only met in Victoria Square under special circumstances.

It was possible, Harry had supposed, that Victoria Square was the chosen venue simply for convenience. Harry knew from his own experience that the Security Service had the benefit of owning a covert flat in the palace mews, and the Square itself was hardly a detour from Harry's normal route home. Perhaps, as the meeting had been scheduled for the late afternoon, Sir Robert's business had taken him to the mews, and he'd thought the Square was mutually convenient for them both towards the end of the working day. The problem was, Harry knew it wasn't true. Meetings at Victoria Square had always been off the record.

'There's been a lot of embarrassment over that fiasco of a trial,' Sir Robert had begun.

Harry hadn't needed to ask which trial; there was little doubt it was that of Quinton Bickley-Morris. It had been rushed. The case had been taken to court only a few months after Bickley-Morris' arrest. Sir Robert's objections had been ignored; he'd been told it was hardly unprecedented and reminded of the Gordon Lonsdale case, which had run to a similar timescale. The fact that the Lonsdale trial had taken place over thirty years earlier had only fuelled his fears that something was amiss. Sir Robert had been incredulous when any chance of the case succeeding had been taken away by the decision not to name or bring to court Anna Slowik, a former high-ranking East German intelligence officer.

Slowik had first met Bickley-Morris shortly after the Second World War. As a young army officer, Bickley-Morris had not fought in the war, but his first posting had been as a liaison officer based in Berlin. His duties had often taken him to Frankfurt an der Oder in the Soviet-occupied zone, where he took the opportunity to expand his black-market operations. Even before the East German state or the notorious Stasi, the Ministry for State Security, had come into existence, Bickley-Morris had brazenly walked into the local Soviet military headquarters' building and offered to provide something "more interesting" than his own black-market goods.

Slowik had been a teenager, displaced from her native Poland in the chaos following the defeat of the Nazi regime. In return for food and shelter, Slowik had kept the local military informed about unrest in the native German community. As a civilian, she saw things kept hidden from the occupying Red Army. She didn't think of it as spying or informing on people; it was simply what she had to do to survive.

Later, Slowik had been relocated to Berlin and had lost contact with Bickley-Morris, or Agent Foder as he became known during the Cold War. She had done well, and in the 1950s, when she was assigned to the HVA, the *Hauptverwaltung Aufklärung* or Main Directorate for Reconnaissance, the Stasi's foreign intelligence service, she encountered Bickley-Morris once again. Over the course of time, Slowik had risen to be second in command of the HVA, and, although not responsible for or involved with Bickley-Morris, she had continued to follow his activities. There had been nothing sentimental about her continuing interest.

Five years after the dissolution of the East German State, with the Stasi no longer in existence, Slowik had sought sanctuary in the UK. She had been walking a tightrope between the unified German state, which was likely to prosecute her, and her former Eastern bloc colleagues and associates, who would prefer that she be silenced lest she should implicate them. Bickley-Morris' arrest had followed Slowik's confirmation that the former parliamentary private secretary to the secretary of state for defence had indeed been an agent of the German Democratic Republic, or East Germany as it had been more popularly known.

Harry had let Sir Robert's remark hang in the air, he knew

15

that his friend and colleague was thinking how to phrase what he really wanted to say.

'It's bad, Harry, and heads are going to roll. Or at least one, and I'm afraid it's likely to be mine.'

'But *you* didn't withdraw Slowik.'

'No.'

'Then why you? Why *your* head?'

'It's complicated, Harry, and to be honest, a bit of a bloody mess. I've never been mainstream, so to speak – you know that. And it's easier to trim the ragged edges to make things look neat and tidy again. When Slowik sought asylum in the UK, it was me she approached. There are those who think the Service should never have been involved.' Sir Robert paused, as if wondering what to say next. 'We knew each other in Berlin. Back then.'

The one time Harry had met Slowik, he had guessed from the way that Sir Robert had greeted her that they were no strangers.

'But that doesn't explain why your head should be on the block. We don't even know why Slowik was pulled as a witness.'

Sir Robert had smiled. 'Oh, there's an obvious answer to that one. They don't want anyone to know we have her. She was never named in the pretrial disclosures.'

'Why "obvious"? Does it matter if the Soviets know we have her? Get them worried. Hope some of their supposed diplomats get recalled.'

'I'm not sure we're supposed to call them "Soviets" anymore,' had been Sir Robert's response, 'but it's not them.'

Harry's look had told his old friend and mentor that he realised there was something more at work.

'It's our allies, you see. Intelligence, counter-intelligence, there are no boundaries. It's a murky world. We all keep tabs on our friends as well as our enemies. Slowik knows a lot about Western intelligence gathering, especially the European agencies. Who we can trust and who we can't. It would really put the cat among the pigeons if they knew we had her and she was telling all.'

Sir Robert had gone on to explain that Margaret Thatcher's Euroscepticism had done real damage to the UK's relationship with the European Community, and the present government's more conciliatory approach could easily be derailed. A scandal, or even just the suspicion that the UK was aware of the covert activities of its own allies, whether in relation to the UK or other members of the European Union, would cause consternation. The post-Maastricht road to integration was hardly smooth as it was; embarrassment and mistrust would not help any European government. Secret intelligence, especially of the type Slowik could provide, was best kept very secret.

It had occurred to Harry that if Slowik was extradited to another country, most likely Germany, she could probably tell a tale or two about the UK's activities. *Hardly helpful*, he thought.

Sir Robert had gone on to explain that he had been given a choice. "Go with grace or go with disgrace" was how he had phrased it. Harry had protested that there could be no disgrace without evidence, but Sir Robert had pointed out that, even though no names had been given, Bickley-Morris' defence counsel had painted him as a rogue MI5 agent, intent on bringing down one of the government's trusted and high-ranking civil servants. All it would take would be for

17

someone to leak his name to the press.

'And if grace or disgrace,' Sir Robert had said with a wry smile, 'is synonymous with an enhanced or reduced pension? I'm not that far from retirement age. Can't hang on to the reins forever. Sooner or later, I have to be consigned to history.' A smile had brightened his face, and he chuckled quietly. 'History, Harry, have you ever noticed it's almost "his story"? Good basis for a novel or two. While away my time in a leafy lane in the city of dreaming spires, turning some of it into fiction. I might even give Le Carré a run for his money.'

There had been little doubt in Harry's mind that Sir Robert's actions were unlikely to be swayed by threats about his pension, but he recognised the reality. If the proposal was challenged, then, quite simply, the "go with grace" option would be taken away. In reality, Sir Robert's options were rather limited.

'And Tufton Street?'

Given Sir Robert's own difficult position, Harry had felt guilty about asking the question, but the futures of the members of his team were also at stake. He knew that without Sir Robert's continuing influence, a move to the anonymity of Thames House was inescapable. He also knew that the existence of the Tufton Street office owed much to his boss's friendship with former Director General Sir Patrick Walker and Walker's trust in him. Although Sir Robert could not be described as a loner, it was true that he had always trodden his own path. Not a solitary figure in the Service, but someone who avoided the cabals and alliances that existed within the core of MI5. It was a characteristic that had been very useful when there was a need for a discreet and impartial investigation, especially within the Service or within government departments. A characteristic that had engendered a level of trust and respect that Sir Robert had yet to enjoy with the recently appointed Director General.

'Can't be certain,' had been Sir Robert's reply. He had said this whilst looking towards the northern entrance to Victoria Square at the blue door in the wall of the palace mews. It wasn't that he'd been avoiding Harry's gaze; it was just his manner. 'The way I see it is that the Service is becoming very much focused on – what shall we call it? – "the greater good". Which, in practical terms, means countering the most immediate threats at the expense of active surveillance against future risks. Awful as the consequences of biowarfare or bioterrorism might be, they're not as immediate as the effects of the IRA bombing campaign.'

'Are you saying that, were you to retire, the Bioweapons Counter-Espionage Unit would, in effect, be retired as well?'

For some time, Harry had been quite aware that, following changes in leadership, few saw Tufton Street's activities as central to the Security Service's operations. That had been abundantly clear four years earlier, in 1992, with Sir Robert's relocation to the Curzon Street House registry rather than directly to Thames House.

'Not entirely, Harry. Certainly, your more recent, I hesitate to call it speculative, work, analysing the scientific literature, what is published where, which countries don't publish in certain areas, trying to predict where the new threats are likely to come from, yes, that is likely to be scaled back. What's left, however unfortunate it may turn out to be, is unlikely to be seen as an appropriate use of our best resources.'

Sir Robert had looked directly at Harry when he made that last remark. There was no need to say it. *You, Harry, will be deployed elsewhere.*

Harry's thoughts about where this might be leading had been answered before he'd had time to put them into words.

'I am sorry to paint such a bleak picture of the Service, but the time may be coming when you'll have to make a choice. A choice that, one way or another, will determine your future. You need to know... well... what that future may be.' After taking a deep breath, he had added, 'Things may be worse than we thought.'

Once again, Sir Robert had stared down the street towards the door in the mews wall, saying nothing for a few moments. Harry had known better than to interject. An explanation was coming, one that would make it clear why this meeting was in Victoria Square. Why it was, and had to be, off the record.

Another deep breath had underlined that what Sir Robert was about to say was a serious matter, and his decision to involve Harry had not been taken lightly. Harry had listened patiently, not interrupting, wondering what choices he was going to be offered.

'Something's come to light, something we should have been told about a while ago. She's in danger. Slowik is in danger. I may have to take some action. Action that may not be sanctioned.'

Why Sir Robert seemed concerned about this hadn't been clear to Harry. As a senior member of the Service, his standing allowed him to take action without seeking prior approval. 'The only benefit of being a senior officer,' he sometimes joked, 'is that you only have to ask for forgiveness, not permission.'

'I think we're both aware, Harry, that Quinton would not have been acting alone when he was passing secrets to the GDR. Then that supposed burglary in Cambridge, his own disappearance. They took resources. And he certainly didn't organise his own escape act from that hospital bed – he was under police guard. There's an obvious reason why somebody didn't want him talking, naming names. The question is, who might not have wanted Quinton being questioned? Who wanted him out of our way?'

'But not dead,' Harry added pointedly.

'Oh, I have little doubt Quinton kept a little insurance policy, one which would pay out if he simply disappeared. You know, if Rod Graham was holding the policy details, and someone was helping him – what shall we call him? A hypothetical friend? – if he had found that out, it does point to another reason why Graham's death may not have been accidental. But I digress. The point is, it's hard to believe that this, this shadowy hypothetical friend was not privy to the GDR's operation, and he'll know Slowik may well know enough to damn him.'

'Conjecture, Bob. Is there any real evidence?'

'Unfortunately not. But look at Quinton's trial. His brief presented a lot of detail about our own Cambridge operation. Detail that Quinton couldn't have known.'

'And that, well, all of it really, implies someone senior. Very senior?'

'No, Harry, not necessarily very senior, just with good access to information. Perhaps not even within our own organisation, just close to it.'

Harry had returned to the question of whether or not Anna Slowik could identify this person. There had been a flaw in

Sir Robert's hypothesis.

'Slowik's debriefing has been going on for almost a year, yet she hasn't named him. Perhaps she doesn't know him. If he even exists?'

'Who knows, Harry? Perhaps she has, but the name's not released, or worse – suppressed. Perhaps she's keeping one of her cards, the ace in her hand, in reserve. If all else fails, strike a deal with whoever it is. Guarantee me sanctuary and I'll keep your secret. Of course, that may be something he's unable to do, but regardless, there's only one way her silence can be guaranteed permanently. And there's information suggesting that option is being taken up.'

'But, acting on your own, unsanctioned? If you can't trust, or should I say involve, your senior colleagues, it rather limits the possible suspects in the Service.'

'It's just being careful, Harry. As I say, not necessarily a stalwart of the Service, but someone close enough that I doubt I can follow this up officially without our shadowy friend becoming aware. I can't do nothing. It's not just a matter of duty – I owe it to her.'

Even before Sir Robert had elaborated on his apparent predicament, Harry had been wondering why Slowik had sought out his friend when she needed help. It was no secret that in the 1960s, Captain Robert Hamilton had been stationed in Berlin, but that was all Harry knew. And why did he, now, feel so obliged to help her? If circumstances were different, it would be risking his career, but given what Harry had just heard, there wasn't much of that left. Yet, taking that into consideration did not explain why Sir Robert felt obliged. Harry had asked the question, but the answer had not been as helpful as he had hoped.

'She helped us. In Berlin. Things were still quite volatile, and you had to tread carefully. It was often easier for the East to clear out its own operatives than for us to go through the rigmarole of detention. Then what? Trial? Expulsion? Tit for tat? You know how it goes. Slowik...' Sir Robert paused. 'We knew who she was, of course, but she was a useful conduit.'

Harry had reflected for a few moments, trying to digest what had been said, before Sir Robert had drawn the meeting to a close.

'Look, I can't say too much. Nor can I tell the future. But you may have to choose between what you're told and what you believe. And there's a good chance it will be heads you lose, tails you lose. It's better you have time to think rather than be railroaded into a decision you may regret.' Sir Robert had stood up and looked Harry in the eye. 'It's a mess. And you may well be told that it's a mess of my making. I'm sorry, Harry. Trust what you know to be true.'

With that, he had left, leaving Harry pondering over what had been said. It was only later, whilst walking home, that Harry realised Sir Robert had left by the eastern entrance to the Square, towards Buckingham Palace Road. As far as he could recall, Sir Robert, who invariably left first, always left by the northern entrance, towards the palace mews. It was a minor detail, hardly significant in itself, but to Harry it signalled that something, something within the Service, had changed.

And a more disturbing thought had struck Harry. A thought that could explain why Sir Robert felt "obliged". He ran the conversation back in his head. "Easier for the East to clear out its own operatives... We knew who she was...

23

she was a useful conduit." The implications were quite clear. Robert Hamilton had passed information to a known Stasi officer in order that her fellow agents could be withdrawn before they were arrested. It was out of the question that Sir Robert had helped Quinton Bickley-Morris in any way, but could his ultimate loyalties be other than to the Crown? Was the pursuit of Bickley-Morris driven by a need to protect himself? Could this "hypothetical friend" be just an elaborate subterfuge to divert attention away from Sir Robert himself?

There was also a question about Slowik's debriefing. Perhaps she had come forward with a name. Perhaps no one wanted the bad press that putting a senior member of the Service, or possibly the government, on trial for treason would inevitably generate? More than a decade had passed since Anthony Blunt had been exposed and stripped of his knighthood, and Fleet Street would be more than keen to get their teeth into another spy scandal. It cast a different light on "grace or disgrace".

If Harry had to choose between what he was told and what he believed, he needed to be absolutely sure about what he did believe.

Chapter 4

Day one: Monday

As he turned the corner from Montpelier Place into Montpelier Walk, Harry fumbled in his pocket for his front door key. It had been a long day. The matters discussed had not only taken him by surprise but had caused him some considerable concern. If Sir Robert was pushed out, was it just face-saving, or was there something more disturbing at work within the Service? Perhaps involving something in Sir Robert's past?

As he approached his door, he felt alone. He knew only silence was waiting for him. *How wonderful it must be to have a dog,* he thought. *A companion who would greet you enthusiastically, whatever was going on in the world.* He knew it wasn't possible; he had no partner and, even without his often erratic hours, the poor creature would be left on its own for most of the day.

Once inside, his mind went to more practical matters. It was Monday and, breaking with his usual habit of cooking pasta on a Monday, that morning he had decided he would have fish for dinner. He walked through to the kitchen to check the fish had defrosted, but before he could open the fridge door, the phone rang. Not his home phone, but the private line, known only to his colleagues in the Security Service.

'Harry, it's me – Huxley. I'm at Lewisham Police Station.

They've arrested me. They think I killed Ron.'

Four hours later, it was a frustrated and vexed Harry who eventually got to see Huxley. It had taken just over an hour to organise a taxi and get to the red brick Victorian edifice that was Lewisham Police Station. That was when Harry's problems had begun. They had kept him waiting in the reception area and wouldn't let him through to see Huxley. Harry had identified himself as a Security Service officer and confirmed that Huxley was also a member of the Service, but that had served only to increase the resolve to be awkward. It was quite clear that the police felt that this was their jurisdiction, and they were not going to have any other government agency encroaching on their investigation.

Before leaving his mews cottage, Harry had alerted Thames House, and it had been agreed that as Huxley's senior officer he should handle the case until more details were known. As serious as the potential charges might turn out to be, Harry had no more information than the few sentences Huxley had been able to utter before the telephone had been taken away from him. Harry's protestations and requests to talk to Huxley had been met with a brick wall.

'This is not Hollywood, sir. The gentleman exercised his right to inform someone of his detention and chose you. Gives you no rights. End of.'

That, more or less, was all Harry had been told. On arriving at the station, he had been denied access to Huxley on the grounds that he wasn't Huxley's legal representative.

'I don't think you understand the serious nature of the situation, sir,' had been the vocalised opinion of the desk sergeant.

Harry understood the serious nature of the situation all too

26

well and doubted that the police were aware that Veronica had been a Security Service officer too. Nor was he going to tell them that, or the fact that she had been related to a suspect in a terrorism case, who himself had met his end in uncertain circumstances.

Harry didn't like pulling strings, but he had realised quite quickly that this was the only way forward. The desk sergeant had refused to let Harry use a police telephone and he had been obliged to use the public phone in the foyer. His call to Thames House would be followed up by a call to a senior officer in the Met, who would then ensure that clear instructions would be sent to Lewisham Police Station. It all took time, and Harry knew that at the end of it, all he would be allowed was access to Huxley in private. Neither he nor the Service could interfere in a police investigation, though he did hope that they would have the common sense to co-operate.

Harry's first question to Huxley had been an attempt to establish what had happened. His second had been to confirm that Huxley had given the police no further information. Given that several hours had elapsed since Huxley's detention, Harry was relieved to find that Huxley had remembered his training and followed protocol. He had informed his senior officer and then, under questioning, his replies had been to confirm the few details that the police already knew and to exercise his right to make no comment to any other questions he had been asked. Huxley had not taken up his right to have legal representation; that would be part of any further action deemed necessary by his senior officer. Neither Huxley nor Harry had expected the belligerence shown by the local police force, and Huxley had been growing increasingly worried as the hours had elapsed.

Harry knew when to talk and when to listen. He had a myriad of questions, starting with, when had Veronica come back to the UK? Not to mention, why had Huxley not told him of her return? But this was a time to listen. As much as Harry wanted to know all the details, he had to insist that Huxley restrict himself to what had happened at the house: what he had seen, what he had heard, not what he had presumed was happening.

Huxley had spent the morning tidying his flat and doing some food shopping, planning to invite Ron to dinner that evening. That afternoon, he had gone to her house in Blackheath, hoping to surprise her. There had been no reply when he knocked on the door, and that had been when he noticed that the door jamb was damaged next to the lock. Huxley's first thought had been that there had been a break-in, but the door wouldn't open. It was jammed somehow, or still locked. Concerned for Veronica's safety, he had banged loudly on the door and called her name, but there had been no response. Looking through the door light, he had seen a body at the bottom of the stairs.

'I saw her, Harry. Ron. Crumpled, at the bottom of the stairs.'

Harry's response was to ask him how; how could he have seen her? Harry had visited the house the previous year, when Veronica had disappeared, and his recollection was that the glass panels in the door were frosted.

'The door panels. They're not clear. How could you see through?'

Huxley explained that the glass panels were of a rectangular design with clear glass at the bevelled edge of

28

each panel. Barely a centimetre wide, just enough to squint through.

'There was somebody else there. I saw them. Trying to hide. Pressed up against the spandrel.'

Harry didn't know what a spandrel was, but Huxley explained.

'The panelling under the stairs. I don't think he thought I could see him, not with the angle.'

Harry recalled that the front door was opposite the bottom of the stairs, and it would indeed be difficult to look along the length of the hallway.

Huxley had known he had to call the police and had no option other than to head to Charlton Road to find a public telephone box and call nine-nine-nine. Having been told to wait at the telephone box, he did so. Then, somewhat to his surprise, the attending officer had arrested him and brought him to the police station for further questioning.

From what he had been told, a neighbour, alarmed at the sight of the police, had approached them. She had told them the lady who owned the house had been away but was expected back that day. Hearing noises, she had assumed her neighbour, Mrs Blakeridge, had returned. About twenty or thirty minutes before the police arrived, she had seen a man leaving. The description she gave fitted Huxley. Although he had been told no details of what the police had found at Ron's house, his worst fears were confirmed. What he had not expected was being arrested on suspicion of having unlawfully killed his friend.

'It's a consp—' Huxley began, but Harry cut him short.

'No theories, no speculation. Not here.'

Harry knew what he needed to do, even if he didn't think

it was the most honourable way to act. In the absence of any evidence, Lewisham police would be able to hold Huxley for only twenty-four hours. That was enough time for Harry to implement his plan. If the police applied for an extension to the initial twenty-four-hour limit, Harry knew it would be blocked. Immediately after Harry left, Huxley was to demand his right to legal representation and insist upon a solicitor from within the Service's legal department. That would take a little time to arrange, deliberately eating into the time that Huxley could be held. It would also provide some relief for Huxley as the police could not then question him further in the absence of his legal representative. At the end of twenty-four hours, Lewisham police force would be instructed to release Huxley on unconditional bail but would not know that his release was anything *but* unconditional.

Given that both the suspect and the deceased were members of the Security Service, the investigation would be transferred from the Lewisham force to a senior officer at the Metropolitan Police to minimise the risk of any exposure of the Security Service's activities. A deal would have been struck that, in effect, released Huxley into the custody of the Security Service. Not that Huxley would be off the hook – far from it – but the Service could deal with the situation in their own way, in their own time. A covert guarantee would have been given that, should there be any evidence of a case to answer, Huxley would be returned into the hands of the police.

CHAPTER 5

Day two: Tuesday

'What the hell happened?'

Quinton Bickley-Morris was not used to being on the receiving end of a tirade. The man who had called him clearly did not believe what Quinton had just told him.

'If you've killed one of Nevile's team, I won't protect you. They'll be relentless in their pursuit.'

Things were not going well. Quinton's plan of retribution was being derailed, and he was still trying to piece together exactly what had happened. Yesterday, he had been expecting a simple confirmatory phone call, a code word confirming that Kilsdale had been dealt with. What he had then heard threw everything into confusion. Rather than ringing the police to give them an anonymous tip-off, he had found himself trying to contact Kilsdale. It had taken several attempts, but when he did pick up the call, Kilsdale claimed that when he had got to Blackheath, there was a police car across the street, and the police seemed to be stopping anybody wanting to gain access.

* * *

There had been a lot of activity going on outside one house in particular, and Matthew Kilsdale had checked the numbers of the houses close to where he was standing. Counting down the row, it seemed, as far as he could tell, that all this activity was outside the address he had been heading towards: the address that Bickley-Morris had given him. Realising that standing and staring was likely to bring him to the attention of the police on duty at the barricade, he turned and strode away. Hector Alexander, Quinton Bickley-Morris or whatever he chose to call himself, was not going to be pleased. He was hardly likely to say, "Oh, that's OK, not your fault," but all Matthew could do was to wait with increasing trepidation. He'd had no way of contacting his intimidator. Although when he'd recovered from the shock of Bickley-Morris' first phone call, he had tried the one-four-seven-one code to discover the number Bickley-Morris had used to call him. The number had been blocked.

* * *

The news that a woman's body had been found at a house in Blackheath had broken very quickly. That news had now reached the man who had phoned Quinton, the man who was berating him. A man he had never met and knew only as Reid. Quinton had always known that he wasn't the only agent in the UK passing information to East Germany, but the "don't know, can't tell" ethic meant he knew very little about the breadth of activities in the UK. Reid was an exception. Reid was not his handler; Quinton did not have one as such, and he had always regarded Reid as, for want of a better word, an umbrella; an overarching guardian who kept a weather eye open for possible trouble and provided warnings. Sometimes warnings to be cautious, sometimes warnings to curb errant behaviour. Quinton had an uneasy feeling that, even before the closure of the East German Embassy, Reid had been the man who dealt out retribution to those who transgressed or threatened the network. Who he was or what he was remained a mystery, though it hadn't been for lack of trying on Quinton's part. What was certain was that Reid seemed to have free access to information about the current interests of both the Home Office and the Metropolitan Police. Whether that meant he was a Home Office civil servant, a member of the Met, or indeed part of MI5, Quinton had never discovered. Whichever it was, information seemed to flow in his direction. Following Quinton's car accident in Cambridge in 1991, when Rod Graham had effected Quinton's escape from hospital whilst he was under police guard, it had been Reid who had orchestrated the plan and supplied the car Quinton had used to escape to the continent.

Kilsdale's fate had been sealed during Quinton's long months in detention, during which he had given much thought to how Hamilton could have known his whereabouts in Greece. And to who could have betrayed him to MI5. The link to DCM Ltd was glaringly obvious. The managing director, Jack Poulter, was a fool, the marketing director, a nobody. That left only the finance director: Matthew Kilsdale. He was a different proposition, more directly involved with Rod Graham than the others, and Graham's opinion had been very much that Kilsdale was a man who would sell his own mother to save his skin. Unsure though he was of quite how much Kilsdale knew, Quinton was not prepared to take a risk. If he had been responsible in any way for Quinton's arrest, then he deserved what was coming. Even if he hadn't been, Kilsdale knew too much; he was a threat to Quinton's security. A threat that Quinton intended to remove. Kilsdale, however, was now a problem that would have to be resolved later. More urgently, Quinton needed to find out what had happened in Blackheath and to turn it to his own advantage.

The fact that Kilsdale still had to be dealt with was an inconvenience and an annoyance to Quinton, but he realised he still had one opportunity. The dead body in Blackheath. It had to be the worthless bitch who lived there; she must have come back. The bitch who worked for Harry Nevile and who had tipped off Rod Graham. Therein lay a motive that Quinton could exploit: Nevile avenging some past grievance. It may not have been his original plan, but Quinton felt certain he could still implicate Nevile in the death.

The problem was that it had been Reid, on hearing that Quinton intended to silence Kilsdale, who had suggested Kilsdale should meet his end in Veronica Blakeridge's house in Blackheath. Reid had told him it would be mutually beneficial.

It had come as no surprise that Reid knew her address; no more so than the fact that he had known that Quinton had been arrested in Greece and ultimately brought back to the UK for trial. The barrister who had represented Quinton in court had been appointed under Reid's quite insistent guidance. Motives and allegiances may have changed since the unification of Germany, but Reid was clearly still in the business of ensuring no one endangered the former network. Quinton had little doubt that he was also still an active conduit of information for those who could not access it by legitimate means.

At first, Quinton had been puzzled by Reid's continuing interest in his predicament. There was no longer an East German state running a network in the UK, but the remnants of that network remained, and there were secrets to keep and scores to settle. Was Sir Robert Hamilton closing in on Reid? Quinton's impression was that Reid's interest was partly to ensure that he, Quinton, had not disclosed the few details that he knew, but the other part seemed to be a genuine common interest in closing down Hamilton and his Tufton Street team. For Quinton, it was revenge, a simple, if morally impure, motivation. Although there was a clear element of self-preservation in Reid's actions, Quinton had the distinct impression that vengeance was also high on the list.

"Those who betrayed us shall pay," Reid had told Quinton. It had also been made clear to Quinton that he should not get in the way of Reid when it came to dealing with Sir Robert Hamilton. He had been warned off. Reid clearly had a score of his own to settle. Not that it bothered Quinton. Whatever dispute Reid had with Hamilton, he didn't care; it was one less matter that he needed to deal with himself.

'I have my own rat to trap,' Quinton had told him.

'Nevile?'

'No, he's high on the list, but let's say there was a rat in the mouse house who needs dealing with.'

That was when Reid had suggested the Blackheath plan to Quinton.

'Why not catch two rats in the same trap?'

Quinton had been intrigued as to what Reid was suggesting. The proposal that Reid had made was that if something unpleasant was going to happen to Quinton's "rat", then there was an empty property where a trap could be set. Reid had laid out the storyline. A suspect in a case Nevile had been working on, a suspect never brought to justice, suffers an unfortunate accident in a house belonging to one of

Nevile's people; one who had mysteriously vanished, yet any investigation into their disappearance had been suppressed. The common link was Harry Nevile, a rogue officer in the Security Service, operating out of a remote office in Tufton Street, shutting down risks and protecting his own back. A narrative that would be all too believable if Sir Robert Hamilton had become the focus of an MI5 investigation.

Whatever Reid was planning that might cause Sir Robert to be investigated, he had kept secret. "Don't know, can't tell." Even so, the logic of the proposal had appealed to Quinton: Nevile panicking when his mentor and guardian was about to be exposed.

The fact that the plan had gone disastrously wrong was worrying enough, but now there was Reid to worry about. Quinton recalled Reid's words: "I won't protect you". Hidden behind that was the concern that Reid may now consider Quinton a loose end that needed tying off. "I won't protect you" was rather an understatement of what Reid might do. It was possible, Quinton argued to himself, that a simple explanation would be that Reid had set him up. Yet, it was an argument that didn't really hold up. If he had been set up, then no doubt Reid would be arranging to have him arrested. Why do that? If that happened, there was a risk that Quinton would turn on Reid and implicate him in the killing. Quinton may not know Reid's true identity, but with what he did know, the police could narrow the search. If they started to shake the tree, who was to know what they might dislodge? No, it was a risk Reid would not take. Reid did not take needless risks; Quinton was sure of that. The problem was that, currently, Quinton himself was a risk to Reid. A risk that Reid may well decide to eliminate.

The man Quinton had engaged to deal with Kilsdale was one of Rod Graham's former IRA contacts. "A triggerman" in Graham's parlance. Reid had been quite incredulous. "You used a fucking amateur?" as it had been put to Quinton.

Not so much of an amateur that he had hung around. Although he had called Quinton on the day of the debacle, to tell him things had gone awry, Quinton could no longer contact him. He had disappeared and more than likely was now out of the country. His claim to Quinton, the story that, in turn, Quinton had relayed to Reid, was that the body had been there when he arrived. A woman, clearly not the target. Whilst deciding what to do, the target had turned up early.

'Early, yeah?' the man had said angrily. 'Well, I'd locked the door. He couldn't get in, and I wasn't hanging around to see if you were suckering me in. But if you were...'

The threat was left unfinished. Fearful that he may have been set up, the man's preferred option was not to wait around but to get out whilst he still could. A decision no doubt helped by the fact that he had Quinton's upfront, partial payment. Non-refundable.

Quinton hadn't told Reid about the target turning up early. After hearing Kilsdale's version of events, Quinton was smart enough to register the disparity in their stories. If the road was cordoned off when Kilsdale arrived, it could not have been Kilsdale who had turned up at the door. He needed to find out exactly what had happened, and that wasn't going to be easy. Kilsdale almost certainly knew little, if anything, more than he had already told Quinton. When it came to information, the man most likely to be holding the cards was Reid himself. There was little chance that he would forewarn Quinton of any approaching danger, be that from the established forces of law and order, or from himself.

Chapter 6
Day three: Wednesday

Huxley had managed to get some sleep, unlike his previous night, in the police cells. When he drew the curtains in the secure third-floor flat that he had been brought to the previous evening, he was astonished to see that he was gazing out on the familiar aspect of Tufton Street. Nothing seemed real anymore. The past thirty-six hours or so had been an ordeal he hoped would not be repeated, but compared to what had been waiting for him in Blackheath, they were an irrelevance, an annoyance, just something that had to be endured. Ron was dead; he was certain that she had been killed. Nobody seemed to understand, or want to understand, the significance of that.

She hadn't been just a colleague. Huxley had always been attracted to her. Even though his awkward attempts to get to know her better had come to nothing, he had always felt, known deep down inside, that there was a connection between the two of them. When she had disappeared, seemingly alongside Rod Graham, and had been suspected of having passed on information about Tufton Street, their work, their suspicions and investigations, he knew there had to be a rational explanation. She was no traitor. She could not have been a party, in any way, to the vicious attack that had almost killed their colleague Margaret. That had been the reason he had taken such a risk to find her that day on the island of

Aegina, the day of Quinton Bickley-Morris' detention. He had to know the truth, and the truth had vindicated her.

Knowing the truth had not been enough. Huxley had wanted to be with her. Even though he had never told Harry that he had met her that fateful afternoon, Harry seemed to know. Nor had he ever told Harry where she was living. The family restaurant in Perdika was his secret. Since that meeting, they had kept in touch, and he'd been back there. Only twice, only fleeting visits for a couple of days, but enough to convince him that she was The One.

Harry had learned the truth from Veronica's story, written on the computer disk that Huxley had carried back to the UK for her and posted anonymously. Having read the contents of the disk, Harry had no intention whatsoever of pursuing a case against Veronica and even suggested he would be happy for her to rejoin the team.

Huxley knew life was more complicated than that. There would always be some doubt, in some people's minds, that Ron wasn't a security risk. If he were to marry her, something he dreamed about often, Huxley knew he would have to resign from the Security Service. "So be it" was the only thought he had on the subject.

Now he knew for certain that he would be leaving the Service – he was being investigated for murder; mud sticks. He wouldn't leave immediately, but in due course. He was pretty damn sure he knew who was behind Ron's killing, and he wasn't going to let them get away with it. But who could he turn to for help? Who else might be involved?

Harry had bought him time at the police station, and Huxley had used it to figure out what his options were. His biggest problem was that he had no evidence, and there could be little doubt that whoever was in Ron's house two days ago was after only one thing: the evidence that she was bringing back. The evidence that Sir Robert Hamilton was a traitor. Any uncertainty in Huxley's mind about Sir Robert's allegiance had evaporated the moment he had seen her body. It could not be a coincidence; either directly or indirectly, Hamilton was responsible for her murder. Huxley's logic acknowledged, but did not dwell on, the one flaw in his argument. How could Hamilton have discovered that she knew his secret?

The first problem was how to tell Harry of his suspicions. He had almost blurted out that it was a conspiracy, and Hamilton was behind it, when Harry had first been allowed access at the police station. Since then, many conjectures had gone through Huxley's mind, and he was grateful that Harry had interrupted him. He was, however, no longer sure about how much he could trust Harry.

The more he had thought about it, the more Huxley had been convinced that there had been something different about Harry at the police station. Something distant, dispassionate, calculating almost. Surely, Harry could not believe that he was capable of something as unspeakable as murder. If it wasn't that, it had to be something more worrying. Could Harry have been trying to hide his own sinister secret?

Huxley was all too aware that protocol demanded he take his suspicions to his senior officer. Protocol, however, made no allowance for circumstance, and Harry had a close relationship with Sir Robert. Harry had been recruited by Sir Robert, not just recruited, head-hunted. Huxley had not forgotten that Harry and Hamilton had known each other as students. When Harry had been in his final year at Durham,

Bob Hamilton, as he was known then, had been at the same college studying a one-year intensive course in Arabic. At least that was the story that Huxley had been told, though he knew of no service that Sir Robert had undertaken in the Middle East.

Then there was Nicholas, the concierge at Tufton Street. Huxley remembered Harry saying that he, too, had been a member of the same Durham college. "We are all old, Grey men", he had joked, referring to the fact that they were, all three, alumni of Grey College. Hamilton had even been allocated the same room that Nicholas had occupied two years earlier. Coincidence? Huxley was no longer very sure – it all seemed a rather cosy arrangement.

Huxley knew he could not avoid telling Harry of his concerns. It wasn't an issue of cutting him out and going over his head. Above that of Sir Robert too. Protocols could be broken. Huxley had considered it seriously, and it was not an issue, even though the lack of trust would make it impossible to work at Tufton Street if either Sir Robert or Harry proved to be innocent. He was, as he had joked to himself, resigned to his own resignation; he would be leaving regardless. Wherever the truth lay, Ron's death was a result of her having been in the Service. Huxley wanted no more of it. He would stay long enough to see justice done, whether that be through official channels or by his own hand.

Huxley had given much thought to how he could raise his concerns in a way that meant neither Harry nor Sir Robert could block any further investigation. Without the evidence that Ron had brought with her, that was not going to be an easy matter. His only hope lay with Mr Rose, whom the Service's legal department had assigned to his case. Huxley knew no other details about Mr Rose, not even his first name or his position within the organisation. Yet, if any part of the Service was impartial and independent, it had to be the legal department. If that were not the case, Huxley realised, his case was sunk before it had even started. His only option was to tell Harry in the presence of Mr Rose, and he would be meeting with them both that morning.

CHAPTER 7

Day three: Wednesday

It wasn't the fact that Harry had not visited Thames House for a while that was making him uncomfortable. Nor was it the rather bleak, dismally bare room that he had been ushered into: one desk, three chairs, little else.

When he had arrived at Tufton Street that morning, he had been intent on phoning Sir Robert. He had tried to contact him the previous day, without success. He had used Sir Robert's direct line, but the phone had not been answered. Sir Robert was notorious for spending as little time in his office as possible, but Harry had thought it odd that his answering machine hadn't cut in. He had told himself that there was nothing suspicious about a short absence. Ringing Sir Robert's secretary was the obvious option but bearing in mind what had been said just two days ago, however, Harry was hesitant. It would only attract attention. He would wait; Huxley was neither in any kind of danger nor was he likely to be going anywhere. It was routine in serious cases, such as murder enquiries, that the police would apply to keep a suspect in custody for more than the usual twenty-four hours without charge. The Security Service had a parallel protocol.

The fact that he had received no greeting from Nicholas, the concierge, when he arrived at Tufton Street that morning had been Harry's first warning that something was amiss. There may have been no greeting, but caution and concern had been written all over Nicholas' face. It was then that Harry noticed the two gentlemen who had been waiting in the vestibule and stepped forward.

'Mr Nevile.' Not a question, they knew who he was. 'Perhaps you would be good enough to accompany us to Thames House. There is a small matter that needs attention.'

The visitors had their backs to Nicholas and missed the small nod that told Harry not to argue but to comply without asking any questions. A nod that also conveyed reassurance. *Whatever this is, it will be dealt with. Stay calm.*

It had been barely a ten-minute walk from Tufton Street to Thames House; no words had been spoken, giving Harry just enough time to organise his thoughts. His first thought had been for his staff. Thankfully, as was his habit, Harry had arrived at Tufton Street before any others from his team, so they had been spared the sight of him being led away. His absence would soon be noted; the team were already on edge, having been told about Veronica's death and Huxley's detention. At least Harry could rely on Nicholas to provide some reassurance that all was well, though if he failed to return before lunchtime, real concerns would begin to arise. Margaret, his closest and longest-serving member of the team, would not be fooled by Nicholas' reassurances for more than a couple of hours. Harry was also concerned about Huxley, who was expecting to meet Harry that very morning. Although the ever dependable Nicholas had not been formally advised of the meeting with Huxley, Harry had little doubt that he would know of it, and have the foresight to get a message to Huxley, assuring him that all was well.

The man who was now sitting opposite Harry was the opposite of the taciturn duo who had escorted him from Tufton

Street. On entering the room, he had introduced himself as Francis Buckingham and apologised that Harry had been left on his own for almost fifteen minutes. Even though it was barely 9:00 a.m., he had asked Harry if he would like a tea or coffee to drink. Harry had declined. Although Buckingham's manner could not be described as anything other than warm, welcoming and friendly, Harry doubted that his presence was because of some minor administrative issue. Neither did he think he had been summoned in response to Huxley's arrest. It was very rare that any kind of formal interview was conducted on a one-to-one basis – there was usually at least one other person to act as a witness. Harry had an uneasy feeling that this meeting had to be connected to what Sir Robert had been saying to him, not quite forty-eight hours ago.

The conversation took him by surprise.

'Mr Nevile. I'd like to talk to you about your new role. Here at Thames House.'

This was not something that Harry had anticipated.

'I'm sorry… New role? Thames House…?'

'Mr Nevile.' Buckingham's tone had switched from pleasant to businesslike. 'We need to focus our resources where they are most needed. And this biotechnology stuff? Well, it's hardly our most pressing problem.'

Harry, still recovering from being caught unawares, reacted instinctively by defending his work.

'Perhaps that's because we've been successful in our vigilance.'

'Oh, come, Mr Nevile.'

Harry sensed that the die was cast, and there was going to be no discussion. Francis Buckingham continued.

'Hardly an outstanding track record of late. A lot of fuss over what seems to have been a perfectly legitimate project to stabilise a chicken virus. Then there was the case of that virus with such a low mortality rate that our Porton Down experts considered it not to be a threat. Especially as it's difficult to catch and takes some time for the symptoms to appear.'

'Has it occurred to you,' Harry countered, 'that the purpose of terrorism is not to kill but to induce terror? To disrupt a country through fear?'

Harry, who was holding Buckingham's gaze, paused for a moment. Although he was certain that his reply would make little difference, Harry did not think this was a time for meekness.

'Do you not agree that a six-week wait, not knowing whether or not you're infected with a virus that could kill you, would cause you, shall we say, just a little anxiety?'

Harry wasn't entirely successful at suppressing the sarcasm in his voice.

'And how many bombs could they plant on the underground in that—'

Buckingham, realising he had risen to Harry's goading, did not finish the sentence and lifted the thumb and forefinger of his left hand, as if to silence himself.

'We focus our resources where we most need them,' he repeated, softly but firmly.

Harry's mind went to the contaminated ice cream incident in the United States the previous year. One batch of pre-mix contaminated with Salmonella; two hundred thousand people affected after nationwide distribution of the product. Did they not understand the risk? How easy it could be? One small team in Tufton Street was indeed a disproportionate allocation of resources. Too little rather than too much.

Harry wanted to ask Buckingham if he had ever wondered why the IRA issued bomb warnings instead of just killing people, but he knew there was little point in continuing to argue his case. Francis Buckingham was an enforcer, not a decision-maker. Sir Robert's words had come back to Harry: "Heads are going to roll." Harry doubted Sir Robert had been consulted on the reassignment of duties and thought it likely that his interviewer was all too aware of that.

'And Sir Robert is in agreement?' he asked, curious as to what his response would be.

'Robert Hamilton is no longer responsible for the Bioweapons Counter-Espionage Unit.'

Harry noted that Sir Robert's title had been dropped before the realisation of what he had been told registered in his mind. For a moment, he was caught off guard, once again, before his rational mind kicked in.

'I beg your pardon. What? And nobody had the courtesy to tell me?'

'I *am* telling you, Mr Nevile. That is the purpose of this meeting.'

'And Sir Robert?' Harry purposefully used his colleague's title.

'Does not concern you, Mr Nevile.'

Yet again, Harry knew that no discussion would be allowed. He turned to more practical matters.

'And the rest of my team – how are they affected?'

'They will be offered other duties.'

There was, Harry realised, no commitment to keeping the team together.

'When will they be told?'

'In due course, Mr Nevile. In the meantime, you are to say nothing to them. Nothing at all about this matter.'

Harry resisted the temptation to swear, though the first word that had come into his head was *bastards*.

'You're disbanding my team. I'm not allowed to tell them. Then, what exactly is it that you expect me to do? Other than deceive my colleagues, of course.' This time Harry made no attempt to hide his sarcasm, though he regretted it as soon as the words had left his mouth.

Buckingham closed the file that was open on the desk in front of him and looked Harry directly in the eye. Harry registered Buckingham's annoyance: his defiance had not gone unnoticed. Nor, he was sure, would it go unnoted.

Buckingham looked away for a moment and took a breath.

'Mr Nevile,' he said, once again focusing on Harry, 'I think we should bring this meeting to a close. Your first duty is to identify the body that was found in Blackheath. The police are concerned that there has been no formal identification. There appears to be no family, and we can hardly ask Mr Huxley. Given the circumstances.'

Harry was unsure as to whether Francis Buckingham was suggesting that Huxley might be guilty of murder.

CHAPTER 8

Day three: Wednesday

Harry's instinct was to call in to Sir Robert's office, but he was in a hurry. Regardless of what Buckingham considered his priority should be, Harry was due to meet with Mr Rose in twenty minutes and interview Huxley. Had the meeting at Thames House, he wondered, been a deliberate attempt to confound and distract? Timed perfectly so that his mind would not be focused fully on Huxley's plight?

In fact, Harry's mind *wasn't* fully on what he was doing, and ten minutes later, he found himself back at Tufton Street. The fact that Nicholas waived the usual security measures and let him pass straight into the lobby suggested that he was aware of the subject of Harry's meeting.

'You know?' Harry ventured.

'The gentlemen didn't enlighten me, sir, but the presence of your escorts suggested it was hardly trivial. Given recent events, changes are inevitable.'

Nicholas' reply left him wondering. Serious though the matters discussed had been, did they merit the escorts or the early morning meeting? There was no urgency, especially given the instruction to say nothing to the team.

'And Sir Robert?' Harry asked, wondering if Nicholas would, or could, enlighten him.

'Incommunicado for the moment, but more importantly, sir, Mr Huxley...?'

Harry's suspicion that Nicholas would know of the meeting was confirmed. Quite how he knew was a mystery, though it came as no surprise. He had recognised, several years ago, that Nicholas' role in MI5 went far beyond his duties as concierge of the Tufton Street front offices.

Harry cast a glance towards the second lift entrance, the lift that the rest of his team believed to be a disguised holding cell, for use in the unlikely event the unit had unwelcome visitors. Harry knew that it connected through to the Security Service's other offices, those hidden at the rear of the building.

'Best use the Barton Street entrance, sir. Mr Rose's level of clearance, you understand.'

Harry understood it was Nicholas' polite way of advising that he didn't have clearance to use the covert entrance. The one time Harry had been allowed through was in the company of Sir Robert Hamilton. Harry had always known that there must be another entrance, but it was only the previous evening, when arrangements for the upcoming interview had been made, that he had been told its location. Harry had been surprised to find that one of the doorways in Barton Street connected through to the MI5 offices. He had passed that way many times, and to all intents and purposes it looked like a doorway to one of the houses.

'I believe he is waiting for you.'

* * *

Harry and Mr Rose had barely got out of the lift that connected to the secure flat, two floors above Harry's offices, when Huxley blurted out, 'It was Sir Robert Hamilton! He must have found out that Ron has the evidence.'

'Whoa, Huxley!' Harry, who was used to Huxley's outbursts, reacted more quickly than Mr Rose. 'Sit down. Let's just sort out where we are before we embark upon any speculation.'

It was Harry's standard modus operandi when faced with something unexpected. Step back, establish what you do and do not know before examining any speculative thoughts or suggestions.

The Service's legal officer, although a little slower to react, was calm and pragmatic.

'And please explain – who is this person "Ron"? Where does he fit into this sorry episode?'

Harry realised that Mr Rose did not know Veronica's pet name, but was more concerned about his use of the phrase "sorry episode". *What exactly does he mean by that?* Harry wondered. Surely he didn't think that Huxley had killed his former colleague? Perhaps that was why Mr Rose had been so keen to check that Huxley would be kept in a secure flat following his release. It had seemed a sensible suggestion, a less stressful environment for Huxley whilst ensuring that Huxley's eventual testimony remained uncontaminated. Perhaps it was also a rather convenient way of keeping Huxley in detention. Before Harry could explain who Ron was, Huxley, impatient as he always was when excited, carried on.

'He's not who he says he is. Well, he is but he isn't. He's a spy – it all has something to do with that Slowik woman. You remember that meeting we had after Margaret recognised Black Rod in my photograph? Hamilton mentioned the name and then told me to forget I had ever heard it. Now I know why.'

'Huxley! Just stop. Right there.'

Huxley's mention of Slowik's name had triggered an avalanche of concerns in Harry's mind, all of which arose from the thought that Huxley was opening a can of worms. Anna Slowik's defection had been kept secret; officially, that was the reason that her testimony had been withdrawn from Bickley-Morris' trial. Harry was reasonably confident that, as a serving Security Service officer, Mr Rose's discretion could be guaranteed, but what if Huxley wasn't talking nonsense? A few moments earlier Harry would have said Huxley had it all wrong if he thought that Sir Robert could, in any way, be involved in Veronica's death. The mention of Anna Slowik's name had changed all that. It wasn't that Harry felt Sir Robert could be involved, but if Veronica had discovered something about Slowik, and he couldn't think how else Huxley would have come up with the name, that changed things. Sir Robert had said she was in danger. Had Veronica unwittingly become involved in something sinister? Something that had led to her death? But how?

There was also the fact that Sir Robert was, quite clearly, prepared to take unsanctioned, unilateral action to protect Slowik. He owed it to her, he had said, for something that had happened in Berlin. There was clearly more to his association with Anna Slowik than had been disclosed. What if the facts did indeed cast some doubt upon Sir Robert's past?

Harry could see a real problem on the horizon. What if Huxley's defence relied upon Slowik? Given that Quinton had been allowed off the hook to preserve her anonymity, Harry had little doubt that Huxley would be thrown to the wolves if it were deemed to be in the national interest.

'If I might just say.' Harry was looking at Mr Rose. 'Miss Slowik…' Harry was struggling to find a suitable form of words. 'Miss Slowik's name is not to be bandied about. Her file is classified at the highest level.' He wasn't sure how Rose would react.

'Perhaps then, Mr Nevile, I should ask you to leave the room.'

Harry shot him a quizzical glance.

'Do you have the highest level of security clearance? You must appreciate that my duty in this instance is to establish the truth. In order to do this, I need to hear everything. If that requires Mr Huxley to discuss Miss Slowik, then so be it. If that will compromise your integrity in some way, then perhaps you should leave the room.'

'Mr Rose, I am Mr Huxley's senior officer; it is *my* duty to be here.'

Although he didn't say so, Harry had been a little taken aback by Rose declaring he was present to establish the truth. Not to defend Huxley, whose innocence Harry had taken for granted.

'Please, just listen to what I have to say.'

Huxley, who had little patience at the best of times, succumbed to the stress of his own doubts and worries and gave voice to what he was thinking. 'Mr Rose this. Mr Nevile that. I don't need this. We're all on the same side here. Or are we?'

The tone of voice made Harry realise that Huxley had probably had even less sleep than he had himself. It was getting too tense. A confrontation between himself and Mr Rose was not in Huxley's best interests. Harry apologised, saying he had never meant to doubt Mr Rose's integrity and added, more pointedly than he had intended, that he was sure the truth would confirm Huxley's innocence.

Harry could see that Huxley, too, had been stung by Rose's declaration about seeking the truth. He knew that the strain of keeping himself under control, being polite for the last thirty-six hours, would have taken its toll on Huxley's emotions. It came as no surprise that what little remained of Huxley's self-restraint finally crumbled.

'Of course I'm fucking innocent! Jesus Christ! I couldn't kill anyone. Especially her. I've not been charged with anything, just helping them with their bloody enquiries. But nobody is listening to me, you are all too busy telling me what to do or worrying about bloody protocol.'

Huxley collapsed into an armchair, his head in his hands and tears, finally, streaming down his face.

What happened next took Harry completely by surprise. Mr Rose squatted down in front of Huxley and took him by the wrists, pulling his hands away from his face.

'James, look at me. We've been protecting you. *I've* been protecting you. We also have to protect the Service. Mrs Blakeridge is, or rather was, an officer in the Service. The police have their job to do, but much as they might wish it otherwise, knowing our business isn't part of that. We didn't really get the chance to talk yesterday, and I didn't know if there were things we could not discuss with them present. It was clear they had no evidence against you, and the easiest option was simply to let them run out of time. My job was to make sure your right to remain silent was not abused. Trust me, others are working with the police, but not at ground level. You won't be going back to Lewisham, but in order to ensure that, we – I – now have the job of finding out exactly what has been going on.'

Rose glanced up at Harry, who, recognising the compassion on his colleague's face, just nodded.

'Now, my name is Rose, Michael Rose. Just call me Michael.'

Huxley lifted his head, looked into Rose's eyes and smiled. There was a sort of half-laugh in his voice.

'Huxley, call me Huxley. Nobody calls me James.'

CHAPTER 9
Day three: Wednesday

It was almost two hours later when Harry and Michael Rose left the secure flat. Huxley had been open and honest, and much of what he had said had settled several of Harry's suspicions.

Huxley had explained that last year, on the afternoon after Quinton was detained, he had visited Perdika on the slim chance that Veronica had fled there. She had once said to him, "It's one of those places where you can escape. You know, leave the world behind". His hunch had been correct. When she had told him her story, the story that had been on the computer disk she had asked Huxley to post anonymously to Harry, it hadn't brought the episode to a conclusion. Huxley hadn't wanted it to, and he was overwhelmed by the fact that Veronica didn't seem to want it to either. The feelings that Huxley had for her, had always had for her, blossomed, and they had stayed in touch. Much to Harry's surprise, he learned that Huxley had even visited her on the island of Aegina a couple of times. It wasn't the only thing that Harry had learned.

* * *

In a very strange twist of fate, given the ambiguous nature of Rod Graham's death, Veronica had been his sole heir.

Graham's parents were dead, his wife had divorced him many years earlier and there had been no children. As the only legitimate daughter of Graham's cousin, Veronica had inherited his estate. She had wanted none of it. Especially his house on Aegina, the house he had bought to taunt her mother, to make it difficult for her to see the daughter she had borne as a teenager before meeting Veronica's father. A daughter adopted by a Greek couple and whom her mother had kept secret until her husband's death. Veronica had decided to sell the house and give the proceeds to a deserving cause. Probably, she had thought, the only good that would ever come out of Graham's tainted life.

It was whilst clearing the house that she had come across the files. Some of the names on the files were familiar to her: Susan Horne – her mother, Quinton Bickley-Morris, Robert Hamilton, Harry Nevile. Years of intimidation had taught Veronica that these files would contain nothing but vitriol and Graham's distorted view of the world. Opening them, she knew, would be a mistake. The only decent thing to do was to burn them. Veronica already had a fire burning in the garden, incinerating everything that reminded her of Graham. Her hands were trembling as she started tossing the files into the fire, and she had dropped one of them. A photograph had fallen out in the process. Throwing the remaining files onto the fire, she had stooped to pick up the last one, and one of the figures in the photograph seemed familiar. Without thinking, she had turned it over and read on the back *Robert Hamilton with his controller/mistress Anna Slowik. Berlin, 1963.* Turning it back over, she looked again. A couple standing next to each other, about to board what looked like an underground train. The man, who she now recognised as a younger Robert Hamilton, was looking towards the camera as though something had just caught his attention. When she had looked more closely, it seemed as though the woman had her hand in the pocket of the man's overcoat.

She had kept the file. Knowing she would be coming to London soon, she had told Huxley about it. Wanting his advice on whether she should destroy it or whether there might be some substance to the allegations. Graham, she knew, was adept at using information against people, but as far as she was aware, he did not fabricate a story. He may have twisted and distorted the reality of a situation, but there had always been an element of truth that his victims could not deny.

Veronica was taking a flight from Athens, arriving home mid-afternoon, and Huxley had decided to surprise her at her house. That was why he was there. The problem was that a man had been seen entering the house, and a man had been seen walking away. Different witnesses, descriptions sufficiently vague that it could have been Huxley. There had been a delay between Huxley leaving the house and calling the police. He had been shocked and disoriented and hadn't been focused on looking for a telephone box. The police were suggesting that, realising he had been seen leaving, Huxley had been using that time to concoct his story.

As Michael Rose had pointed out, the police had no evidence against Huxley. No one disputed that the circumstances surrounding Veronica's death were unclear, but she had been a serving Security Service officer. The truth needed to be established, and isolating Huxley in a secure flat ensured his testimony could not be contaminated by others.

Downstairs, in the entrance hall of the covert MI5 offices, Harry and Michael Rose had been planning their next meeting with Huxley.

'There's one thing that puzzles me,' Harry had begun, 'and that is why they arrested him rather than just detaining him for questioning.'

Harry never got an answer as the desk guard had approached them.

'Mr Nevile. An urgent message from Brigadier Newcomb. He asks that you return to Tufton Street without delay.'

Harry recognised Nicholas' formal title and was a little perturbed. He had already told Nicholas of his intention to go directly to the mortuary to identify the body. An unwanted and unpleasant task, but one he knew he should not put off.

'Did he say why?'

'I'm afraid not, sir.'

Harry cast a look in the direction of the direct access from the premises into the Tufton Street offices, but the guard shook his head and glanced at Mr Rose. Clearly, Michael Rose was not to be made aware of the access, which Harry thought a little odd. If one knew about the Tufton Street offices and these premises at the rear, it was hardly a great conjecture to assume that the two were connected. Harry knew there was little point in debating the matter.

A few minutes later, as Harry closed the blue outer door to Tufton Street, his concern grew as Nicholas overrode the elaborate security system. Something serious must have happened in his absence.

'Nicholas, what is it?'

'It's Mrs Blakeridge, sir.'

'Veronica?' Harry wondered what on earth could be so urgent that he had been asked to return to base. 'What about her?'

'She is upstairs, sir.'

CHAPTER 10

Day three: Wednesday

Harry bounded out of the lift, his face lit with a huge grin. Veronica was alive.

Whatever Harry had been expecting, it was not a quiet, empty office. He could see three people through the frosted bands of the meeting room's glass wall. Two, whom he took to be Veronica and Ben Chowdhury, his computer analyst, were seated opposite each other at the desk. Margaret was standing by the door. Andrew and Thomas, the other two members of the group, affectionately known as the Disciples, were in the back office, serious looks on their faces.

Before Harry had time to take this all in, he was halfway across the room.

'Veronica. Am I pleased to…'

Margaret had turned as Harry began to speak and shook her head, warning him that all was not well.

Harry reached the entrance to the meeting room. Veronica was sitting at the desk, her back to him, her head in her hands, sobbing. Ben had his hand on her arm, trying to comfort her. Margaret took Harry by the arm and led him back into the office. She spoke quietly, bringing Harry's euphoria crashing down.

'The body, the one that Huxley saw. She thinks it might be her cleaner. She's upset. She feels responsible.'

Harry had been so pleased to hear the news that Veronica

was upstairs, which meant she was alive, that it hadn't registered with him that there was still the matter of a body that had been found in her house. He also expressed some surprise that Veronica had a cleaner, but Margaret explained.

'She was coming back to the UK, and the place had been empty for the best part of a year. It needed a spruce up. Especially as she was planning to put the house on the market.'

'And does she know about Huxley? His arrest?' Harry guessed that she also planned on spending some more time with her former colleague.

'Yes, she does. She says it wasn't him.' Margaret's voice then took on a more perplexed tone. 'Harry, she says Hamilton is behind this. Sir Robert Hamilton.'

It was the second time in the space of a few hours that Harry had heard that accusation. Deep down, he was certain it couldn't be true, but at the back of his mind there was a niggling doubt. Sir Robert, himself, had unsettled Harry with the conversation they'd had two days earlier. The choice between grace and disgrace, the Tufton Street team being deployed elsewhere, and the suggestion of taking unofficial action to protect Slowik. That very morning, it had also been confirmed to him that the Tufton Street team wouldn't just be deployed elsewhere; the team would be disbanded. If that was not bad enough, this depressing information had been followed up, twice now, by the claim that Hamilton, the man who had recruited him into the Security Service, had himself been recruited by the East Germans. By Anna Slowik, perhaps? It would certainly be a reason why he might be prepared to sacrifice his career to protect her.

It can't be true, surely. He wouldn't kill to protect Slowik?

63

To protect his former mistress? To protect himself?

Harry had been warned that a time might come when he had to make a choice. It seemed that the time had come. If there was one thing Harry was certain of, it was that Sir Robert would not have taken him into his confidence unless there was some hidden truth, a truth that would explain everything, why Harry's world was being turned upside down and shaken apart.

The choice, Harry realised, was whether to trust his friend and mentor when the evidence against him was beginning to mount. It was clear to Harry that the only way to choose was to discover the truth, and there may be those who would try and obstruct him in that. Hopefully, he would not have to take unsanctioned action himself, unless it was the only path available to determine what was fact and what was conjecture. With that resolve, he nodded to Margaret and went into the meeting room.

'Veronica. I'm so sorry.'

Ben stood up. 'Perhaps I should leave.'

Harry motioned for him to stay. 'I don't know what's going on, but I'm going to need you all if we're to sort this mess out.'

It seemed to have taken Veronica a few moments to register that Harry had joined them, but as soon as she did, there was only one question she wanted to ask.

'Where's Huxley?'

The reassurances that Harry gave her that Huxley was OK, being well cared for, but being kept in a secure location, did little to ease Veronica's distress.

'I need to be with him. Tell me, what's happened to him?'

Margaret and Ben had already given her the bare bones

of the circumstances of Huxley's arrest, but they knew no real details either. Harry gave them all a summary of the discussions he'd had at the police station and his meeting with Huxley that morning, though he couldn't reveal that the secure flat was above their heads, on the top floor of the Tufton Street building.

Veronica butted in. 'I don't understand. If he's innocent, why is he still being detained? He has rights, you know.'

'I can understand your concern,' Harry began again, 'and I know you've grown close.' Margaret and Ben looked at him and then at each other. This was a surprise to them. 'But this is standard procedure. Even though the police have released him, there are still questions to be asked. In these circumstances, you know, a...' Harry stopped himself from saying "murder". 'Well, in such circumstances, you know, a serious crime, it would be quite usual for the police to seek a magistrate's warrant to keep a suspect for up to ninety-six hours. His current location is preferable to a police cell. We're looking after him—'

'Well enough?' Veronica snapped.

Sensing that Veronica's distress could prove to be a barrier, alienating her even further from the team she had been an integral part of, Margaret spoke up.

'I think we need to hear Ron's side of the story, don't you?'

'Yes, starting with why you disappeared so suddenly.'

Ben had voiced what most of the team had been wondering about for quite some time. Harry had told them that he understood she was safe and well looked after, but he didn't expect her back. He had not disclosed what was on the disk that had been sent to him, the story that Huxley had so recently told to Michael Rose.

It was Veronica's turn to put her hand on Ben's arm.

'Graham had been blackmailing me. It was over something he had forced my mother to do. I needed to get away.' Veronica paused, though it was clear that Margaret's intervention had been successful. The tension between Veronica and Harry had evaporated. 'It's going to sound strange, but I went to the one place that I suspected was his bolt hole. I have family there.'

Harry noted the look of surprise on Ben's face and he guessed that, like most of the team, Ben thought she was an only child whose parents had both died.

Veronica smiled. 'It's a long story, but I thought that if I found him there...' She wondered how best to describe her feelings. 'If I could find him there, then somehow, I could help. You know, help in getting him arrested. Then he was killed.'

It was obvious from the look on Veronica's face that there was something about Graham's death that troubled her. She put her head in her hands, her fingers pressed against her eyes, clearly struggling with her emotions. After a minute or two, she seemed to pull her thoughts together.

'To cut a long story short, it turned out I was his only living relative. He had a house there, on the island. Things need sorting out. Anyway, I found some files, most of which I burned. Without reading. Didn't want to know. Then I dropped one and recognised a photograph of Sir Robert Hamilton. Younger then but unmistakable.'

She looked briefly at Harry, who nodded to indicate she should continue, holding nothing back.

'The file suggested that Robert Hamilton had been

recruited by the East Germans. Years ago. When he was in Berlin. I thought I ought to bring it over here, show Huxley. Decide what was best to do.'

Ben was puzzled. 'Why Huxley?'

Veronica gave him another smile and squeezed his arm. 'Oh, Ben. That day, in Aegina, when Quinton was arrested. Huxley came to find me. Since then, it's as Harry said, Huxley and I have become quite close.'

Veronica continued her narrative, explaining that she had decided to sell her house. Even though she wasn't sure if she would stay in the UK or return to Greece, the house brought back too many memories. It had been her parents' former home and reminded her of the dark shadow Graham had cast over her mother and herself. She had taken an early morning flight and planned to meet Huxley at her house, later in the day.

It had been a dreadful journey. The flight had been delayed by almost an hour, and then there had been an issue with unloading the bags – some kind of problem with the cargo hold door. When she eventually arrived home, the road was sealed off with police tape, and people in white Tyvek suits were coming out of her house. Clearly, some sort of crime had taken place. At first, she had assumed it was a burglary; somehow Hamilton must have found out about the files and had been looking for them. Identifying herself, she realised, could put her in danger if Hamilton found out she was in London.

Harry interrupted her, asking how many people knew about the files. When she said only herself, Huxley and her sister, Eliana, not even the rest of the family in Aegina, Harry pointed out that it was unlikely Hamilton was aware that the files existed. He didn't voice the thought, but he felt certain the files were not genuine; some kind of a plot to incriminate Sir Robert. Veronica agreed it was unlikely, pointing out she had been tired from the flight, stressed by being late and worried about what to do. She hadn't really been thinking straight; she just wanted to get hold of Huxley. When she couldn't contact him, she had panicked. She had phoned Huxley's house several times, but there was no reply. Her instinct had been to go round to Huxley's house, but then she'd had second thoughts. It was unlikely Hamilton was aware that Huxley knew about the files, but if she went to his house, would she put him in danger?

'Where are the files? Now?'

It was obvious to Harry that Veronica didn't have the dossier with her, but it was clearly going to be key to any investigation Harry carried out. There was an ongoing police investigation, and Veronica would have to be interviewed by the police; that much was clear. The question was, how much should the police be involved in any wider investigation? If there were issues relating to a Security Service senior officer, they were not for investigation by the police. On a practical level, if someone had killed her cleaner, thinking it was Veronica, then clearly, she was at risk, and the police could do little to protect her. The bottom line was that she was one of his team, despite her disappearance. Harry had a choice to make. Difficult though the choice that Sir Robert had suggested may be coming Harry's way promised to be, this was far more challenging. If Slowik truly was in danger, then the threat was likely to be from within the intelligence community. Who else would know about her? Was that the real message that Hamilton had wanted to convey? A forced retirement, the closure of the Tufton Street office, disbanding of the team; could these be indicative of a high-level cover-up?

Harry didn't want to consider the alternative: that Sir Robert Hamilton was, and had been for some time, a double agent working for the Stasi. Now causing confusion to cover his own back? As much as Harry could not believe that was true, he knew it was a possibility that had to be investigated.

'Veronica. Where is this document?'

Veronica hadn't brought anything to Tufton Street with her. She had been unsure of the reception she would receive. The dossier was in her luggage, left at the hotel where she had spent the night. She was due to collect it before 4:00 that afternoon. Harry's brain clicked into gear.

Regardless of whatever the files would reveal, because of what had happened at Blackheath, Veronica's safety was the number one priority. Harry lacked the authority to requisition a safe house or the additional security that would be required. Sir Robert could, but not only was he no longer in charge of the team, Nicholas had said he was uncontactable. It hadn't been made clear to Harry who was now in charge of the group; however, it was clear that a safe house was not an option. Awkward though it was, Harry knew that Veronica would refuse any option that involved Sir Robert himself. It was a case of telling the truth but not the whole truth, and Harry told the people in the room that, given the circumstances, he could hardly approach Sir Robert, and he could not see how he could arrange some form of protection for Veronica at short notice. It was Margaret who solved the dilemma, simply by insisting that Veronica should spend the night at her house. Who would know, apart from the people currently in the meeting room? Ben reminded her that, just in case it was known Veronica was at Tufton Street, they would need to ensure she wasn't being followed. He was happy to help there and to pick up her luggage if necessary. Harry would be too obvious.

Harry's next concern was identifying the body. Now that he knew it wasn't Veronica, there was little point in his attending the mortuary that afternoon. When he asked Veronica how well she knew her cleaner, he was relieved to discover she had never actually met her. A neighbour had made all the arrangements for her. Harry could spare her the ordeal of identifying the body; it would be sufficient to pass on the details to the police. The lady's disappearance was likely to have been reported to the police already, though it was too soon for them to have opened a formal case. It was not lost on Harry that he would have to inform the police that he had been in contact with Veronica, but at least the Met were more likely to respect his confidentiality than the somewhat antagonistic officers he had met at Lewisham. With luck, they would accept his word that he had been in contact with Mrs Blakeridge, that she was alive, and that the only person known to have been in the house was her cleaner. Veronica's neighbour would be able to provide more details to help the police establish whether the deceased lady was indeed Veronica's cleaner. The police, he knew, were aware that Huxley had visited the house in Blackheath in order to meet Veronica. That may be a complication, but Huxley's presence had been perfectly innocent. At some point, the police would need to interview Veronica, but hopefully, he could delay that for a day or two, buying time to establish more of the facts. Given that she may have been the intended victim of the murder, he could claim that Veronica was in the protective custody of the Service. Though not official, it was not untrue.

That was when it struck Harry. Sir Robert had warned him there was a time coming when he would have to make a difficult choice, and it seemed that now he was making that choice. He was choosing to ignore official channels and protocols. Harry really needed to speak with Sir Robert, but was he still an active member of the service? That hadn't been made clear to Harry earlier in the day. He certainly couldn't tell Veronica of his intention; if he did, she would bolt. He wasn't even sure about how much he could or should tell his, now, former boss. He would decide that later. Difficult as it was proving to get in contact with Sir Robert, Harry was certain that, if it was necessary to get a message to him, Nicholas would know how.

A plan was put together – hardly a perfect plan, but under the circumstances, one that would have to suffice. Ben, who would pick up Veronica's luggage, would leave the office shortly after Margaret and Veronica, and follow them to St James's underground station, checking that no one else was following them. Margaret and Veronica would do a full circuit of the Circle Line, changing trains once or twice just in case they were being followed and meet up with Ben again to pick up the luggage before going to Margaret's house. Harry had felt a bit guilty, as his unease about Veronica staying with Margaret had been borne of concern for Margaret's safety. She had, however, advised him that following the attack on her in the street, almost a year ago, her home security was now second to none.

CHAPTER 11

Day three: Wednesday

Matthew Kilsdale was considering his options. It wasn't as though he was spoilt for choice: he had very few.

His first thoughts on seeing the police presence in Blackheath had been that Bickley-Morris was not the only person interested in the documents. Potentially, there was another party. Perhaps there had been a burglary. Once he had begun to calm down, he realised that such a heavy response had to signal something more serious than a burglary. There had even been an ambulance in the road. When Bickley-Morris had phoned him, demanding to know exactly what had happened, it only confirmed his suspicions. The following day, he had returned to Blackheath, not to visit the house – he knew that was too risky – but to buy both the local and City newspapers. That was when he learned that a woman's body had been found in the house.

Matthew had understood that the person who would meet him there was a man. It was possible, he had argued to himself, that the woman had been a would-be thief, searching for the same documents. Bickley-Morris' man had turned up – or had been there already – and whatever had ensued, the woman had been killed. It wasn't an explanation that satisfied him – too much of a coincidence.

Hector Alexander, he knew, was just an alias, though one that Bickley-Morris had continued to use. Why continue to hide his identity? There was only one reason, and that was to ensure Matthew could not identify him. Then a more sinister thought entered his head. Bickley-Morris had never specified exactly what it was that he was to look for. Matthew had assumed that was why there was to be an accomplice – someone who knew what Graham had taken from the man he now thought of as Quinton Bickley-Morris rather than Hector Alexander.

What if there were no documents? What if Bickley-Morris was setting him up? Framing him for murder? He arrives at the house. There is no accomplice, just a dead body. Had the intent been to photograph him entering and leaving the house? Or worse still, for Matthew to be found at the house with the body? It was quite likely that Bickley-Morris had contacts within the police. After all, he had known Graham, and Matthew doubted Graham was the only bad apple in the Metropolitan Police force.

Why had the police been there when he arrived? He had been late, but not that late. Only about twenty minutes or so, something he hadn't mentioned to Bickley-Morris. The fact that the police were there when he arrived meant they must have been alerted before he was due to arrive. There was no scenario that he could think of which explained that anomaly. Whichever way he looked at it, he was trapped. If Bickley-Morris had been trying to frame him, this would not be the end of the matter. If what had happened was somehow unconnected with his visit, Bickley-Morris would still want his documents. There was no way he would give up or let Matthew off the hook, and Matthew had no intention of returning to Blackheath to look for documents, or anything else for that matter. It would be asking for trouble.

There was another scenario that troubled him, even though it didn't quite fit with what had happened. What if he had been the intended victim and there had been some sort of awful mistake?

The only option he could think of was to contact the two MI5 officers who had initially posed as police officers at DCM Diagnostics. They had shown him photographs of Bickley-Morris and Rod Graham, linking them both to the possibility of a terrorist attack. They had also threatened to link Matthew and his fellow directors to the plot if they didn't co-operate. The names they had used were Superintendent Hamilton and Sergeant Neville, possibly not their true identities, but something Rod Graham had said suggested their names, if not their titles, were authentic. Matthew recalled Graham's boast that the person who had tipped him off had been "one of Hamilton's own". He also recalled Graham speaking disparagingly about a Robert Hamilton. When Bickley-Morris had talked about the files Graham had stolen, he had said, "She must have them". She. The body was that of a woman. There was a good chance that "she" had been the same person who had tipped off Graham. One of Hamilton's team. It seemed likely that the bogus Superintendent Hamilton had been using his own name, even if his police rank was an alias.

It had been obvious back then that Hamilton had Bickley-Morris on his radar as a suspected terrorist, and now Matthew could tell him that one of his own team had been working for Graham. And it appeared likely that "she" had files which would incriminate Bickley-Morris. Hamilton would have to listen to him. Of course, Hamilton might also search the house in Blackheath, and if he found the files, it would get

Bickley-Morris off his back. For the moment at least. It would be even better if the stolen files really did contain information that could lead to Bickley-Morris' arrest and imprisonment. Kilsdale would be free of him.

Chapter 12

Day three: Wednesday

It was quiet in the Tufton Street front office. Margaret, Veronica and Ben had left, and all Harry could do was hope that they were being overcautious. Harry needed to talk with Sir Robert Hamilton. They hadn't been in contact since their clandestine meeting two days ago. Harry wondered if Sir Robert knew of the death in Blackheath and Huxley's arrest. He could not know that Veronica wasn't the victim, nor that she had been to Tufton Street. Not unless Nicholas had somehow updated him. It was certain that Sir Robert would not be aware of Veronica's assertion that she thought he was a traitor. Now he had to decide how much to tell his friend and senior officer. Harry did not believe for one minute that Sir Robert could be a Stasi mole, but he knew he had to look at the evidence objectively. Perhaps that part of the story could wait until tomorrow when he had seen the contents of Graham's file. There was, after all, the not insignificant matter of the conversation, if that was the right word, with Francis Buckingham. Could it really have only been that morning? It had been quite some day, and Harry suspected it might not be over.

A quick glance told him that Andrew and Thomas were working at their desks in the back office. He could make the call from his desk; no need to use the phone in the meeting room. Harry dialled Sir Robert's direct line and was greeted by the monotonous sound of the number-unobtainable tone. *Time to talk to Nicholas.*

As Harry exited the lift, Nicholas intercepted him.

'I have taken the liberty, sir, of advising the police.'

Caught off guard, Harry gave Nicholas a questioning look.

'About Mrs Blakeridge, sir. Not being the victim.'

'Thank you, Nicholas, I'll have to advise them that it's likely the body is that of Veronica's cleaner. I have some information upstairs.'

'Leave that to me, sir, just give me the details. I assume, sir, that you will not be visiting the mortuary to identify the body.'

Harry mouthed, rather than spoke, 'No', shaking his head as if to confirm his intent.

'I will let them know that too, Mr Nevile. The police do, of course, wish to interview Mrs Blakeridge, but they have agreed to wait until tomorrow.'

Harry expressed surprise that the police didn't think it was a matter of urgency, and the concierge explained that he had told the police that there were concerns that Veronica may indeed have been the intended victim.

Harry smiled. 'My thoughts, exactly.' It was almost as though Nicholas had read his mind, and Harry wasn't sure whether that surprised him or not.

'I told them we are keeping her under our protection whilst we debrief her fully,' Nicholas added.

'Are they aware that she visited her house yesterday but failed to contact the local police?'

'I told them that Mrs Blakeridge has been away and that, on discovering the police cordon at her home, she had come here. As would be appropriate for an officer on leave. I may

77

have forgotten to mention that it was yesterday when she went to Blackheath. Besides, sir, my contact at the Met is… How might I put this? Empathetic? Understanding? She was one of my junior officers. Before I joined the Service, that is. Done rather well for herself.'

'Thank you, Nicholas. I couldn't have done better, though perhaps it's stretching the truth a little to say she was an officer on leave.'

Nicholas smiled. 'Oh, I never said Mrs Blakeridge was on leave, sir. I just mentioned that it would be appropriate behaviour for an officer on leave.'

When it came to telling the truth, nothing but the truth, but not quite the whole truth, there were few as skilled as Nicholas.

Harry brought the conversation back to the reason he had come down to the lobby. 'I need to discuss all of this with Sir Robert. His phone at Thames House seems to have been disconnected.'

'Already,' Nicholas whispered, as though to himself. It was rare for Nicholas to be caught unprepared, but it told Harry something he was dreading.

'I assume there would be little point in my going to his office.'

Nicholas recovered his composure. 'No, sir, I suspect there would not.'

Harry did not respond. He could tell Nicholas was deciding what to tell him, though Harry had little doubt that it would not be everything he knew. What had been Sir Robert's parting words? "Trust what you know to be true." Nicholas was a good, honest and reliable servant of the Crown, Harry had no doubts about that. Nicholas would tell him what he could, beyond that, Harry would have to trust him.

'I think it is probably fair to say Sir Robert has taken a leave of absence.'

From the way that Nicholas had said "taken", Harry was certain that this was what Sir Robert had meant when he had said, "I may have to take some action. Action that may not be sanctioned".

'And there is no way of contacting him… directly?'

'No, sir. Not *directly*.'

Nicholas' inflection told Harry there was almost certainly a way of making contact, *in*directly. A way that was equally certain to be via Nicholas.

Harry looked Nicholas straight in the eye. 'Well, if he were to find out about the events of today, I would be happy to discuss them with him.'

There was no need to say anymore; Nicholas understood.

'You have had a busy day, sir. Why not take the opportunity to go home? It's almost four o'clock, and I don't think anything else will be happening here today. If we need to contact you, we'll ring you at home.'

Harry wondered if that meant Sir Robert would be in touch later that evening, but the phone call he did get was not the one he had been expecting.

Harry had taken Nicholas' advice and left early, something that would have rung alarm bells with Margaret or Huxley, had they been in the office. It was a little early for him to start cooking his dinner, so he decided to sit, listen to the radio to catch up on events elsewhere that day, then put some music on and try to figure out what was going on. It wasn't just the disturbing news about the future of the Bioweapons Counter-Espionage Unit that was bothering him, nor his

79

anxiety about what Veronica's file might contain. There was something about Veronica's story that was troubling him. He had barely settled in his armchair, and the strings had just taken up the melody a few minutes into the music, when the phone rang. It was Nicholas.

'Thought I should let you know, sir. The pathologist has completed his initial report.'

Harry's mind went back to the body that had been found in Blackheath. 'Yes?' he said cautiously, wondering what had been found that might cause Nicholas to phone him.

'The lady had a condition known as ARVC, sir.'

Harry was none the wiser and asked Nicholas to explain.

'The full name, I believe, sir, is arrhythmogenic right ventricular cardiomyopathy.' Despite feeling no further explanation was really necessary, Nicholas added, 'A heart condition, though I imagine that is obvious to you.'

'Yes. Thank you, Nicholas, though I have no idea what the condition is. Does it mean the unfortunate lady… died of natural causes?'

It seemed a strange term to use for what was clearly a heart condition that may be natural, but hardly an unremarkable or common cause of death.

'That, sir, is not clear. Apparently, it is a weakening of the heart muscle. Overexertion can bring about a heart attack, but so-called "sudden deaths" are not unknown.'

Harry's mind was running through the possibilities. 'Could a shock, or perhaps fleeing an assailant, be a cause of death, do you think?'

'That, sir, I don't know. There are some test results awaited. Perhaps they will shed more light on the circumstances.'

Harry thanked Nicholas for letting him know. The

possibility of death by natural causes had to be good news for Huxley, though the uncertainty did not help. He switched off the CD player; he would return to the music again later. For the moment, however, it was time to cook his dinner.

As he took the defrosted beef medallions from the refrigerator, his thoughts went back to what was troubling him about Veronica's testimony. She had, apparently, been burning a number of documents, without reading any of them beforehand. Yet the one she dropped, the only one she dropped and the one she read, concerned Sir Robert. It was far from unknown for people to be caught out by slip-ups or accidental findings, matters of chance, but to Harry's mind, it still seemed a bit of a coincidence. And Harry just did not like coincidences.

CHAPTER 13

Day four: Thursday

Back at his desk in Tufton Street the next morning, Harry's anxiety was exacerbated by his disappointment that Sir Robert had not been in touch. The rational part of his brain told him that there had hardly been enough time, and it was quite possible he had overinterpreted what Nicholas had said to him.

The truth was, he was still unsettled, but he was looking forward to a quieter morning. Margaret and Veronica would come in later; it seemed sensible for them to wait until the rush hour was over. That way, it would be easier to check if anybody was following them. Paradoxically, Ben, who would also not be in the office until later, had volunteered for an early start. He was taking the Tube out to Gunnersbury, one station closer to the city than Kew Gardens, Margaret's nearest station. The plan was for them all to try to catch the same train back into central London, having already agreed which part of the train they would be sitting in. It wasn't a cast-iron plan. It required Ben to be early and wait until he saw Margaret and Veronica in the penultimate compartment. He would then board and sit at the very end of the train. Margaret and Veronica would alight at Stamford Brook station and catch the next train through. Ben would do the same at Ravenscourt Park, then follow them on their ten-minute walk from St James's Park station to Tufton Street.

If the ladies failed to appear in a half-hour window, Ben was to call it in.

It was barely 9:20 a.m. when Nicholas rang Harry from the vestibule.

'It's Thames House, sir. They say there is a Mr Kilsdale insistent that he sees you.'

Nicholas explained that Matthew Kilsdale had turned up at the Millbank HQ asking for a Mr Robert Hamilton. On being told Mr Hamilton was unavailable, Kilsdale had asked for Hamilton's associate, Mr Neville. Looking in the staff directory, the security guard on reception had found a Harry Nevile operating from the same branch as Sir Robert Hamilton. Hence the call.

This confirmed to Harry that Sir Robert was indeed absent from his duties. Whatever was known about Sir Robert's absence from Thames House, Harry could only hope that there had been no flag on the system that escalated the enquiry to a higher level. The fact that the call had come through to Tufton Street on the switchboard number suggested that, for the moment at least, there was no general alert regarding Sir Robert's activities.

Harry recalled Kilsdale's name from his dealings with DCM Diagnostics Ltd, the investigation that had led to Quinton Bickley-Morris' detention. Something Harry was unlikely to forget. But what on earth could Kilsdale want? And today of all days, when Veronica was due to produce the file she had found. Alarm bells were going off inside Harry's head. There was too much happening in too short a space of time. Sir Robert's obscure warning, the body at Veronica's house, Huxley's detention. Veronica claiming she had a file that exposed Sir Robert as a traitor, and the accused, himself, being uncontactable since yesterday, his whereabouts unknown. The damning file had belonged to Rod Graham, and now, here was Matthew Kilsdale. There was no question that Kilsdale had been involved in Graham's suspect dealings, probably more so than he had ever admitted.

The circumstances of Graham's death had never been fully established. On the face of it, an accidental death, and that was what Harry was now thinking with regard to the death at Veronica's house. Were they accidental, or could they be connected in some sinister way? Two deaths and Matthew Kilsdale seeking out MI5; was it possible Kilsdale feared for his own life?

The timing could not have been worse, and meeting Kilsdale again was not something that appealed to Harry. Yet he knew he had no option, and he knew also that he had to keep it as low-key as possible. Stoking interest in a case that had been Sir Robert's, one that involved a terrorist threat and a former senior civil servant turned criminal, was probably not a good idea in the circumstances. Harry wanted some time to evaluate Veronica's file himself before deciding what to do.

Bringing a member of the public to Tufton Street was out of the question. Harry did his best to sound calm, disinterested even.

'Tell him I have somebody with me at the moment, and I'll be about twenty minutes, if Mr Kilsdale would care to wait. And perhaps find a vacant interview room. A cup of coffee too?'

Harry was committed and asked Nicholas to tell his team, when they arrived, that he had been called to Thames House at short notice. That, at least, Harry told himself, was true.

As Harry had hoped, Kilsdale had not been admitted to the main part of Thames House but had been shown to one of the interview rooms outside the secure zone. Many thought of them as holding rooms rather than genuine interview rooms, but Harry was just grateful it would help keep his meeting low-key.

'Good morning, Mr Kilsdale. I understand you wish to speak with me.'

'And your colleague Mr Hamilton.'

'Sir Robert is unavailable at the moment. I'll have to do, I'm afraid.'

Harry had used Sir Robert's title deliberately. Partly to gauge how much Kilsdale might know and partly to try and put him on the back foot by emphasising Sir Robert's seniority. It had the desired effect; clearly, the knighthood was news to Matthew Kilsdale. Harry handed over his card, not that it bore any information other than Harry's name and the crown logo.

Harry took the seat behind the desk.

'What is it that you want to talk about?'

No more pleasantries, Kilsdale got straight to the point as his uncertainty gave way to bravado.

'I have information about your colleague's murder.'

'Murder, Mr Kilsdale? I'm not aware that any of my colleagues have been murdered?'

Kilsdale was in no mood for playing games. He didn't want to be talking to MI5; it was only his fear of what Bickley-Morris might do that had brought him there. Anxiety overcame him; the dam burst, and he was riding on a wave of anger.

'Don't bullshit me, Nevile. Or whatever your name is.

85

Blackheath. Three days ago. Your colleague's house. It's in the newspapers.'

Harry was quite aware that the press had carried the news of the death in Blackheath, but Kilsdale had to have another source of information. It was the only way he could know whose house it was and that the owner was, or had been, one of his team. It wasn't clear if he knew Veronica's identity or the reason why Veronica had returned to the UK. Harry didn't reply. He let Kilsdale's exasperation reveal what else he knew.

'I was told she was away. He tried to set me up. I know who did it.'

'And you're going to tell me? Or is there something you want in return?'

'I want that bastard off my back. In jail. Where he belongs.'

'And who is "that bastard", Mr Kilsdale?'

Harry was going out on a limb, hoping that a combination of Kilsdale's anger and whatever need had brought him to Thames House would yield a name. It worked.

'Alexander, or Bickley-Morris, or whatever he calls himself. He's the one.'

Harry had had no idea what name Kilsdale might give him, but he certainly had not expected to hear the name Bickley-Morris. A thought flashed through Harry's mind. "A fiasco of a trial", Sir Robert had said. "Heads are going to roll." Something else that had been said in the same discussion came to mind: "Bickley-Morris would not have been acting alone". The fight was never-ending. No amount of arrests or deportations could fully eradicate the rot within. Quinton could still have contacts – contacts who would be only too happy to help him exact his revenge.

Harry listened to Kilsdale's version of events, comparing each aspect with what he had been told by Huxley. There was a file that Quinton wanted, one that Graham had stolen. Could it be the same file that Veronica had discovered? According to Kilsdale, Bickley-Morris had been sure that Graham had hidden the file before he fled to Greece. Harry knew that Graham had been coercing Veronica, and it was possible she had been pressured into hiding the document. Veronica claimed to have found her file of documents only recently, and Harry could think of no good reason why she should claim that if she knew the material was still in Blackheath. It could be a ploy, but if it was, that meant she had known about the file before she fled to Greece, and it was not the sort of file you would leave behind. If so, though, why hadn't she disclosed the fact earlier? Any threat of retribution from Graham had evaporated with his death, and disclosing the existence of the documents then, whether or not she was fully aware of the contents, would have substantiated her claim that she had been acting in fear of Graham. Harry could see where his argument was leading. Either Quinton was wrong about the documents – it was a lie, possibly to lure Kilsdale to the house – or Veronica had been acting in collusion with Graham. He hoped it was the former, but the similarity of Kilsdale's story to Veronica's claim made him very uncomfortable. Harry dragged his mind back to the current interview.

'Are you suggesting Mr Bickley-Morris was in the house and had killed… the occupant?'

'That's a strange thing to say. "Occupant?" She was one of Hamilton's team, just like you.'

It was obvious that Kilsdale was unaware of the structure of the team based in Tufton Street.

'It's an ongoing investigation, Mr Kilsdale. You've just admitted you were present at the house, so excuse—'

'Outside. I never went in. The police were there.'

'Excuse me for being cautious, Mr Kilsdale. This is a police matter, not a Security Service matter. I have to be careful—'

'Yeah. One of your people is murdered, and you just stand back and let the police get on with it. Oh, come on. I'm trying to help you here.'

Recognising that antagonising Kilsdale would not be helpful, Harry rephrased his question.

'Are you suggesting that Mr Bickley-Morris has committed murder?'

'No. Not Bickley-Morris. Oh, I don't know. Maybe. Maybe him. Maybe not. All I know is I was told to meet somebody there. Bickley-Morris doesn't do his own dirty work.'

That much is true, thought Harry, and it was clear that Kilsdale knew more about Quinton Bickley-Morris than he was admitting.

From what Huxley and Kilsdale had told Harry, it seemed that Kilsdale had arrived at the property about an hour to an hour and a half after Huxley. Sufficient time for an initial police attendance, with a full team being called in after confirming that there was a body. That fitted with what Harry had been told by Huxley and Veronica. Kilsdale had been told the house would be empty, apart from the unknown person he was to meet. Had this unknown third party or his actions brought about the death of the unfortunate lady? Whatever had unfolded at the house that afternoon, the presence of the cleaner would have been unexpected, and her death, most likely, unplanned. There was one option that could not be ignored. Had Quinton planned something rather unpleasant for Kilsdale? Perhaps he thought Kilsdale had betrayed him to save his own neck? But why Veronica's house? Some kind of bizarre plan, perhaps, to discredit Harry's team at the same time? Kilsdale could be linked to Harry via the investigation at DCM Diagnostics. Harry to Veronica. Veronica to Graham and then back to Kilsdale, or perhaps more importantly, the plot to attack the government at their party conference last year. Revenge against Sir Robert and Harry for Graham's death? For foiling the plot? Or simply for pressurising Bickley-Morris to hand himself over to the authorities? As the latter had claimed in court, the other option was an indeterminate stay in the notorious Korydallos Prison in Athens.

Kilsdale was claiming that Quinton had sent him to the house to retrieve a document, one stolen from Quinton, by Graham. Could it be the file that Veronica was now claiming exposed Sir Robert as an agent of East Germany? Could there be two files? If not, how could Quinton know Veronica had the file, or was planning to return to the UK? There was no option that made sense, and that troubled Harry.

And it wasn't the only thing. He needed to get back to Tufton Street. Veronica would have arrived by now with her file.

'Why not go to the police, Mr Kilsdale? If you have information relating to a murder and suspect Mr Bickley-Morris as being an accessory?'

'Yeah, right.' Kilsdale's anger was returning, and he

lapsed into a sarcastic rant. 'Oh, officer, I was just going along to burgle this house, but someone got murdered. It wasn't me, guv, honest. Happened before I got there.' They going to take me seriously when I tell them it was Bickley-Morris? Pat me on the head and say, "Thank you, you've been a great help, off you go now"? Come on, I'm not a bloody fool.'

An old proverb, one that was not unique to English, came to Harry's mind: "Tell me with whom thou goest, and I'll tell you what thou doest." Kilsdale had a point.

Harry realised he was unlikely to get anything more useful out of Kilsdale at the moment and decided it would be best to let him stew for a little longer. Hopefully, his anxiety would get the better of him, and he would come back prepared to give Harry some more information.

'Give me your contact details. I will look into it. No promises, though.'

'That's it? Your colleague's been murdered, and "No promises"? Have I wasted my fucking time?'

'No, Mr Kilsdale, you have not wasted your time. But I can't go charging into ongoing police investigations like a bull in a china shop. Bickley-Morris has already evaded one prosecution, we must be careful if we want to bring another.'

Kilsdale just stared at him.

'Even so, I would be failing in my duty if I did not advise you to go to the police. Not Lewisham.' Harry tore a page out of the small notebook he had and wrote down a name. He handed the piece of paper to Kilsdale. 'New Scotland Yard. Tell them that you've been talking to me.'

Harry doubted that Kilsdale would take his advice. A thought that was confirmed by Kilsdale shaking his head, as if in disbelief.

'I'm sorry, Mr Kilsdale. That's all I can offer for now. You have my contact details.'

Despite all the uncertainty about the events that had unfolded in Blackheath, Harry had picked up one piece of useful information. Matthew Kilsdale had just confirmed Huxley's claim that there had been a second person inside Veronica's house. A claim that, as far as Harry could tell, the police had discounted. As Kilsdale had just reminded him, Quinton was not in the habit of doing his own dirty work. There was an upside, however, if Kilsdale's claims were true, then it was unlikely that Veronica was in danger. Things were beginning to fit together. It seemed reasonable to assume that whoever had been in Veronica's house was there to meet Kilsdale and not to do harm to Veronica. That was consistent with what he had learned from Huxley: that very few people had known about Veronica's return to the UK.

Chapter 14

Day four: Thursday

'I'm afraid you have just missed them, sir.'

For a moment, Harry didn't register what Nicholas had just said. His mind was still grappling with the possibilities that his interview with Kilsdale had generated. Especially the assertion that Quinton Bickley-Morris was somehow involved in recent events.

'Sorry, Nicholas. My mind was elsewhere. Who have I missed?'

'Mr Huxley and Mrs Blakeridge, sir. They left about ten minutes ago. Mr Huxley is in need of some clean clothing.'

Harry struggled to grasp what Nicholas was saying, his mind alternating between the fact that Huxley must have been released and that Veronica had left without waiting for him.

'Erm, Hu… Huxley?'

'Yes, sir. Mr Rose arranged his release this morning. He came straight here. They will have asked him not to say where he has been staying.'

'Oh. Thank you, Nicholas. I'd better go upstairs then and see what's what.'

Harry still had not fully come to grips with what Nicholas had just said and, on his way across the lobby towards the lifts, he stopped and returned to Nicholas' desk.

'Mr Kilsdale. He claims that our friend Bickley-Morris

was somehow involved with what happened in Blackheath.'

It wasn't anything that Nicholas needed to know, but Harry was certain that somehow the message would be passed to Sir Robert Hamilton.

Nicholas's response was a simple nod. He understood why Harry had just imparted this piece of information.

In the solitude of the lift, Harry took a deep breath and composed himself. As the door opened and he stepped into the office, he saw Margaret at her desk. The fact that he dropped his coat over the back of his chair, rather than hanging it on the stand, told Margaret that whatever meeting Harry had been in at Thames House, it had been far from trivial. Harry spoke first.

'Well, it looks as though you've had a busy morning. I understand Veronica's left. Where does that leave us with the file?'

Margaret updated him on what he had missed. She and Veronica had looked at the damning file yesterday evening, and Veronica had brought it with her to Tufton Street. Whilst waiting for Harry, Huxley had turned up.

'I'm not sure how to put this,' Margaret said with a slightly embarrassed smile on her lips. 'Let's just say the reunion was – what shall we say? – as affectionate as it was unexpected?'

Harry couldn't resist a smile either.

'Are they coming back? And what about this file?'

'Yes, possibly later today, if not, then tomorrow. We've arranged an interview for her with the police, this afternoon. There's a lot to sort out.

'About the file, as I said, we looked at it yesterday evening. She wouldn't leave it, but don't worry, Ben has copied it to the computer somehow. With that new piece of equipment he has – the one Huxley calls his spanner.'

Harry smiled again. 'I take it you mean his scanner.'

'Yes, but tell me. Another visit to Thames House? Is there something we should know?'

Margaret might just as well have punched him in the head as the shock of what he had been told only yesterday, that the unit would be closed, hit him once again. Harry recovered quickly.

'I've just seen Matthew Kilsdale. You remember him?'

Harry had no need to add "from that DCM Diagnostics mouse plot". Margaret had not forgotten her visits to Pitsea and, though she had met only briefly with Matthew Kilsdale, she was quite aware of his nefarious dealings that had lined his own pockets at the expense of his colleagues.

'He's just told me Quinton is involved in the business at Veronica's house.'

Margaret's eyes widened in disbelief.

'Claims it has something to do with a stolen file,' Harry added.

'What the hell is going on, Harry?'

'That's what I intend to find out.' Harry nodded towards the small meeting room. Words were unnecessary.

'Shall I get Ben?'

'Yes. Please.'

Harry had taken the decision, yesterday, to involve both Margaret and Ben fully in investigating the death at Veronica's house. He was going to need his team. Whatever had happened, it was not a simple case of an unexpected death. Harry also recognised that he was going to have to be more open and honest with them than he had been so far.

Harry asked Ben to close the meeting room door. A sure sign that something very serious was about to be discussed.

'As you know,' Harry began, 'Ron has some information that casts doubt upon the integrity of Sir Robert Hamilton.' Even saying it made Harry uncomfortable. 'Before we take a look at it, there are a couple of things I need to say. Yesterday, we wondered if the unfortunate death at her house was in some way connected with the file she has brought with her. I now firmly suspect that is true.'

Harry held up his hand to stop both Margaret and Ben from interrupting. He had no doubt that Huxley's appearance had signalled that the police were inclined to the view that the death was due to a heart attack rather than something more suspicious.

'I know about the unfortunate lady's heart condition, but there's other information that I need to share with you.'

Harry outlined his meeting with Matthew Kilsdale that morning. The revelation that Kilsdale had implicated Quinton surprised Ben as much as it had Margaret and Harry.

'Do you believe him?' Margaret asked the question that was in Ben's mind as much as hers.

'I'm not sure, but he certainly has information that's not available to the public. But let's not lose sight of the fact that Kilsdale's account confirms Huxley's belief that there was another person in that house.'

'Quinton?' Ben and Margaret both spoke at the same time.

'I doubt it. As Kilsdale reminded me, Quinton does not do his own dirty work.'

Margaret was quick to pick up on the implication. 'Was Kilsdale the intended victim, then?'

Harry shrugged. 'It would explain why Kilsdale's running scared. There's one other thing. Both versions mention a file that Graham had. I think I need to see what Ron's file contains.'

Ben opened a folder he had with him and went to remove the contents, but Margaret stopped him.

'Harry, I'm not sure how much Ben has read, but there's a name in here. One that perhaps shouldn't be bandied about.'

'Slowik. I know. Huxley told me.'

Ben looked at them both. 'Who's Slowik?'

Harry knew that if he was to get Ben's full engagement, he could not hold back information. Slowik's name was in the file, that much Huxley had told him, albeit indirectly, so there would be no hiding it. He had thought long and hard the previous evening and had made his decision. He turned to face Ben, knowing he was almost certainly overstepping a boundary.

'What I'm about to tell you is known to very few. Parts of it, Huxley knows and may have told Veronica. The rest is not to be repeated.'

Harry explained that Slowik was a former high-ranking Stasi officer who, in the years following the war, had dealings with Quinton. She was the person who had confirmed he had indeed been an agent of the East German government, a traitor to the Crown. Both Margaret and Harry were aware that Slowik had defected to the UK a little over a year ago. Harry wasn't sure how much Huxley knew. Anna Slowik's name had come up, but Huxley had been told to forget it. Following the unification of Germany, she was not only an embarrassment to the new German government but was also at risk of prosecution. Her former Stasi colleagues still at

96

large viewed her as a potential threat, so whichever way she turned, she was *persona non grata*.

'There's something else you need to know, both of you. Sir Robert and I met a few days ago, and he was concerned that there are people seeking to harm Miss Slowik. I don't know if they're within the Service or not, but Sir Robert felt certain she was in danger. So much so that he was prepared to take unofficial action to protect her.'

'That suggests someone within—' Ben began, but Harry cut him short.

'Or has access to Service information. What I need to tell you is that I haven't been able to contact Sir Robert for a day or two now. Yesterday I was told he had taken a leave of absence.'

'But that means—' Margaret stopped herself. 'Ron has a file that says Sir Robert is, has been, working for the East Germans. He suggests he's going to take some unsanctioned action to protect Slowik, a Stasi officer. Someone is killed, dies, whatever, at Ron's house, where Quinton, at least, believes there's a file containing evidence against Sir Robert.'

Ben was quick on the uptake. 'And there's no love lost between Quinton and Sir Robert, so maybe he wanted to get to the file before anyone else.'

The implication had not been lost on Harry, but he pointed out the incongruences. Both Sir Robert and Quinton would need to know about the file and to think it was in Blackheath. Yet Veronica had only found the file in the past two weeks and, certainly, she had only brought it to the UK two days earlier, the day Huxley had spotted the body. Both would have to know Veronica's house was unoccupied and, even more unlikely, attempt to steal the file on the same day. Sir

Robert had known about Veronica's move to Greece and had colluded with Harry in keeping the fact confidential. Neither Sir Robert nor Quinton was likely to share intelligence with the other, which implied that a third party was involved. "Probability decreases as complexity increases" was one of Harry's well-known mantras.

Ben raised the possibility that if both were Stasi agents, they could have been working together, but quickly dismissed it. Even if they were, and bad blood had developed between them, why had Quinton not denounced Sir Robert when he was detained? The obvious answer was he didn't know, at least not until recently, if indeed he knew at all. If indeed, Sir Robert had in fact been working under cover for the Stasi.

'Or, of course, Quinton could be innocent,' Margaret added, but it was clear from her tone that she did not, for one minute, think it could be true.

Harry put a stop to the conversation. They were getting sidetracked. They simply did not have enough information to distinguish fact from conjecture, and Harry was keen to see what was actually in the file that Veronica had so curiously dropped.

Ben took out the contents of his folder and, whilst they examined it, Margaret summarised the discussion that had taken place between Veronica and herself the previous evening. The evidence was far from substantial. Most of the file was conjecture, typed in the main, and Ben was fairly certain that most of the documents had been printed from a computer, using an inkjet printer. That, he suggested, gave them a timeline, though quite a broad one, of the last ten years.

Some of the pages seemed to contain conclusions drawn by

the author, possibly Graham himself, and could be discounted as conjecture. What might be considered harder evidence was of two types. The first was various photographs showing two people in a city. There was one taken in an underground station. Even though the station's name was partly hidden by the couple, the distinctive lettering suggested a Berlin U-Bahn station. Harry recognised another of the photographs as the bridge where Friedrichstrasse crossed the River Spree. He couldn't remember its name, but it was one of the few bridges that had survived the bombing of Berlin. Margaret and Ben were puzzled by Harry's reaction to the photograph until he explained. It was a bridge in East Berlin.

They all agreed that the man was almost certainly a young Robert Hamilton, but only Harry had met Slowik face to face.

'Is the woman this Slowik lady? Has anybody actually met her?' Ben wasn't the only one wondering about the woman's identity.

'I met her once, briefly.' Harry was reluctant to admit it, but he had taken the decision to be open and honest. Both Margaret and Ben looked at him in surprise. Harry felt a little embarrassed. 'Last year,' he added, 'as I say, only briefly. She's much older now, of course.' He felt silly stating the obvious.

'And?' Margaret had known Harry long enough to tell when he was about to say something that made him feel uneasy.

'Yes. It could be. Something about the eyes.'

The second line of evidence was documentary. There was a photocopy of what appeared to be a log of dates and places. None of them understood enough German to fully understand the heading, but Harry, who had spent a couple of years working in Germany, thought it translated as log, or list, of meetings. They all recognised the name *Kapitän* Hamilton, and the phrase "*mit Kapitän* Hamilton" told them what the list was. Some of the dates had been highlighted on the copy. Another document, seemingly unofficial, was in English and titled "Suspects Escaping to East Berlin". It contained a list of German-sounding names, and a set of dates, some of which were also highlighted. The selected dates had corresponding entries in the German document, although these were generally a few days earlier. Ben drew the obvious conclusion.

'So Hamilton meets someone and, a couple of days later, a suspect flees to East Berlin. Sounds like Hamilton was passing information to the East Germans.'

'And Sir Robert takes a leave of absence as the evidence comes to light.' Margaret drew another obvious conclusion. '"Leave of absence?" A convenient euphemism, Harry? For what?'

Harry, too, was quite sure that "leave of absence" was a euphemism, not for the detention of Sir Robert, but for the fact that he had gone off the radar. An action that many would, no doubt, see as an admission of guilt. Once again, Harry was haunted by the warning he had been given in Victoria Square: "You may have to choose between what you're told and what you believe." The file seemed to condemn Sir Robert, and Sir Robert himself had implied he had indeed passed information to the East Germans. It may have been something which would be denied officially, but the implication had been that Sir Robert's actions in Berlin had been sanctioned. They were a matter of convenience. Something else Sir Robert had said that day came back to Harry: "I owe it to her...

She helped *us*." If there was a debt of honour to be paid, Sir Robert would not shy away from risking his own reputation. He would do what he felt was morally right, regardless of personal cost. Harry had no doubt that if Sir Robert was taking unsanctioned action, then he felt it was the only way he could protect Slowik; yet two things puzzled Harry. Had the intelligence services lost their own moral compass and been prepared to abandon Slowik when she was no longer of any use? And why, when Sir Robert had forewarned him, had he mentioned his activities in Berlin? He couldn't possibly have known about the dossier, could he?

'Harry?' Margaret brought him back to the matter at hand. 'Any idea what's going on?'

The truth was, he didn't know what was going on, so he had little hesitation in simply confirming that all he had been told was "a leave of absence". Ben asked if Slowik had taken a leave of absence too, but Harry reminded him that he had no way of knowing. Tufton Street had never been party to Slowik's debriefing and, officially, knew nothing of her defection.

'What about Huxley? What can we tell him?' It was typical of Margaret to think about the practicalities of working together and how difficult and divisive working in a small group on confidential matters could be.

'My meetings with Sir Robert and with Kilsdale, nothing. Same with Slowik, other than what's in this dossier.' Harry put his hand on the folder as if to remove any doubt. 'Veronica's read it, there's no further risk. But, as I've just said, this office is not aware, officially, of Slowik's existence, and we must respect that. The little that Huxley knows about Slowik is confidential – he knows that. As for Sir Robert...'

Harry paused as if reassessing his decision. 'Sir Robert's leave of absence is – whatever is going on – either official, or an official explanation at least. I suspect his absence has been noted and is the source of curious gossip in Thames House. I see no reason why we should keep it from Huxley.'

CHAPTER 15

Day five: Friday.

'He'll have to be dealt with. He's been talking to Nevile.'

'Who is this man Kilsdale?'

The two men strolling around the fountain in St Thomas' Hospital's riverside garden were oblivious to the crowds on the other side of the wall, taking their memento photographs of Parliament across the Thames.

'He's a nobody. A crooked director of that company Bickley-Morris used as a front out in Essex. Or rather, he was. Had a close shave with our friends in the Security Service. He was also in cahoots with that bent copper Bickley-Morris relied on. Since he... well... copped it, Kilsdale seems to have taken fright. Cut himself off from the company. Moved into one of those new developments – Poplar – Limehouse way.'

'A nobody? You're too slack, Reid, not sharp at all. Gives up his job, moves house. I dare say those new developments are expensive. I wonder how "a nobody" can afford to do that? Has he got friends? Connections? People who might come looking if something happened to him?'

'Quite the reverse, more likely. He was supposed to have been dealt with. That farce in Blackheath, I was hoping it would have done for Bickley-Morris and Nevile too, but the fat oaf fucked it up. Got in some useless cretin, ex-IRA supposedly. Irresponsible Reckless Amateur more like. Hit the wrong person. Kilsdale's probably wondering what was really planned. The fact that he went to Nevile yesterday makes him a liability. There's no knowing what ex-detective sergeant Graham told him. I don't know, as yet, what was discussed – that will have to wait for Mr "Do it by the Book" Nevile's report, but I doubt it was the price of potatoes. But you know what needs doing.'

Reid took a deep breath as if weighing up the options. 'And make sure the body's found, somewhere near Bickley-Morris' place.'

His companion, Tobias Tschesche, gave him a look that said, "Don't tell me how to do my business".

The two men paused for a moment, stopping to admire the view of Big Ben, caught through the eye of the fountain sculpture.

'Why not just take care of him directly? Your blunderbuss friend himself, Mr Bigotry-Morris, I mean. He's caused more than enough problems for you in the past few years.'

'Not for the moment, Tobias. In time, he'll have to pay. But I think our friends in MI5 might take care of him for us.'

Tobias looked questioningly, almost disbelievingly, at Reid, who continued.

'Bickley-Morris knows what will happen if he doesn't keep his mouth shut. That's why he told them nothing they didn't already know, whilst he was in detention. Kilsdale doesn't – that's why he's been talking. That's why we have to deal with him, but bodies attract attention in this country. Kilsdale's demise is a risk in itself, but if Bickley-Morris is taken out as well, that would only set off alarm bells. Almost certainly, Kilsdale has implicated Bickley-Morris in the Blackheath business, and that we can use. Even our friends in MI5 will see it as a motive for silencing Kilsdale. They can ensure the police take Bickley-Morris down for Kilsdale's demise. Especially with a little help. It won't take a lot to stitch him up, and we can focus on the real threat. Hamilton will never give up, especially now he's got Slowik.'

'They knew she'd come to the UK, that's why they sent me. She may be no real threat to your network, being counter-intelligence in Berlin, but our people have asked questions. It was lax not to pick up on the fact she'd slipped into this country. You know she's a threat to them. They want her silenced, and I have a job to do.'

The two men resumed their walk around the garden. The man known to his companion only as Mr Reid stopped at a bench, and they both sat down.

'As you know, we were asked to find her, and we did, a few weeks ago. I kept my promise, I kept you informed. You can't blame me for her disappearance. Yes, we leaked some information, but that worked – she was pulled from the trial. By all accounts, she isn't the only one to vanish; Hamilton, too, it seems, has gone AWOL. That's madness on his part, and not something we could have foreseen.'

Whilst thinking over the implications of what Reid had just told him, Tobias looked up. His attention caught by a plane to the south of them, en route to Heathrow.

'They say there were rumours about them in Berlin. Thirty years ago, maybe, but is it possible they've fooled us all?'

'They knew each other, at least knew *about* each other, that's true. I've heard the rumours that there was more; could explain why Hamilton was pulled out, but I can't imagine it was anything the Ministry for State Security didn't know about. If it wasn't useful to us, it wouldn't have been allowed. If indeed anything happened.'

Both men looked up as a couple of nurses came into the garden. In true British fashion, they sat themselves on the other side of the garden, as far away as possible from Reid and Tobias, even though it was shaded by the hospital buildings. Reid continued the conversation. He told his colleague that Hamilton had got quite close to finding the network when he was investigating leaks from the MOD a few years earlier. 'Fortunately,' a word he chose carefully, 'Bickley-Morris was up to his usual meddling and diverted attention towards himself. Damn nearly came unstuck, too, with that stupid stunt in Cambridge.'

Reid was far more worried than he dared let on to his associate. Bickley-Morris had been reckless with the business in Blackheath, hadn't listened to Reid, hadn't just acted too early but had done so at the worst possible time. He was a loose cannon, always had been. But not for much longer. Two more deaths were unthinkable, attracting too much attention. Even one was a risk Reid would have preferred not to take, but Kilsdale was a threat that could not be contained any other way. Kilsdale's days were numbered, and Reid had recognised this as an opportunity, one that would not be bungled. Unfortunately, now that Kilsdale had talked, it was inevitable that his death would attract Nevile's attention. Reid knew that when you did attract attention, you had to focus it to your own advantage, and bringing Bickley-Morris down over Kilsdale's death would certainly be to Reid's advantage. Even more so if it brought Hamilton out into the open. The key to success was taking your time. Plant suspicion, but let it ferment before you start feeding the doubts.

Slowik was an undoubted risk, but as Tobias had suggested, it wasn't clear what she knew about operations within the UK. She had been involved with counter-espionage, mainly in Berlin. Two things puzzled Reid: even though she had known Hamilton in Berlin, why had she given herself up to MI5, and why had MI5 taken responsibility for her? Slowik's information would be of more use to MI6, which would want to know how far their East German operations had been compromised. There was no doubt that the services would be working together, but it was still a puzzle.

Reid felt responsible for protecting the residual network. His main interest in Slowik was that it was her defection to the UK that had caused all the recent upheaval in his life. It was others who had Slowik in their sights, and they had sent Tobias. Tobias who had tasked Reid with finding her. There had been no option, no negotiation. Reid resented the intrusion, his focus had been on Sir Robert Hamilton, who, in his search for a mole in the MOD, had unmasked Quinton Bickley-Morris. It was open to question as to how close he had come to discovering the network, but his more recent pursuit and detention of Bickley-Morris showed that he was still following up on his investigations. Undermining Hamilton's position in the Security Service would serve a dual purpose: take away a risk to Reid's own organisation, and, with Hamilton out of the way, or at least diverting the Security Service's attention, Slowik would not be so well protected. Now he could use Bickley-Morris' rash vendetta against Kilsdale to get that bungling oaf out of his hair too. The plan had been to use his own position to add credibility to an anonymous tip-off linking Bickley-Morris directly to the Blackheath killing. The problem was that what had been prepared implicated Bickley-Morris in the death of Kilsdale at the Blackheath address, but it wasn't Kilsdale who had been killed. Documents could be changed, new "evidence" prepared, but that would take time, and Kilsdale's meeting with Harry Nevile demanded immediate action. No doubt, fearing for his own safety, Kilsdale had done Reid a service by linking Bickley-Morris to the debacle in south London. The worrying question was, what else had Kilsdale learned from either Graham or Bickley-Morris? It may have been a last resort, but Reid had already reconciled himself to Kilsdale's death. Afterwards, Reid could refocus his attention on the plan to discredit Hamilton. His plan was to have been actioned by others, thereby distancing and protecting himself. Realising that he may no longer have the luxury of time, however, he had already taken steps to set things in motion. Mrs Veronica Blakeridge did not have the only copy of the dossier. Reid had an insurance policy in case she didn't, or couldn't, deliver the goods. There were two other copies of the dossier, and he had made sure that one of them had been delivered to Thames House. To somebody sufficiently senior that it would cause a stir. Whatever Hamilton was up to, there was no way back for him now.

What was worrying Reid most of all was that, within hours of doing so, he had been told that the body in Blackheath was not, as had been supposed, one of Nevile's people.

CHAPTER 16

Day eight: Monday

'Mr Nevile. Do you or do you not know the whereabouts of Robert Hamilton?'

This was the third time that Harry's named but unknown interrogator had asked him that question. Neither he nor the other four members of the investigative panel were satisfied with Harry's indirect responses. It had started with a pleasant "We're growing concerned about Robert Hamilton, who hasn't been in contact for a few days. Have you heard from him?" but each iteration was delivered with less civility and more aggression. Harry sighed. He had foreseen this coming, though not quite so soon.

Veronica and Huxley had not returned to Tufton Street on Thursday. Veronica's interview with the police had taken far longer than anticipated. She had pointed out that the baggage delay at Gatwick had made it impossible for her to have reached Blackheath before Huxley reported the crime. The police, however, had remained sceptical, and their behaviour made Veronica think that she was being considered a suspect.

Last Friday morning, Veronica had repeated her story to Harry about how she had come across the file. Nothing had changed from what she had told Margaret on Wednesday evening and retold in Tufton Street whilst waiting for Harry on Thursday.

Frustratingly for Harry, she had not brought the dossier

with her, pointing out that it was unnecessary as Ben had already made a copy. The original, she had told Harry, was in a safe place, but she wouldn't be drawn into saying where. It was clear that Harry could not just ignore the matter, though how best to move it forward was far from obvious. Sir Robert reported directly to the Director General. It was an unusual arrangement that had arisen quite a few years ago for a project that had never been spoken about. Having an almost independent branch within the Service had proved useful to succeeding Directors General, and the arrangement had persisted. It wasn't yet clear if the current incumbent, appointed just a few months earlier, found it to be of benefit.

A move to Thames House, following the consolidation of the Gower Street and Curzon Street operations, seemed inevitable. Given Sir Robert's own relocation to Thames House, it had puzzled Harry that they remained at Tufton Street. Although a move seemed certain, the news about the restructuring, which he had been given a few days ago, was a bitter pill to swallow. Taking Veronica's file to the DG, as the Director General was usually called, could only support the case for change. Inevitably, it would also raise concerns, no matter how unfounded, about the trustworthiness of Harry and the rest of his team.

The case had to be investigated. Harry couldn't do it – he was hardly independent – but taking it to the DG would be galling. Yet he had no choice and impressed upon Veronica the fact that Thames House would need to see the original documents, not just Ben's copies. Whilst making it clear to his team that an official investigation was unavoidable, Harry sought to buy himself more time and told Veronica that she had no choice other than to bring the dossier to Tufton Street on Monday morning. A few days, and it could only be a very few, would hardly matter, and it was possible that Sir Robert would make contact.

Harry had already let Nicholas know that there were things he needed to discuss with Sir Robert, but could he raise this new matter? If the accusation of treason was true, it was likely that "taken a leave of absence" was a euphemism for fled, and that would also implicate Nicholas. There was little doubt in Harry's mind that the Bob Hamilton he knew, or at least thought he knew, would simply remind him of his duty to bring the file and its implications to the attention of the Director General. The problem would arise if Sir Robert did make contact and if Harry advised him of the file, Sir Robert suggested some other course of action. The simplest solution would be that Harry just gave him advance warning that it really was time to flee. The worst-case scenario was that Harry, through misplaced loyalty, risked being drawn in and implicated himself.

Truth will out. There was only one course of action he could take: the honourable one. But it could wait until after the weekend. If Sir Robert did make contact, Harry would not raise the matter of Veronica's file himself but would ask about his knowledge of the closing down of Tufton Street. He would still hand over the file, but should he hand over his resignation at the same time?

This morning, Harry hadn't managed to get as far as the office; his escorts had been waiting for him to leave his house. One fell into step behind him as he passed Montpelier Place. A second gentleman, whom Harry recognised from a few days earlier, was waiting out of sight, around the corner of Rutland Street. At least it told Harry one thing: they had no evidence against him, or else they would not have allowed him the luxury of waking in his own time and having breakfast. They were fishing for information. Information that he was thankful that he was unable to give them.

Harry took his time before answering, looking around the room that seemed as soulless as most of the panel he was facing. He breathed in heavily before answering, almost sighing as he breathed out.

'As I have said, I am not Sir Robert's secretary. He does not keep me informed of his plans or his whereabouts.' Harry, once again, emphasised the word "Sir". It seemed that the panel had already decided on Robert Hamilton's guilt and had stripped him of his title.

'Take another look at the photographs, Mr Nevile. You know who these people are. You know how serious this matter is.'

Harry took another look at the photographs. The images were the same as the ones that Veronica had brought with her from Greece. He could only presume that the Service had a copy of its own – he just wondered for how long. His answer was deliberately long-winded.

'As I have already told you, these are the same photographs that a former member of my team discovered in the house of a deceased and disgraced member of the Metropolitan Police's Special Branch. Their authenticity has yet to be established, I believe.'

'Look at the photograph in the U-Bahn station. Remind us all of the station name.'

'Well, I can't make it out fully – it's partially blocked by people on the platform. It looks like "Friedri—", something like that.'

'Friedrichstrasse, Mr Nevile. A crossing point. Rather curious crossing point, entirely within East Berlin. Why do you suppose Robert Hamilton is there? Talking with a known Stasi agent.'

'You tell me she's a known Stasi agent, but I can't be sure it's Anna Slowik, whom you say it is. I have met her only once, briefly, a year or so ago, and this photograph must be, what? Thirty years ago?'

When Harry had first seen the photograph, the lady talking to Sir Robert had looked familiar. It wasn't until Veronica had turned the photograph over that he recognised her. According to the note on the back, the lady was Anna Slowik. With hindsight, he had seen the similarity. Veronica hadn't known who Anna Slowik was, but Huxley had told her.

'But you do recognise Robert Hamilton. Thirty years ago.'

'Well, yes. But that's hardly surprising. We had rooms on the same corridor at college. Early seventies. He was a mature student, doing a one-year language course.'

'And you have been friends ever since. How curious. Perhaps that's why you're being so evasive? Or worse, perhaps? Did he recruit you into his little cabal?'

'Oh, for goodness' sake!' Harry was genuinely exasperated by the suggestion.

The chair of the panel intervened. Harry knew him by name, recognised his seniority, but was not familiar with his service record. 'Perhaps this would be a good time to take a break.'

Fifteen minutes later, Harry was not back in the interview room where he had expected to be. He was sitting facing the

Director General across a surprisingly modern and functional desk. The chair of the interview panel was sitting to one side.

'Quite the revelation, Mr Nevile. One of your former colleagues having a copy of a damning dossier. Did it not occur to you to report the matter?'

Harry was unsure as to whether there was a hint of sarcasm in the Director General's voice.

'With respect, Director, I knew nothing about the dossier until last Wednesday and only saw the contents last Thursday. That was a copy. I have yet to see the original documents, nor was I able to interview the lady concerned until Friday. As I'm sure you're aware, there was an unfortunate death at her house, and one of my people was arrested. Wrongly, I should point out. The lady's attention, and ours, has been focused on helping the police.'

'Quite the bloody shambles in Tufton Street at the moment.' The Director General was quite forceful. 'And quite the coincidence that Robert Hamilton chose last week to stage a disappearing act. What the hell is going on, Mr Nevile?'

The DG was staring at Harry. It was clear he wanted more by way of an explanation.

'I *have* written a report.' Harry defended himself, explaining that he had intended to bring the matter to the DG's attention that very morning and would have done had he not been, as he put it, "invited" to Thames House.

It was only a couple of days ago that Harry had told himself that "truth will out", but he had done a great deal of thinking over the weekend. He knew that the version of events that he was about to tell the Director General was the truth, nothing but the truth, but not the whole truth. He couldn't help but think of Nicholas, but this was more serious. There was no doubt he would be putting himself at risk, but what was worrying him more was that he could be putting Margaret and Ben at risk too. He had told both about Sir Robert's concerns that Slowik was in danger and of the course of unsanctioned action that had been mentioned at the Victoria Square meeting. Ben had picked up, quite quickly, that there was a possibility that Sir Robert's proposed unilateral actions suggested that Slowik may need protecting from someone very senior in the Security Service itself. It wasn't the only possibility they had discussed, but it was clear the risk had to be associated with somebody with access to high-level intelligence. For that reason, Harry had asked that those discussions remain confidential to the three of them, and no mention had been made the following day when they had discussed the file with Huxley and Veronica. Nor had Harry mentioned Sir Robert Hamilton's disappearance in those discussions.

Harry ran through the course of events of the last week, starting with Huxley calling him from Lewisham Police Station on the Monday evening. As he came to his conclusion, he decided that he needed to show some mettle.

'You may consider that I have behaved inappropriately by waiting until this morning to bring the dossier to your attention, but given other developments last week, I'm not alone if I have.'

Both the DG and the panel chairman looked at Harry, not sure what to expect.

'Last Wednesday, before I knew anything about this dossier, I was summoned to Thames House by Francis Buckingham. Only to be told Sir Robert Hamilton is no longer responsible for Tufton Street, that my team is to be disbanded – not that I'm allowed to tell them – and I'm to be assigned to a new role. Beyond being told to identify the body in Blackheath, I was given no role, no instructions and no reporting structure. To coin a phrase, Director, "a bloody shambles". What the hell is going on here, if you don't mind me asking?'

As soon as the words had left his lips, Harry regretted his final outburst. He had not intended to go beyond a statement of facts, nor to ridicule the DG. The stony silence that followed only served to confirm Harry's fears.

The Director General turned to the chairman of the panel. 'Mr Nevile and I need a word in private. Would you leave us? I think Mr Nevile's business with the investigation is over for today. No doubt his report will confirm what he has told us.'

As the Director General's office closed, Harry decided to push his luck once again.

'She's gone missing too, hasn't she? Anna Slowik.'

It had never been mentioned during Harry's interview with the panel, but Harry had no doubt that if Sir Robert had gone into hiding, he had done so to protect Anna Slowik. He wanted to be sure, and this might be his only chance to find out. The Director General stood and looked at his office door, as if to check it was properly closed.

'Harry, I can't tell you everything, not even I know that—' the Director General stopped himself, a wry smile crossing his lips. 'We – no, I – I have to be seen to be taking Sir Robert's absence seriously.'

It struck Harry as a somewhat curious admission for the DG to make. It was something that should be taken for granted. He also noted a change in the DG's manner. Not just "Harry" rather than "Mr Nevile", but he detected a more relaxed, less formal tone of voice.

'This file that has appeared rather complicates things. Just let me say that there are reasons to believe it's a subterfuge designed to damage Sir Robert's standing.'

It seemed rather obvious to Harry that it was designed to damage Sir Robert's reputation, but he was relieved to hear that the DG had reason to doubt its veracity. Before Harry had time to say anything, the Director General asked him to explain, fully, how Veronica had come into possession of a copy. The DG listened without comment, stroking his chin from time to time. When he had finished, the Director General told Harry he should send him a copy of his report via the normal channels and try to secure Veronica's original copy voluntarily, but not to arouse suspicion by being insistent. If Harry could avoid further discussion with his team on the matter, he should, but in no circumstances should he or his team disclose the existence of Veronica's copy to anyone beyond those who were already aware. Neither should Veronica be made aware of the Thames House copy before she handed over her own set of documents.

Once again, Harry was struck by the DG's choice of words. "Normal channels" would be via Sir Robert Hamilton.

'If you don't mind me asking,' he said, 'what *are* normal channels, given Sir Robert's unavailability and Francis Buckingham's comments?'

The Director General smiled. 'You've cleared up one "bloody shambles" for me, let me clear one up for you.' He paused for a moment before adding, 'As far as I can.'

Harry was told that, yes, a restructuring was being

considered and that, in the fullness of time, it was likely that his team would be transferred to Thames House. The Director General didn't think any of that would be a surprise to Harry, given Sir Robert's age and the need to plan for his retirement.

'On the matter of Mr Buckingham, I need you to bear with me. It's not a name I recognise, but then again, I can hardly be expected to know everyone who works at Thames House. I will look into it, but why he acted how he did, when he did, is a matter which concerns me and not you. The immediate future of your team is safe – let me leave it at that. I shall let Mr Buckingham know we've spoken and that, given the issue with Sir Robert, a new direction is necessary. Which brings me to something important that will affect you.'

The Director General told Harry that one of Sir Robert's duties was to act as a liaison with Whitehall's Joint Intelligence Committee. A role which could not go unfilled, and to Harry's great surprise, the DG expressed his intention to appoint Harry to the position with immediate effect, reporting directly to the DG. The JIC calendar dictated the schedule of regular digest reports, but in Sir Robert's absence, some interim files had already been sent to the JIC via a fail-safe but unorthodox route that had raised some eyebrows.

'It makes sense, Harry,' the DG told him. 'You reported to Sir Robert, Sir Robert reported to me. We don't need to fill the gap; we just shorten the chain. And speaking of shortening the chain, if there are any further developments, you can contact my office directly on this number.' The Director General handed over a business card that bore only the crown logo, his name and a telephone number. 'It's my private office number, so needless to say, be discreet when using it.'

It was clear to Harry that this new role was a foregone conclusion, not an offer he would be given the luxury of considering. He would have some additional duties and was likely to spend more time at Thames House. Perhaps there was some element of truth in what Francis Buckingham had told him.

Owing to the extremely sensitive nature of the information that Harry would both pass to the JIC and also back to the Security Service, there was a need to ensure secure access to the files. In addition to his standard username and password, Harry would require an additional identifier. One that was never to be written down or spoken about, nor would ever appear on any screen it was typed onto, not even in redacted form.

The DG had a grin on his face. 'Not my system, Harry, but one of Sir Robert's making. It may sound silly, but we use Vatican names. Your identifier is Innocentius Tertius.'

'Innocent the Third?' Harry asked, bewildered both by the realisation he was, for the immediate future, Sir Robert's successor and by the absurdity that, at one of the highest levels within the Service, officers were given papal names as security identifiers. 'Was he not,' Harry asked, scraping the barrel of his own memory, 'one of the anti-popes?'

'I prefer to think of him as an alternative to Alexander Tertius,' the Director General quipped back.

Why, Harry wondered, had the DG, in effect, told him what Sir Robert's identifier was? It was also clear to Harry that this appointment was not something random, nor something chosen on the spur of the moment. This was something that had been planned.

Chapter 17

Day eight: Monday

Unsurprisingly, Harry's unexpected absence that morning had been a cause for concern amongst the rest of the team. When Harry arrived back at Tufton Street, Nicholas advised him that he had taken the liberty of informing upstairs that Harry had, once again, been summoned to Thames House.

Harry shot him a glance that made it obvious that he was surprised that Nicholas knew where he had been.

'They were kind enough to let me know, sir. Otherwise, I would have had to raise the alarm.' After the briefest of pauses, Nicholas then added, 'Protocol, sir,' as if to reassure Harry.

'Did they say why?'

'The purpose of the meeting, sir, was not my concern.'

Harry wondered if Nicholas did know but was being his usual soul of discretion. Not so the people upstairs, who descended upon him as soon as he stepped out of the lift. An unexpected summons to Thames House for the third time in a week rather suggested something serious. Harry sought to allay their concerns.

'We have been discussing the dossier, yes.'

Harry knew he couldn't mention the existence of a second copy of the dossier with Huxley in the room. It was no secret that Veronica had been staying at Huxley's flat, and there was something niggling away in the back of Harry's mind. Two copies of the dossier appearing, possibly in the same week, a coincidence he didn't like. Although Veronica had found her copy in the past few weeks, it was still odd – both copies causing a stir in London within days of each other.

Not wishing to invite further speculation, Harry advised them that there was another reason he had been at Thames House. There was little point in hiding the fact he had been assigned a new duty: liaison with the Joint Intelligence Committee. Harry had not been aware that Sir Robert had occupied that role, so there was little chance that anyone else in the team knew either. Only Margaret and Ben were aware of the concern about Sir Robert's whereabouts, though it could only be a matter of time before rumours started.

'That's interesting. But the dossier, what did they say about that?' Huxley was his usual impatient self, going directly to the core issue. Harry's new role seemed an irrelevance to him.

'They're considering it. What more can I say?'

Harry knew that would not be an answer that satisfied Huxley, but the investigation was out of his control. No one else in the room was yet aware of the second copy of the file, so Harry knew that Huxley and the others would assume that he himself had disclosed the existence of the dossier to Thames House, based on the electronic copy that Ben had made.

'You know as well as I do that no action will be taken until it's been established if the documents are fabricated or not. Which means they do need sight of Ron's original, not just the copy that Ben made. Please arrange for that, Huxley. And, by the way, where is she this morning?'

Harry was mindful that nothing fully added up, and it was

still possible that Veronica was in some kind of danger.

Huxley told them that Ron had come into town with him this morning, arguing that it would be more difficult to plan a second attack if they could not predict her whereabouts. Staying at home, by which he meant *his* home, alone, only increased the risk that she could be targeted. Huxley, who was unaware of the Kilsdale revelation, was even more concerned than Harry for Ron's safety. He also pointed out that she needed to meet with the Met, who were now handling the case, in order to know when she could access her own home once more. Explaining that to the team seemed only to increase Huxley's impatience.

'In the meantime, what's our next step? We can't just ignore the evidence.'

'We, especially you, Huxley, are not going to do anything.'

Harry pointed out that the matter was now in the hands of Thames House and, in any case, Huxley would be excluded from any discussions, be they at Thames House or Tufton Street.

Huxley's exasperated reaction took no one by surprise, and Harry pointed out that anyone involved in the discovery of the documents could not take any active part in the investigation, other than as a witness. Knowing that Huxley would still not be satisfied, he added, quite forcefully, 'Let's face it, there's also the small matter of your relationship with Veronica. You are not, I repeat *not*, independent.'

It was unusual for Harry to be either forceful or formal with Huxley, usually accepting that his foibles were the price to pay for the benefit of his inciteful mind. To everyone's further surprise, Harry continued.

'Now, I expect you do know of her planned activities this

morning, so your job, the one thing you can do to help, is to go and bring her and the original documents back here to Tufton Street.'

With that, Harry turned to Ben and Margaret. 'You two, I need a word in private, now.' He pointed to the meeting room and led the way in, leaving a bewildered and unhappy Huxley standing alone in the office.

As soon as the meeting room door was closed, Margaret turned to Harry and expressed her surprise.

'That was harsh, Harry. It wasn't necessary, and that tells me there's something else. Something you're not saying.'

There were few people who could, or would, speak to Harry like that. Despite feeling that Harry had indeed been unfair to Huxley, Ben held his silence. Harry slumped into one of the chairs and motioned for Ben and Margaret to do the same.

'I know it was, but it's for his own protection.'

Harry's deep breath was an unfailing signal to Margaret and Ben that he had more to tell them. He wasn't sure where to start, but he justified himself by saying that those responsible for the dossier may well be monitoring Huxley, if only because of his relationship with Veronica. It was better that he knew nothing.

Margaret was unsettled, not by what Harry had said but by his manner of speaking. There was a clear implication that Ron could be involved, possibly Huxley too. She did not hold back and told Harry of her concerns, repeating that it sounded as though Harry had some new information which he hadn't shared with them.

'This is not to be shared outside this room,' Harry began, 'especially with Huxley or Ron. I haven't shown a copy of

Ron's dossier to anyone.'

Both Margaret and Ben looked confused, wondering what had been discussed at Thames House that morning and why Harry would have lied.

Harry explained that he had not shown his copy of the dossier to the people at Thames House because they had a copy of their own. How it came into their possession he did not know, but as a result, he had been summoned to headquarters. He had not gone there of his own volition.

'I also had a meeting with the Director General,' he told them. 'He says he has reason to believe the documents may not be genuine.'

Harry paused for a moment. The phrase that the DG had used was "a subterfuge"; he had not described them as fake or fabricated. Harry wondered if he was just overthinking the conversation. So much had happened in the past week, and so little sense could be made of any of it.

Ben looked as though he was about to speak, but Harry held up his hand to stop him.

'There's something else, something that occurred to me on the way back here. It's a little... Excuse me a moment.'

Harry had noticed, through the frosted banding of the meeting room's glass wall, Huxley sitting and looking disconsolate at his desk. He got up, left the room and approached his colleague. In a much more conciliatory tone, he explained to Huxley that the one thing he could do to help matters was to find Ron and persuade her to hand over her original dossier so that Thames House could evaluate it.

'It's a serious accusation, Huxley. They're not going to act on hearsay, nor are they going to be satisfied with the copy that Ben made. I can't see any reason why Ron wouldn't hand it over. Why else come here?'

He reassured Huxley that the matter was being dealt with at the highest level, adding that he had even had a brief meeting with the DG. 'There will be no whitewash, Huxley,' he added, squeezing Huxley's shoulder to give some reassurance to his words.

Huxley nodded, stood up, put on his jacket and made towards the lift.

Back in the meeting room, the door once again closed, Harry told Ben and Margaret of the thought that had occurred to him. It was not a comfortable thought. The fact that a second copy of the file had appeared was troubling in itself, but the circumstances suggested something Harry would have preferred not to consider. Veronica had claimed she had found the file at Rod Graham's house and was going to bring it to London. Which she had done, but then there was the business at Blackheath, and, for a while, everyone believed that she had been killed. A second copy had been sent to Thames House. Harry did not know when that had happened, but why two copies? Could it be that someone wanting the dossier to be seen, and thinking Veronica was dead, had sent the second copy directly to Thames House? The weight of the implication cast a shroud of silence across the room. It was Margaret who spoke first, slowly and carefully.

'Well. It would fit with a conspiracy to denounce Sir Robert, regardless of whether the accusations are true or not. But it says that...'

Margaret couldn't finish the sentence. It was Ben who gave voice to the thought that was troubling all three of them.

'Ron is part of the conspiracy.'

'Worse, I'm afraid.' Harry's words cemented their worst

125

fears. 'If the accusations are true, why didn't the person who had the second copy let Thames House have the information directly? Why involve Ron at all?'

Ben followed the line of logic. 'Possibly to lay a smoke trail, or because, if the accusations came from within Sir Robert's own group, they would be given more credence?'

The inference they all drew from that was that both options suggested the accusations were unfounded: the dossier had been fabricated.

None of them thought that it was likely that Huxley was involved, at least not in the plot, though it was a possibility that had to be considered. Distasteful though the thought was, it seemed more likely that Ron was simply using him to find a way back into Tufton Street.

'There's something else that you need to come completely clean about, Harry.' Margaret's look told Harry that whatever it was, she was not going to be put off. 'Veronica's disappearance last year.'

At the time, little had been said. Rod Graham was believed to have been behind an attack on Margaret, and it had been assumed that Veronica had fled in fear for her own safety. Something she had perhaps found difficult to get over, hence her decision not to return. Last week, it had become common knowledge that she had fled to Greece, inexplicably to the same island where Graham had a property, and that Huxley had visited her a couple of times. Although Harry agreed that, on the face of it, there was a possibility that she had fled with Graham to avoid detection, he pointed out that the family she had mentioned, living on the island, was her half-sister and her only relative. On the other hand, where better to hide from Graham than right under his nose?

Margaret wasn't letting go until she had followed the idea through.

'Graham's death, the unclear circumstances. Huxley's visits, which we now know about. A damning dossier appearing, not to mention a death at her house. Surely, Harry, even you must find it suspicious. Something bigger that we've missed?'

Suspicion, Harry reminded them, was just a thought that something *may* be possible. Although he did not say it, Harry knew that suspicion was insidious; once it was awoken from its slumbers and raised its head, it never slept again.

'Let's not go too far down this road,' he warned.

They were in danger of spiralling into unfounded speculation. He did not like coincidences – the whole team knew that, but what he had said was conjecture. He could well be wrong. Productive decisions could only be made on the basis of fact.

'Speaking of facts, let's dig out some more, then, shall we?'

Margaret was not letting go; there was more that Harry wasn't telling. She knew him too well, and Harry was quite aware that she did. He tried to deflect the question.

'Do we know any more?'

'Bigger picture, Harry. Sir Robert Hamilton and Slowik, the people the dossier is about, don't seem to have been mentioned at all this morning. One thing we do know is an accusation that's being made against Sir Robert, and he takes a leave of absence. Suspended? Possibly before anyone had seen the documents? Then again, he told you he might take unsanctioned action to protect this woman Slowik. I don't suppose she's on a leave of absence too, by any chance?'

Harry knew that the taunt wasn't there to provoke him but to tell him that Margaret would not be satisfied until he had told her all he knew. Although the Director General had not answered directly when the same question had been asked of him, Harry had taken it from the response that his supposition had not been wide of the mark. Now the same thought had occurred to Margaret. Unsettled though he was about the possibility that Ron was somehow involved in all of this, Harry still had to consider that either Ron or Huxley, possibly both, could be in danger. There had, after all, been one death, and whether or not it had been a murder, both Huxley and Kilsdale had mentioned somebody else being at Veronica's house that afternoon. Getting to the bottom of the mystery was going to be easier if there were three brains working on it.

'There is some truth in the story that Sir Robert passed information to the East Germans when he was in Berlin.'

The expressions of surprise and bewilderment on the faces of Margaret and Ben confirmed Harry's revelation had had the impact he had expected.

Half an hour later, Harry had told Margaret and Ben everything he knew about the events of the past week, including what Sir Robert had told him about Berlin. Nothing was left out, yet they had a perplexing problem; was there anything useful that they could do?

The investigation into Veronica's dossier had already been taken up at a more senior level, as was appropriate both for the seriousness of the accusations and the independence of the investigators. Harry reminded the team that, given there had already been a death, the safety of both Huxley and Veronica had to be uppermost in their minds.

Were it not for the fact that the pair of them would be needed in London for the ongoing police and Security Service investigations, Harry had considered offering them the use of his mother's house in North Yorkshire. It had lain empty since Harry's mother had died, about five months earlier, and Harry's application for probate was taking a long time to work through the legal system. As a small market town, close to but not on the local tourist routes, Loftus could provide for their immediate needs whilst being sufficiently distant, at two hundred and seventy miles away, to frustrate any attempts to find them.

'There was a third party in that house, remember.' Harry gave voice to his main concern. 'Both Huxley and Kilsdale agree on that, though it seems that whoever it was, was there to meet Kilsdale. At least according to Kilsdale, that is. If there's any hint that they *are* in danger, I'll offer them the house. And, if I deem it necessary not to, I won't tell the police or Thames House. Their safety is more important than convenience. If they want them back, then they'll have to provide proper protection.'

Harry realised that what he was proposing bore a marked similarity to the actions Sir Robert had proposed. There would be consequences, but Harry was prepared to take them.

Margaret thought Harry was being slightly overdramatic, reminding him that this was real life, not fiction. Yes, there had been a death, which may turn out to be from natural causes, but even if it was suspicious, people did not go on the rampage, killing every person who could potentially identify the guilty party. There was, however, one thing that was troubling her.

'Has it occurred to you, Harry, that the third party may

have been Ron herself?'

Margaret's thought was not an option that eased Harry's discomfort.

'But,' Harry said as he struggled to organise his thoughts, 'it was a man. He was a man.'

'No. Nobody has ever said that. At least not from what you've told us.'

Harry thought about it. Margaret was right, though it was something else that did not make any kind of sense. Why would she want to kill a cleaner she had never met, and if it was an unfortunate accident, why not answer the door? Why hide from Huxley?

'I am as perplexed as you Harry,' Margaret continued. 'But as you say, we need some facts. That's why I'm going to see the airlines tomorrow.'

'Airlines? Why?'

Harry knew why; he was just reluctant to admit it.

'To find out exactly when she did arrive. Hopefully, it will confirm that she couldn't have been home before Huxley arrived.'

'Let's do it. There can't be that many airlines. We can do it over the phone.' Ben was as keen as Harry and Margaret to find some evidence that would show their concerns were unfounded.

Margaret voiced a note of caution. 'No, not today. If Ron hands over her originals, she'll come back here with Huxley. Besides, people tend to be more co-operative when we turn up in person, and you know how Huxley's mind works. If one of us isn't here, he'll be impossible till he knows why.'

'OK, and we can ask Ron which airline she flew with.'

'No, Ben, better not. Just in case.'

'I think I can help you there.' Unsettled though he was by Margaret's "Just in case", Harry was pleased he had something positive to contribute. 'When she came in last Wednesday, her shoulder bag still had the hand luggage label on it.'

CHAPTER 18

Day nine: Tuesday

Given the tumultuous events of the previous week, the rest of Monday afternoon had been relatively uneventful. Harry had reminded Margaret and Ben that they all had other matters to deal with still. Last week had been disruptive, but it had not been as though they had all been sitting around twiddling their thumbs, waiting for something to summon them to action.

There was one awkward problem that Harry knew he had to deal with: he could no longer keep Nicholas in the dark about Veronica's dossier. It had been a fine balance: present guilt at not having spoken with Nicholas before versus future guilt. Part of Harry hoped that Nicholas was in contact with Sir Robert and the information would be passed on, even though it would be a unilateral and unsanctioned disclosure.

'Nicholas,' Harry had said, 'there's something I need to discuss with you.' Harry had felt remarkably awkward and, not knowing where to start, had continued, 'My meeting this morning. Raises certain issues.'

Nicholas' reply had come as no surprise.

'Ah, yes. The documents that have been sent to Thames House. Rather puts all of us at Tufton Street under the microscope.'

Quite how Nicholas seemed to be aware of everything that affected the Tufton Street team had long been a mystery.

As had his uncanny ability to defuse an awkward situation. In a couple of sentences, he had acknowledged that he knew about the dossier and was quite aware it would point the finger of suspicion at all in Tufton Street, himself included.

'There's one thing you may not be aware of.'

Harry had told Nicholas that there was a second copy; it had come into Veronica's possession, and that was the reason why she had returned. Nicholas had indicated that he thought her action was "quite proper" and asked if people at Thames House were aware. Harry had confirmed they were and then tackled another awkward issue.

'Mr Chowdhury and Miss Millard are aware that there are two copies.' Somehow, when discussing the team at Tufton Street with Nicholas it always seemed appropriate to adopt Nicholas' own style of formality. 'Mrs Blakeridge and Mr Huxley are not. For the moment, I would like to keep it that way.'

Harry had felt uncomfortable, but his concern had been that if Veronica knew of the existence of the other copy, she may be reluctant to hand over her own. As he had said it, he had felt more than uncomfortable – he had felt guilty. At the back of his mind had been the thought, *especially if it's a falsification.*

Nicholas had pointed out that operational decisions were not his to make and thanked Harry for having the courtesy to let him know. 'Perhaps, sir, in order to avoid continuing difficulties…' he had added. It had been a sentence that did not need finishing.

It had been awkward and difficult not to have kept Nicholas fully informed over the past week. Keeping Huxley in the dark about the second copy could only cause equal discomfort. Veronica was no longer an active member of the Service and, thus, there was no obligation to update her about the Thames House copy. He could ask Huxley not to tell her, but that could introduce difficulties in their relationship. When measured against national security, Huxley's social life was not an important consideration, but Huxley was the only direct link to Veronica. A potential source of information that needed to be kept live. If informing Huxley was informing Veronica too, Harry had thought, *why not?* Shake the tree and see what falls out. Even if you are hoping there is no tree to shake.

Huxley and Veronica had turned up in the early afternoon with the dossier. Veronica had seemed quite happy to pass it on. Harry had made a phone call to the Director General's office, using the number he had been given, and arranged for Huxley and Veronica to be met when they arrived at Thames House. He also made it clear to Huxley that there was no need for him to return to Tufton Street afterwards.

As nothing had been said about Thames House already having a copy, after the pair had left, Margaret and Ben tackled Harry as to how they should handle the matter. 'I don't like game playing,' he had told them, whilst wondering if that was exactly what he was doing. There was no need, he had continued, to keep the existence of the other copy secret. Neither was there any reason to make a point of telling Huxley. If it came up in conversation, let it. There was no benefit in being furtive. Given Huxley's sporadic absences over the past week, they could be forgiven for forgetting he didn't know of its existence.

'Besides,' he had added, 'none of us knew about its existence until today, and Huxley doesn't know when today.'

It was barely 2:30 in the afternoon and, although Harry was uncomfortable misleading Huxley, he asked Ben and Margaret to go along with the story that he hadn't been able to tell them about the second copy until it was confirmed that Veronica had handed over the Graham version.

Shortly thereafter, there had been a call from Thames House, though it had nothing to do with Veronica or the Hamilton accusation. An appointment had been made for Harry to meet his contact at the Joint Intelligence Committee the following morning. Harry had thought it unnecessary as his role seemed to be little more than acting as a single point of contact between the Service and the Committee, and his main duty was no more demanding than forwarding files, albeit in strictest confidence. Needing a distraction, however, Harry had looked up Mr Giles Martin Linthorpe Gifford. As far as could be deduced from the record, Mr Gifford was a dedicated and effective, if a little uninspiring, career civil servant whose role was more secretary than decision-maker.

Nevertheless, Tuesday morning saw Harry in Whitehall, entering the Cabinet Office building. His first impression of Giles Gifford was a symphony in grey: greying hair, charcoal grey suit, white shirt, silver-grey tie, with matching links through his embroidered, mitred shirt cuffs. Even the well-polished black shoes toned well with the caliginous grey cloth of his suit. Somewhere in the back of Harry's mind, the name James McNeill Whistler popped up. Was there a painting *Symphony in Grey*? Harry wondered, before Gifford's opening remark caught him off guard.

'Ah, you must be the new pope.'

From what the Director General had told him yesterday morning, Harry had the distinct impression that neither the name nor the theme of his additional security ID was known outside of a very small circle within the Security Service. Harry decided to let it go. 'Most people just call me Harry.'

An hour later, Harry was none the wiser about the purpose of his visit. He had not warmed to Mr Gifford, who had impressed upon him the importance of the Joint Intelligence Committee's work, to what degree they were supported by the Joint Intelligence Organisation, and the role they had in assessing and reviewing intelligence reports. All of which Harry already knew. Part of Harry felt he had been treated like a school-leaver applying for his first job. There had been no attempt at rapport. Gifford had been remote and overbearing. Clearly, Mr Gifford had not been at all happy with the unorthodox method of the last update, but Harry thought it hardly merited his haughty manner. It had been as though he was suggesting that the Security Service was subservient to the JIC. Harry had the feeling that it was also an attempt to aggrandise Gifford's own position in order to impress.

Harry's overall opinion of Gifford was that of a meddlesome busybody with too much time on his hands. A monotonous man in grey, memorable for only two reasons. The first was that he was left-handed, the second, that Gifford had certainly known more about Harry's own position than might be expected. As Harry was leaving, Gifford had asked if he was walking back to Tufton Street. It wasn't so much that it seemed a stupid question – the short walk hardly merited a taxi – it just seemed odd that Gifford knew where Harry's office was. *Perhaps he has nothing better to do?*

On his way back to the office, Harry knew that he would have to find something to divert Huxley. The need had been made abundantly clear that morning when, unsurprisingly, Margaret's absence had triggered Huxley's curiosity. Harry's attempt to deflect any questions by maintaining it was due to matters that he could not discuss with Huxley had not gone down well.

How to keep Huxley occupied was something Harry had given much thought to the previous evening. Concern was rising, once again, regarding the Iraqi government's intentions with respect to the Kurdish civil war, and there were concerns that Saddam Hussein's regime may be planning genocidal attacks. Despite the sanctions and protestations of innocence, there was uncertainty as to whether a bioweapons programme had been re-established. To what extent were UK universities and research institutes being duped into providing knowledge and training to supposedly bona fide students who would then go on to become the regime's weapons specialists? It was a legitimate concern, one that Sir Robert had discussed several times with Harry, and that they had plans to investigate. All Harry was doing was to bring those plans forward. Asking Huxley to re-evaluate the records and provide a guidance document on potential threats would not only keep him occupied but would require him to spend time in the archives, which meant he would be out of the Tufton Street office on a frequent basis. It was also something that Harry could claim was being brought forward as a result of his visit to the JIC that morning.

As Harry stepped out of the lift into the Tufton Street office, he thought it odd that Margaret hadn't returned, but his thoughts were diverted almost immediately. Huxley sprang up from his seat and, with one arm raised, greeted Harry as only Huxley would.

'Is this a gentleman I see before me, or is it the prince of darkness?'

Harry suppressed a smile. It was good to have Huxley back to his normal self.

'I'm not sure Shakespeare used those quotes in the same play, let alone the same sentence.'

'Perhaps, but methinks thou hast kept me in the dark.'

Harry knew what was coming but asked anyway.

'About what?'

'Oh, nothing much. Just the small matter of another copy of Ron's file?'

With that, Harry signalled Huxley to join him in the meeting room. He had never been in any doubt that once he had left for his Whitehall meeting, Huxley would be unable to resist bringing up the subject of Veronica's dossier, if only to find out if it was related to Margaret's absence. Harry was also sure that Ben would have had more sense than to tell Huxley the truth about why Margaret was away from the office. In the event, Huxley had asked Ben what he thought Thames House would do with the dossier. Ben had replied, 'Well, compare it with the copy that was sent to them, I suppose.'

'It's quite simple,' Harry began, explaining to Huxley that he had known nothing about the second copy until the previous morning and that he was not allowed to say anything until Thames House had possession of the file Veronica had found. Huxley protested that Harry could have told him that morning, before he left, but Harry pointed out that he did have a meeting to prepare for. Perhaps if Huxley had not been so persistent in trying to discover the reason for Margaret's absence, he may have had the time and inclination to tell him of the developments at Thames House. Even as the words were leaving his mouth, he knew mentioning Margaret was a mistake.

'Oh, where is she by the way?' Huxley asked, as casually as he could manage. By way of an answer, Harry just shook his head and smiled.

'Touché,' Huxley said, adding unexpectedly, 'Well, I'm no prince of darkness. I have some news for you.'

He explained that whilst Harry had been away, Ron had telephoned. The police were no longer considering the death at her house to be suspicious. Harry immediately latched onto the one piece of evidence that suggested the suspicion of foul play should not be discarded lightly.

'But what about the person you saw under the staircase?'

'They think I was mistaken.'

'And you?'

'Not sure... Perhaps I was. I was certain at the time, but then again, I was certain that the body I saw was Veronica's.'

Harry thought it better not to tell Huxley about Kilsdale's claim. There seemed little point. The person had been there to meet Kilsdale and was probably unaware of Veronica's impending return. Although it couldn't be discounted entirely, it was not likely that there was any intent to harm Veronica. *If indeed*, Harry thought, ashamedly, *that person wasn't Veronica herself.* Instead, he surprised Huxley by turning his greeting back on itself.

'Then, let the prince of darkness cast some light onto your future. As you're aware, I was at the Cabinet Office this morning.'

Harry never actually claimed that Huxley's new project was a result of his visit to Whitehall, but was pleased when his colleague's assumption clearly fired his enthusiasm. Harry's pleasure was overshadowed by an abundance of guilt. He was misleading his colleague deliberately, even though it was with the best of intentions. Huxley must not be party to either the current need to establish Veronica's innocence or the investigation into the accusations against Sir Robert. With regard to the latter, Harry still felt much unease. There was too much he didn't know, and if Sir Robert's fear that it could become a case of "heads you lose, tails you lose" became a reality, Harry did not want to drag his colleagues down with him. It may be that they were damned anyway. The Francis Buckingham meeting still troubled Harry. He had the Director General's assurance, but that did not mean Harry could disregard the best interests of his team.

Harry's prior discussions with Sir Robert on the Iraq concerns had provided him with a coherent and plausible case to present to Huxley – a case that Huxley had warmed to. He had often voiced his opinion that the Tufton Street team should be more involved in what he called "the really big issues". After their meeting, Huxley was quickly engrossed and wasted no time in asking for Ben's help in locating where in the archives he could find the relevant information. Ben had looked at Harry when Huxley first approached him, and Harry gave him a simple nod of approval.

With Huxley's attention firmly focused on the computer screen in front of him, Ben felt it safe to attract Harry's attention and pointed to the meeting room. Assuming Ben wanted to be brought up to speed, he started to explain that despite recent events, they still had a job to do, but Ben interrupted him.

'Margaret will be back soon. It's not great news, but more

of an enigma than a worry, she says.' Misinterpreting Harry's quizzical look, Ben explained that Margaret had telephoned him just before Harry and Huxley finished their meeting. She had wanted to know if Huxley was in the office. Ben seemed embarrassed to explain that she had phoned him because the back office was more discreet. Seeing the lift doors open, Ben paused.

'Ah, here she is.' He sounded relieved as he stood and opened the meeting room door to indicate where they were.

Huxley had also noticed Margaret's arrival. 'Ah, the fair maid returns. Whither hast thou been? Kent?'

'No, "to unpathed waters and undreamed shores,"' came the reply. Huxley looked puzzled, but Margaret just smiled. As she passed his desk, she patted Huxley on the shoulder. 'Shakespeare. Good to have you back.'

As she looked towards the meeting room, her demeanour changed from flippant to serious. Huxley's attention returned to his screen, hardly registering Margaret joining Harry and Ben in the meeting room.

'Good news or bad?' she asked them. Harry's spirits sank.

Margaret recounted the events of her day. She had visited the airline's offices, and they had been happy to help. Veronica had indeed arrived on Monday morning last week, but the flight had not been late. Nor was there a record of any issues with the bags. When Harry asked if there *would* be any kind of record, Margaret said the same thought had occurred to her. If there had just been a delay in delivering the bags to the baggage hall, then no, it was unlikely to have been recorded. If there had been a serious issue with unlocking the hold door, that was different. That would have required a maintenance inspection and clearance before the aircraft

141

could take off again. There was no maintenance record.

'Isn't that something the police would have checked?'

It seemed obvious to Harry that checking Veronica's story would have been a priority, but Margaret pointed out that it wasn't that simple. Veronica had not been interviewed by the police until last Thursday. By that time, the case had been transferred to the Met, who were aware that the Security Service was involved and investigating. Also, the post-mortem had revealed the lady's health issue. By that time, it would have been decided that it was death by natural causes.

'Of course,' Margaret added, looking as though what she was about to say was troubling her, 'we only know what Ron has told to us. And we only have her word that she gave the same story to the police.'

Harry was stunned by the suggestion. Were they condemning Veronica based on nothing more than conjecture? He knew that once trust was lost, all options were open for debate, but did they have any reason to doubt Veronica? He felt it necessary to speak out.

'I know it's been a rather strange week, but that's no reason to doubt people on the basis of speculation. There are no grounds to suppose that Ron was in that house before Huxley arrived.' He looked at Margaret. 'I don't even know why you should think that. Huxley himself thinks he may have been wrong about somebody else being in the house, and even if there was, we have no reason to suspect it was Ron. Have we?'

Harry felt a sinking feeling in the pit of his stomach. Partly because of Kilsdale's testimony and partly because Margaret was not given to wild speculation. Had there been something concrete directing her thoughts? Harry wasn't sure that he wanted to know the answer, but the look that passed between Margaret and Ben turned the sinking feeling into a knot.

'No, it wasn't Veronica.'

The assuredness behind Margaret's statement unsettled Harry. Even before Margaret added the word "but", Harry sensed it was coming. And he knew it would be nothing to calm his unease.

Yesterday, Ben and Margaret told him, they had been trying to piece together a timeline whilst Harry had been at Thames House. Based on the expected flight arrival time, they had estimated that Veronica should have arrived home between about 3:00 and 3:30 p.m.

'Before Huxley?'

Harry was confused – there had been no doubting Margaret's certainty that Veronica had not been the other person in the house. It was Veronica's statement that the police cordon had been in place when she arrived that had troubled Margaret and Ben. Huxley had phoned the police at about 4:10, and the police would have arrived ten to fifteen minutes later, and no more than thirty. When they had forced an entry, no third party had been found in the house. Ben wasn't sure how long it would take the police, especially the forensic teams, to arrive, but even with a flight delay and a holdup with the bags, his best guess was that Veronica should have been home about 4:30 to 5:00 p.m. It was just a little too early for the degree of police activity that she had described.

Margaret took up the narrative. If Veronica had bags that needed to be checked into the hold, then it was unlikely she would walk from Charlton station to her house. Ben had found the addresses of a couple of local taxi firms, and Margaret had paid them a visit after leaving the airline office. She had

143

been in luck. There had been an incident that had stuck in people's minds. A fare from Charlton station to Hassendean Road. The road had been cordoned off and, after having a quick look, the lady had asked to be taken back to the railway station. They had joked about it in the taxi firm's office, but when the news had broken about a possible murder, it had stayed in people's minds. The firm had contacted the driver and checked the times. Veronica had not arrived at her home until nearly 6:30. She had misled them about the flight and airport delays. There was no doubting she arrived home late, so what had she been doing that afternoon?

There was more to add to Harry's worries. The airline had checked her booking. It had been a return ticket. The journey back to Athens had been booked for two days ago: Sunday. Veronica had not planned on staying long. When Margaret said that all three had looked through the frosted banding of the meeting room towards Huxley, engrossed in reading his computer screen, the same thought going through their heads: where did that leave Huxley?

Harry mulled over what he had been told. It was a relief, certainly, that Veronica could not have been involved in whatever had happened at her house. The rest was a riddle. It was true that there were a couple of hours unaccounted for, but that was not the main issue. Why had Veronica lied?

Harry gave voice to his opinion. There was no making sense of everything that had gone on: the body in the house; Kilsdale's story; Veronica's lies; the unknown third party; Quinton, even. There was just too much that had happened.

'It doesn't make any sense,' Margaret responded, 'if you try and fit it into one narrative. What if there are two independent strands here, just happening to overlap at Veronica's house

144

last Monday?' Before Harry could comment, she jumped in quickly. 'Coincidences do happen sometimes, Harry.'

'There's another factor too,' Ben was keen to tell them. 'Do we really know the truth about what happened at that house. Lies aside, what if people were just telling us what they thought at the time, only having one piece of the picture? Lies are not the only things that can mislead us. Let's face it, a week ago we all believed Veronica was dead.'

'Which leaves us,' Harry inhaled deeply, 'no further forward.'

Ben drew a square on the whiteboard and in it he wrote, "Kilsdale. Quinton. ANO(?)". He drew a circle, and in that he wrote "Ron's house", and connected the square to the circle with an arrow. He then drew a second square in which he wrote "Ron, Huxley", and connected that to the circle. Inside a second circle, he wrote "Dossier".

Holding the marker pen against the dossier circle, he said, 'This connects to that' and drew an arrow to the box containing the words "Ron" and "Huxley". 'It's nothing to do with Kilsdale or Quinton. If it has anything to do with what happened at the house, it does so indirectly, only through Ron. Possibly Huxley, but this is what we need to focus on.'

Ben tapped the word "dossier" on the whiteboard and then drew another square. 'And what's the dossier about?' He wrote two names in the empty square: "Hamilton" and "Slowik".

'Sir Robert,' Harry commented by way of confirmation, but Ben had a different thought.

'No. Slowik. She's at the centre of this. "Cherchez la femme", as they say.'

'Better rub that out,' Harry told him, casting a look

towards Huxley in the main office. 'But you're right.'

They agreed that the only concrete link they had to the mystery was the dossier – the reason why Veronica had returned to the UK. It was the only starting point that they had. At present, they had no idea if it was genuine or not, nor did they know its relationship to the copy that had been sent to Thames House. How did that copy connect to the story? Although it was getting late in the afternoon, Harry felt it worthwhile to ring the Director General's private office number and try to make an appointment for the following morning. Veronica's copy had been delivered to Thames House twenty-four hours ago; there must be some preliminary information on its authenticity.

Giving due regard to the Director General's call for discretion, Harry didn't make the phone call from the office or his desk. He preferred that there was no chance Huxley might overhear or interrupt. Even though it felt disloyal to Margaret and Ben, he went down to Nicholas' vestibule to make the call.

The response was not what he had expected. After he identified himself, the call was muted, as though a hand was being held over the mouthpiece. He thought he could decipher 'It's Mr Nevile', followed by another voice with what sounded like an expletive, but he didn't catch anything else. The line cleared, and the response from the DG's secretary was quite firm:

'You are to attend the Director General's office. Immediately.'

CHAPTER 19

Day nine: Tuesday, late afternoon

'The way I see it, Mr Nevile...'

Harry wondered if the Director General was deliberately parodying Sir Robert Hamilton's manner of speaking. The mood of the DG was distinctly different to the last time that Harry had met with him. This afternoon, there was no bonhomie, no pleasantries whatsoever – the DG seemed almost remote. Not surprising, perhaps, in light of the news that Harry had been told upon arrival. A body had been found yesterday in Pimlico. Sir Robert had been Harry's first thought – it would explain the urgency of his summons to Thames House so late in the afternoon. To his relief, but also his great surprise, the body had been identified as that of Matthew Kilsdale.

The body had been found in the grounds of Pimlico School, close to Chichester Road. Even before he was given any more information, Harry had wondered if Quinton was involved somehow. Harry was not that familiar with Chichester Road, but he knew it was close to Dolphin Square, and Quinton Bickley-Morris was one of the residents of the upmarket blocks of flats, which had been associated with intrigue and scandal.

The Director General was quite blunt in his assessment of the situation.

'I have been presented with a number of events. A senior

member of the Service has gone – how shall I say this? – unexpectedly absent without leave? At the same time, a former member of your staff, who, may I remind you, did a similar disappearing act last year, reappears, bearing documents that incriminate our newly missing colleague. And, quite by chance, on the day she returns, there's an unexplained death at her house. A current member of your staff, who was known to have been present at the house, was detained by the police in relation to that death. Subsequently, you have had a meeting with a Mr Kilsdale. A meeting at which, you say, he implicated Mr Bickley-Morris in the Blackheath death. You appear not to have informed the police, nor taken further action of any kind. Mr Kilsdale is now dead, almost certainly murdered, and his body was found with your business card in his pocket. On the back of that card was written "QBM, 8:30". The way I see it, Mr Nevile, is that the common link between all of these events is your good self. Perhaps you have an explanation?'

Harry's explanation about his card was quite simple: he had given it to Kilsdale when they met, though he had no knowledge of the details written on the back. As for everything else, he had as little idea as any of the others in the room.

'I know Bickley-Morris lives close by, but that's *all* I know.'

Whilst Michael Rose explained that the police had already interviewed Mr Bickley-Morris and, unsurprisingly, wished to speak to Harry too, Harry was digesting the few facts that he knew. Matthew Kilsdale had quite clearly been both frightened by and angry with Quinton, thinking Quinton had arranged the killing in Blackheath and had planned to set him up to take the blame. So why go alone to a meeting with Quinton at night? It was true that Kilsdale had said he wanted "that bastard" off his back, but Harry thought it unlikely Kilsdale would have gone intending to harm Quinton. Especially at Dolphin Square. Given its proximity to Westminster, Thames House and Vauxhall Cross, the Square not only had more than its fair share of dignitaries but was also becoming popular with senior members of the intelligence services.

Harry recalled what Sir Robert had said about Quinton not acting alone but having what he described as "a shadowy hypothetical friend". If, as Sir Robert had suggested, this hypothetical friend feared that Slowik knew enough to identify him, then it could explain why Sir Robert felt it necessary to take unsanctioned action to protect her. That unsanctioned action being their apparent joint disappearance. Although the DG had not confirmed Harry's suspicion that Slowik, too, had disappeared, he had not denied it either. But where did Quinton fit into this? Something clicked in Harry's brain.

According to Kilsdale's account, Quinton had blackmailed him into going to Veronica's house, but he had not been able to enter because of the police presence. Whatever Quinton's intention had been, something had gone wrong with his plan. Whether or not the death was intentional, accidental or, as it seemed, an awful happenstance, did not matter; Quinton had attracted the attention of the police. Kilsdale, almost certainly, had known more than he had ever admitted about the money-laundering scheme that Quinton ran before he was arrested in Greece. Had he tried to blackmail Quinton? Or did he just know too much? Enough that Quinton would lure him to Blackheath, intending to do him harm? Why Blackheath? Harry doubted that Quinton could have known that Veronica had found some of Graham's papers; as far as he was aware, only her sister and Huxley knew of the discovery.

It also puzzled Harry how Quinton knew Veronica's address. *He* wouldn't, but would his hypothetical friend? Ben had picked up quite quickly on the possibility that Slowik may need protecting from someone very senior in the Security Service. That meant someone who could quite easily access details such as Veronica's address, and the fact that Veronica had left the Service under unclear circumstances and was suspected of having left the United Kingdom. It would not have been difficult to confirm that her house was unoccupied.

Was Kilsdale's death a second and, sadly, successful attempt to eliminate a growing risk, whilst at the same time seeking to frame Quinton? *No, not frame him.* This was someone who would be smart enough to know that, without further evidence, Quinton would go free. Not frame him then, but certainly distract him, give him a warning perhaps? "We can make life very difficult for you, should we choose."

Harry also realised that, with Kilsdale's death, he had lost the only witness who could confirm Huxley's assertion that there had been somebody else in Veronica's house that ill-omened afternoon.

'Mr Nevile! Perhaps we are mistaken in thinking that you take this matter as seriously as we do?' The Director General's sharp reprimand brought Harry's attention back to the room.

'Apologies, I was just trying to find a connection between these events.'

'And?'

'Nothing, I'm afraid. Not that I can see.' Harry didn't want to play his hand yet; it was all supposition, and there were some senior members of the Service present.

There was also the mystery of the two copies of the dossier and Veronica's direct involvement in that peculiar business. Sidelining Sir Robert Hamilton, who seemed more involved in the Slowik business than Harry might have supposed, could be a ploy to make her more vulnerable. That fitted with the arguments Sir Robert had put to Harry just over a week ago. Harry already had his doubts about the probability of Veronica finding the dossier by accident and had discussed the possibility that the second copy had been necessary, given the belief that Veronica had been killed before she could hand over her copy. Had her unknown movements been to pick up the dossier in London, and that was how they knew she had not had time to make the delivery? Whoever "they" were.

'Mr Nevile. Pay attention. I will not remind you again.'

Harry was subjected to close questioning about Veronica, about his relationship with Sir Robert, about Huxley's version of events and about his meeting with Matthew Kilsdale. The one item that was not brought up was his meeting with Francis Buckingham, and it was clear to Harry that he was there to answer questions, not to raise concerns of his own. He was worried, however, that by sticking assiduously only to known facts, he was giving the impression that he was hiding something. That he was complicit in Kilsdale's death. The Director General seemed to confirm Harry's concern by insisting he surrender his passport.

'I am sure Brigadier Newcomb will take adequate care of it,' the DG added. It took Harry a moment or two to

151

register that the DG was referring to Nicholas. The Tufton Street concierge seemed an odd choice of custodian, but Harry's main reaction was a feeling of relief. This suggested convenience as much as security. A reasonable precaution seen to be taken rather than serious concern about Harry's involvement. Odd, though, that the DG referred to Nicholas by his former army rank. It was only rarely that Harry heard anyone other than Sir Robert Hamilton refer to Nicholas as Brigadier Newcomb

The Director General then excused himself and for the next hour or so, the questioning became more aggressive and intrusive. Harry felt drained after the meeting closed, and he was excused. Thinking he could catch a Tube home, he started walking south along Millbank. As he passed the end of Thorney Street, he changed his mind. It would be about fifteen minutes on foot to Pimlico Underground and about the same from South Kensington station to his house in Montpelier Walk. By the time he changed lines at Victoria, he wouldn't save much time compared to walking. He knew that he could cut through from Thorney Street to Page Street, at the rear of Thames House, and then make his way towards Belgravia via the back of Victoria station. Almost certainly, he would pass somewhere to eat, and perhaps he could indulge himself with a pint of beer and a pub meal, considering the events of the day.

As Harry turned the corner to the rear of Thames House, he noticed a parked car with a man, presumably the driver, holding the rear passenger door open. A figure emerged from one of the doorways and looked around. The man seemed to pause and give a brief nod of acknowledgement in Harry's direction before getting into the back of the car. The driver took his seat, and the car sped away so quickly that Harry thought the engine must already have been running. It was dusk; the light wasn't good, and although Harry was by no means certain, he had a feeling he recognised the person.

It was Sir Robert Hamilton.

CHAPTER 20
Day nine: Tuesday, evening

As Harry was walking home, his was not the only mind dwelling on the death of Matthew Kilsdale. Reid was considering his options. Part of him regretted sanctioning the killing, though another part of him knew that, had he not, it would have made no difference. It was becoming increasingly clear that Tobias, and the people who had sent him, regarded Reid as subservient. He was increasingly worried that he was becoming a pawn whose fate depended upon how helpful he was towards Tobias.

Even though it seemed that the death at Blackheath was no longer being treated as suspicious, it was still a death. It was inevitable that Kilsdale's death would set alarm bells ringing, though it was a bonus that it was now linked to Harry Nevile as well as Bickley-Morris. Tobias was resourceful, thorough and quick-thinking. He had checked Kilsdale's pockets, planning to leave his own cryptic note implicating Bickley-Morris and had come across Harry's card. The police would recognise the card as belonging to a member of the Security Service and involve Thames House. It had been an opportunity not to be missed. With both Nevile and Bickley-Morris under suspicion, it may well tempt Hamilton to break cover. Reid had no plans to harm Sir Robert physically; the evidence that he had been working for the East Germans would be sufficient to compound the doubts that had been raised by the debacle of the Bickley-Morris' trial. A sham trial to absolve one of Hamilton's fellow agents. Even if nothing was proven, the doubts would finish Hamilton's career. Undoubtedly, Hamilton was the key to finding Slowik again, a task that would be easier with her protector out of the way.

Reid also knew it was time to plan his own departure. The network had functioned smoothly when there was information flowing through it. Now it was becoming fragmented, ragged and uncontrolled. The fiasco in Blackheath was clear evidence of that. Whatever the circumstances of the death, Bickley-Morris had not listened and had acted too early. In the uncertainty that followed, Reid had taken his own actions. If rumours were true, it wasn't only Hamilton who had disappeared but Slowik too. If nothing was done, the chances of finding Slowik could evaporate completely. Why not capitalise on the inevitable uncertainties and doubts? There was an opportunity to go beyond discrediting Robert Hamilton, by having MI5 searching for their own man. Who better to flush him out? It was too good an opportunity to be missed. After all, Reid was quite certain that some of the evidence against Sir Robert must have come, originally, from within the intelligence agencies. The way the case had been handled made the intention clear: bury the story to save embarrassment. Reid's plan was simple: bring it out into the open to make sure they couldn't. Those who had been complicit in trying to avoid a scandal would be the loudest in denouncing Hamilton in order to deflect attention and cover their own backs. They would be relentless in seeking him, diverting attention and resources away from Slowik.

Reid had no direct interest in finding Slowik, but in

helping those who did, his hope was that he would be left alone. It was time not just to consider his own future but to secure it. He now knew the dead woman had not been Nevile's former colleague, who, according to the news he had been given yesterday evening, had now handed over her copy of the Hamilton file. Too much was slipping out of his control. Too many changes were having to be made. Reid's contingency plan had always been to escape to Canada, a country sufficiently expansive and empty for him to disappear. Cyprus was now looking like an attractive alternative. Since the dissolution of the Soviet Union, Reid had noticed a growing influx of Russian émigrés, who were not finding the new Russian Federation to their liking. Here was a chance to find like-minded people who could be sympathetic to his background and security. He just needed to wait a little while. Running out on Tobias might prove to be a fatal mistake. Quite literally. His only hope was that when Tobias returned to Germany, he would be able to slip away himself. Surviving long enough to do that meant keeping on the right side of Tobias.

* * *

Just over a mile from Reid's flat in Eaton Mews, Quinton Bickley-Morris was looking out of his window, watching the red sky and the setting sun. A whisky and soda in his hand. He was fuming. Reid. It had to have been Reid.

The first that Quinton had known of Kilsdale's death was the police knocking on his door, midmorning. On being asked if he knew a Matthew Kilsdale, his initial reaction had been to deny he knew anybody with that name, and then one of the officers, who had identified himself as a detective sergeant, had asked him, "Then, do you know anybody by the name of Harry Nevile?" That was when the alarm bells had started to ring, and he refused to answer any more questions until they told him why they were asking. He needed to figure out what was going on, and to do so rather quickly. He had tried to browbeat the officer by pointing out that he was a former PPS to the secretary of state for defence and, without knowing the reason for their enquiry, could not answer for fear of disclosing confidential information.

'Oh, we know who you were and something of your more recent activities,' the officer had retorted. That had been when the officer had suggested Quinton accompany him to New Scotland Yard. Quinton recognised that as a ploy to intimidate him rather than a genuine request but put the detective on the back foot by accepting the invitation, suggesting that perhaps it would be the most sensible course of action. It bought Quinton time to think. Not wanting to give the impression that he may have something to hide, Quinton had waived his right to have a solicitor present.

At New Scotland Yard, Quinton had played a skilful game, piecing together the events that had led the police to his door. A body carrying bank and credit cards in the name of Matthew Kilsdale had been found, close to Dolphin Square. A business card in the name of Harry Nevile had been found on the body, and written on the back was "QBM, 8:30". Quinton knew the format of Security Service business cards and was quite certain that the police did too. That would have led the police to Thames House. Harry would have been identified as one of their officers, and somebody had been smart enough to recognise QBM as his initials.

Possibly Harry himself, but Quinton doubted the police had interviewed Harry – the Service would take care of their own.

Quinton acknowledged that he did indeed know a Harry Nevile. Sticking to the truth, he told them that about five or six years ago he had, to his great surprise, been asked to manage Harry's group. He enjoyed telling them that, at the time, Harry Nevile had been under arrest. It may not have been the whole truth, but it was what he had been led to believe. Quinton then played what he hoped would be a winning card.

'Mr Nevile and his associates have continued to harass and pursue me over a number of years. I have little doubt that you are aware I was brought to trial earlier this year. I was found entirely innocent, and unless you have good cause to doubt the wisdom of Her Majesty's courts, you will treat me as such. Quite frankly, Mr Nevile is not to be trusted.'

Quinton had the good sense to stop short of reminding the officers that only the previous week, some of Harry's team had been involved in a suspicious death in south London. It was not something an innocent man would have known.

Quinton's gambit was not entirely successful; the police officer came back at him:

'Perhaps you would care to explain your involvement with a company called DCM Diagnostics.'

The detective had not mentioned that Kilsdale had been a director of DCM, but it was a trap that Quinton had been sharp enough to recognise.

'I had investments in a number of small companies, including one called DCM, I believe. But if you were to take the trouble of reading the transcript of my court case, you would find that Mr Nevile and his superior officer, the bafflingly knighted Sir Robert Hamilton, used that company to plant fabricated evidence against me. Perhaps you should address your enquiries to them.'

Quinton was hoping that the rumours of Sir Robert's disappearance were true.

'You had an investment with the company, yet you're unaware Mr Kilsdale was a director?' was the detective's inevitable question.

'A small investment, a small company, fifteen hundred miles from my base in Greece? It would be surprising if I could remember the names of the directors. Of course, if this Mr Kilsdale was diligent in his duties, he may have become aware of Hamilton and Nevile's unscrupulous abuse of his company's facilities. That would have given *them* a motive.'

The interview had ended in stalemate, and the police had detained Quinton, quite unreasonably in his opinion, at New Scotland Yard for several hours without further interview before letting him go. No doubt, Quinton had thought and hoped, they were checking with the Security Service. At least it gave him more time to think. Kilsdale's death could only be down to Reid. True, having Kilsdale dead was to his own benefit, in more ways than one, but why had Reid said nothing? And why the dumping of the body so close to Dolphin Square, with a misleading message on Nevile's business card? Following the shambles in Blackheath, the weasel Kilsdale may well have been to see Nevile, worried about his own neck. If the rumours were true, he would not have been able to contact Hamilton. Nevile, however, could not be responsible for the writing on the back of the card, which implicated him as much as it did Quinton. It had to be Reid, who, in any case, could access counterfeit cards. It

159

wasn't a serious attempt to frame Quinton, or indeed Nevile, but it was a clear warning: "Stay on the right side of me. I can make things very difficult for you. Or worse!"

* * *

Harry cleared away the last of his crockery. Tempting though the idea of a pub meal had been, he had decided that he needed something fresher, something lighter, something he would cook at home. Cooking wasn't a problem for Harry – he had a number of Asian recipes that he could cook in ten to fifteen minutes, and dried noodles took only four minutes to soften. His meal over, Harry slid a compact disc into the slot of his new CD player. Not having a car, Harry had never felt the need for a cassette deck; he had plenty of music in his record collection. The quality and convenience of CDs, however, had appealed to him, and he had given in to temptation. It had only been a few months, and his selection of CDs was limited, but it did include his favourite: Smetana's *Má Vlast*. With a little luck, he could escape the turmoil around him for a short while.

Luck, however, eluded Harry. He was certain that the person he had seen getting into the car was Sir Robert, and that meant his supposed disappearance was some kind of deception. Had that been what the DG had meant when he told Harry he was unable to tell him everything? Although several thousand people worked at Thames House, and only a small fraction could know Sir Robert by sight, it would have taken something serious for him to run the risk of being seen. That "something" had to be Kilsdale's death and the link to both Harry and Quinton.

Assuming he was right about Kilsdale's reluctance to meet Quinton, Harry wondered who could have lured Kilsdale to that part of Pimlico. Perhaps the answer was no one, perhaps Kilsdale had been killed elsewhere and his body dumped close to Dolphin Square to give credence to the writing on the business card. Which would mean it hadn't been Kilsdale who put the details of the supposed meeting on the back of Harry's card. A third person. Just like at Veronica's house. Both Huxley and Kilsdale had told him there was a third person. It was a tenuous link, but it was a link between the deaths in Blackheath and Pimlico. If whoever had been waiting at Veronica's house had intended to harm Kilsdale, silencing him was a possible motive. If so, the meeting with Harry could only have increased the danger towards Kilsdale. Harry realised that meant that he too could be in danger; not that Kilsdale had revealed anything of substance, but if it was believed he may have, it would explain why this second attempt on Kilsdale's life had followed so quickly after Blackheath.

Could all this be connected to the hypothetical friend that Sir Robert had mentioned, possibly someone senior, either within MI5 or closely associated? Someone who clearly had access to confidential information. Someone who was now a potential threat to Harry and his team? Nobody had given Harry any information on where the second copy of Veronica's file had come from, but casting doubt on Sir Robert's loyalty fitted with the actions of someone with a grudge against the Bioweapons Counter-Espionage Unit or its members. If Slowik could identify this person, then why hadn't she? Especially if she was in danger from him? The answer had to be that she didn't know. Undoubtedly, if this person existed, they needed to be stopped; to Harry, that seemed sufficient justification for Sir Robert to risk breaking cover.

Above all, Harry regretted that he had not given Kilsdale more time and attention. If he'd listened more and taken some action, Kilsdale might still be alive.

* * *

Sir Robert closed the lid of his notebook computer and unplugged it from the telephone line. Weighing around three kilograms, it wasn't the most convenient device to carry around, but the ability to connect remotely to the office was invaluable. Despite wondering how long it would be before people stopped writing what he thought of as "proper letters", the ability to send and receive messages in real time was critical to his present situation. Without what his junior colleagues called "email", his present operation would have left him isolated and vulnerable. Even so, the events of the past week had caused so much disruption and added too much complexity. He knew he was running a risk visiting Thames House, and he was in no doubt that Harry had seen and recognised him earlier that day. Unfortunately, relations between the Security Service and the Secret Intelligence Service were becoming strained and meeting the Director General had become necessary.

Not surprisingly, the DG had been far from happy to have been kept in the dark. Even though it was becoming increasingly likely that the risk to Slowik was not coming from within the Security Service, a decision had been taken not to forewarn the DG. Ultimately, Sir Robert Hamilton was responsible for Slowik's safety, and he did not answer to the Director General of MI5. The DG had been aware that, should it become necessary to ensure Slowik's safety, action may have to be taken without warning. There was a course of action that the DG himself was required to take in that event, and he had taken it, but not being kept informed had caused some friction. Slowik was now safe, or at least as safe as she could be, and other matters had come to the forefront. Mrs Blakeridge's copy of the dossier had caught Sir Robert unprepared. The original, he knew, had been prepared by the Secret Intelligence Service, MI6, with information supplied by Slowik and Sir Robert himself. It had been Sir Robert who had fed it into the system. It had been an attempt to flush out where the danger lay.

The question was, how had Mrs Blakeridge got hold of a copy? It was a question that Sir Robert could not ignore. Although it was possible that the file had been planted in Rod Graham's house, it certainly hadn't been in Graham's possession. The document hadn't been created when Graham had died. If, as seemed likely, Mrs Blakeridge was involved, then there was the distinct possibility that Harry and his team could be in jeopardy. It was a possibility that worried Sir Robert, and the recent attempt to involve Harry in the death of Kilsdale seemed to legitimise that concern.

Despite the police concluding that there had been nothing suspicious about the death in Blackheath, that too worried Sir Robert. It wasn't so much the coincidence of it happening the day Mrs Blakeridge arrived back in the UK, but the fact that both Huxley and Kilsdale had claimed somebody else had been in the house. Somebody who had never come forward. If the intent had been to harm Mrs Blakeridge, Sir Robert

163

was puzzled. Killing the bearer and leaving the finding of the dossier to chance – was that a sound strategy? It was a puzzle that needed solving. If done properly, ensuring that the dossier was brought to the attention of the police, it would be more difficult to keep the accusations under wraps. Especially if details were leaked to the press. A more immediate need, however, was to protect Harry. There was no real option other than to meet him and bring him into the plan. Harry could be trusted; he had, after all, passed the Buckingham test.

* * *

Anna Slowik was sitting on deck, a shawl wrapped around her thin shoulders, the dark sky scattered with stars. There was said to be a comet in the sky, one predicted to become the brightest in living memory. Anna could not see it, but wondered if it was a portent. One more night and she would step off the boat and into a new identity. An identity she had been practising on her fellow passengers for the last week. She was holding her left wrist to stop her hand from trembling. Her condition would only get worse, she knew that, but she also knew that she would be well looked after and safe. She had Hamilton's word on that, and not once, in almost thirty years, had he let her down. Even though she had been unsettled by the haste with which the short fjord cruise had been arranged, she had been certain he still had her best interests at heart.

She knew that "long-term" was hardly a fitting description of her long-term prognosis, and she was facing progressive deterioration, even with medication. There was time, still, to attend to one outstanding matter. One injustice which, for almost fifty years, she had thought she would never get the opportunity to redress. There had been hope that the British justice system would deliver retribution of a sort; she would have been content with that, but it had let her down. There remained only one option now, one that she had prepared well for over the past few months.

CHAPTER 21

Day ten: Wednesday

How had he missed it?

The thought had given no pleasure to Harry; it had just delivered a kick to his stomach. It was only when you put things together that the full picture emerged. It wasn't conclusive, but evidence rarely was. How many people would look at a brick and see a house?

Harry had woken as usual that morning, without the need for an alarm. As a student, he had realised that whenever he did set an alarm, he was always awake before it went off. He hadn't bothered with one for many years. Ready to leave, putting on his watch, he noticed the date. It had been a month since he had last heard from the solicitor dealing with his mother's estate. He needed to get in touch and check on the progress, if any, of his application for probate. The thought hadn't struck Harry immediately. It was whilst listening to the BBC's *Today* programme and having breakfast that it had occurred to him. There had been a news item stating that work was finally about to start on a new airport in Athens, and it highlighted that discussions had been taking place for almost twenty years. Time, Harry thought, had hardly been of the essence.

Time. Harry's application for probate should have been simple. His mother had left a will, and he was an only child. The will, however, had been written quite a few years ago, and his mother had made some more recent investments that were not mentioned. Harry had been asked to provide additional information, which had not been difficult to do, but it still seemed to be taking a long time to work its way through the probate registry. How much more difficult would it have been if his mother had died abroad, there was no will, and Harry had been a distant relative? The child of a cousin, for example.

Veronica had claimed she had inherited Rod Graham's house. From the searches Huxley had done the previous year, after Veronica's disappearance, it seemed quite likely that Veronica would be Graham's next of kin, but how long would the process take in Greece? Especially if she hadn't pursued a claim. From what Harry could recall, the embassy in Athens had taken guardianship of Graham's estate. When Harry, with Sir Robert and Huxley, had been in Greece, their focus had been on detaining Quinton. He doubted they had mentioned any relationship between Graham and Veronica. Especially as her whereabouts were unknown at the time. The more Harry had thought about it, the less plausible it had seemed that she had inherited the house. At least not in any legal sense. He knew there was no strict legal definition of next of kin under UK law, and he certainly had no idea about the situation under Greek law. Harry couldn't rule out that Veronica may have been rifling through Graham's belongings unofficially, but she would have had to have forced an entry; she would not have had a key. And, if so, she would not have drawn attention to herself by burning his documents on a garden fire. She would have taken what she was looking for and run.

Harry needed to talk to Sir Robert Hamilton. Not just

about his suspicions, but also because there was something else going on – something he wasn't party to. The sighting of his friend and colleague yesterday was testimony to that. Harry had thought about approaching the Director General. That would be the proper route in Sir Robert's absence, but Harry was unsure. The DG's attitude recently had been ambivalent, and if there was a covert operation, the DG would protect the status quo. Harry had not been made privy to the details, and that would continue to be the official policy. He had no option other than to put his trust in Nicholas and hope that his hunch that Nicholas was in contact with Sir Robert was true.

A morning chill was in the air as Harry walked through Belgravia on his way to Tufton Street. There was a slightly shorter route via Knightsbridge and Constitution Hill. Both gave him plenty of time to think, but Harry preferred the route that avoided the most road traffic. He thought over the incident of the previous evening when he had seen Sir Robert. At the time, he had not taken much notice of the driver. It hadn't been Clive, Sir Robert's regular driver – Clive was slim and slight. This driver was more solidly built, more like Nicholas. *Could it have been?*

When he arrived at Tufton Street, before his colleagues as usual, he knew how he was going to approach Nicholas, and Nicholas gave him the perfect opportunity by remarking that Harry looked puzzled that morning.

'Are you by any chance, Nicholas, familiar with the philosophical question of the tree in the quadrangle?'

'The question of does the tree exist if there is nobody there to observe it?'

'Yes. I was thinking. If I'm the only person in the

quadrangle, and I observe the tree, then the tree exists. But if I can see the tree, I too must exist.'

'Yes, sir,' Nicholas agreed cautiously. He had an inkling of where Harry was taking the argument.

'Then, if I exist, I must be observed myself. Yes?'

'The argument would suggest that, sir.'

'And, if I'm the only person in the quadrangle, then if I see the tree, the tree must have seen me.'

'Or God sees both yourself and the tree, sir, as I believe the argument is sometimes put.'

Harry wondered if Nicholas had missed the point or was trying to mislead him deliberately. Even if Nicholas had not been the driver, Harry was sure that he would have been forewarned about the incident by Sir Robert.

'Indeed, Nicholas.' Harry was smiling at the concierge's quick-witted response. 'I could pray for an answer, but if American Indians can talk to trees, perhaps I could too.'

It was Nicholas' turn to smile. 'Perhaps you can, sir, but first, do you have something for me? Something for safekeeping?'

'Damn!' It was about as close to swearing as Harry came, except when he was really stressed. He had forgotten his passport. The sighting of Sir Robert, the realisation that another part of Veronica's story didn't ring true, let alone the revelation and possible repercussions of Kilsdale's murder, had taken up so much of his attention that he had forgotten he had been told to hand over his passport to Nicholas.

'Not to worry, sir. Perhaps you could pick it up on your way back from your meeting this morning?'

Harry wasn't aware that he had any meeting that morning.

'Yes, sir. The police would like to talk to you about Mr

Kilsdale.'

Harry was taken aback. He had rather assumed that, as was usual in these cases, the Met would let the Security Service carry out its own initial investigation. Just in case there were security implications. Wasn't that what yesterday evening's meeting had been about? He double-checked with Nicholas and asked if Thames House were aware. Nicholas confirmed that the meeting had been arranged through the appropriate channels and reassured Harry that it would be an informal meeting; Harry would not need to have anybody from the Service's legal department present.

'Scotland Yard, 12:15. Ask for Detective Chief Inspector Salisbury. Give her my regards, by the way. I think I may have mentioned we served together for a couple of years.'

Harry thought about returning to the subject of his wish to meet Sir Robert but was interrupted by the arrival of Margaret. After exchanging pleasantries, Harry waited until they were in the lift before asking the obvious question.

'In early today. Any special reason?'

'Yes, I need to have a word with you before the others arrive. Didn't want to say anything in front of Nicholas, though.'

Harry was surprised as he knew that Margaret was quite aware that Nicholas was the soul of discretion, though, given the doubts and uncertainties that had engulfed them all recently, perhaps it was not surprising.

'And I'm not just asking about your unexpected call to Thames House yesterday,' Margaret added with a querying look.

Harry smiled. 'Yes, we do have to talk about that. I think I need to include Huxley too, but as you're here early, perhaps

I could ask your advice on that one. But your news first.'

Having hung her coat up, Margaret perched on the edge of Harry's desk. The least interesting part of her news, she told Harry, was that the transcript of Veronica's interview with the police had arrived yesterday, shortly after he had left. Although the baggage delay was mentioned, the flight delay was not. Harry's "Oh, really?" was met with a warning from Margaret not to read too much into the fact. The police were already aware, when they interviewed Veronica, that the deceased had had a medical problem, and the interview had not been particularly probing. By the time Veronica had arrived at New Scotland Yard, they were not treating the death as suspicious.

'But there is one thing that's suspicious, Harry, and that is Nicholas seemed to know about the transcript. My request didn't go through him, but when the envelope was delivered, he seemed to know what it contained. Is there something I should know? Can Nicholas really be trusted? He's close to Sir Robert, and if there's any truth in the dossier...'

Harry chuckled. 'The case is being handled by a Detective Chief Inspector Salisbury.' He did not bother to wait for a reply. 'She served under Nicholas' command in Germany. I suspect that's why the request was dealt with so promptly. I think you can trust Nicholas; I do.' Harry looked Margaret straight in the eye. 'I also trust Sir Robert.'

Margaret wasn't sure what to make of Harry's remark. She still found the suggestion that Sir Robert had been working for the Eastern bloc hard to believe, but she felt the evidence should be weighed for what it was. The essence of being a successful agent was, after all, building a persona of innocence. She avoided any discussion by asking Harry

171

what had happened at Thames House that meant he wanted her advice with regard to Huxley. She was not expecting it to be another death – Matthew Kilsdale's, this time – and a death that was being treated as suspicious. When Harry went on to explain his latest concerns about Veronica's story, she understood the concern around Huxley.

'You're not suggesting, are you…?' Margaret didn't like the direction that her thoughts were taking. 'Ron goes to Greece, and Rod Graham dies. Ron comes back to the UK, and Kilsdale dies. And goodness knows what went on in her house.'

Harry's forehead dropped into the open palms of his hands.

'Oh, shit. I hadn't connected her travels with the deaths.'

The fact that Harry had just sworn, for possibly only the second or third time in her hearing, told her just how worrying he found her suggestion.

'You have to tell him about Kilsdale, Harry. He could be in danger. And if she is involved somehow in Kilsdale's death, and Huxley says nothing… Well, she knows we'll get to hear the news sooner rather than later, and if Huxley says nothing, she may become suspicious of him.'

Much as they didn't want to admit it, they both knew that if Veronica had been involved in the deaths, if she had suspicions about Huxley, she may not have too many qualms about adding him to the body count. Another thought struck Margaret.

'Dear God, Harry. Huxley! She knows he saw somebody else in her house. If it was her, and she thinks he knows… We need to be careful what we tell him, but we need to tell him something.'

Margaret reminded Harry of the reason he had decided not to keep the news of a second copy of the dossier from Huxley. The chances that the two copies had appeared independently were slim. If Veronica really was involved, it would be something she was likely to be aware of, and she would be suspicious if it hadn't been discussed at Tufton Street. Nothing, however, could be said about their suspicions about Veronica for fear of putting Huxley at risk. They both knew that Huxley getting hurt was unavoidable unless Veronica was innocent. If she wasn't, Huxley would be devastated, but all they could hope for was that the damage was limited to his emotions. The poor chap was clearly head over heels in love. Margaret would update Ben with Harry's thoughts about the legitimacy of Veronica's claim to have inherited Graham's house; another meeting with Huxley excluded would not be conducive to goodwill. They would need his feedback on Veronica's actions and movements.

It was decided that Harry would be completely open and honest about his most recent meeting at Thames House. After all, the whole team knew he had been summoned at short notice. That meant something serious. He would not, however, mention his meeting with Kilsdale the previous week. Margaret and Ben were aware of that, not anyone else. If he were asked about how Kilsdale came to have his business card, Harry would be non-committal. They all knew he had visited DCM Diagnostics about a year ago, and Harry could point out that the card could be counterfeit. That would also be a good time to tell them he had been invited to New Scotland Yard later that morning. Verifying the authenticity of his card and checking if the writing on the back was in Harry's hand were good enough reasons for the

Met to interview him.

'You don't think... you know... Huxley? He couldn't be involved too?' Margaret asked the question that neither of them really wanted to ask. They were, however, both firmly convinced that he was not. Yes, he had made some visits to Greece without mentioning it, but if he was involved, surely he would have fled too? Certainly, he would not have passed on the information that Veronica was hiding in Perdika, staying with her half-sister and her family – even to Harry. The awkward fact was that Huxley had chosen to remain silent, even when it was clear that Harry had decided to take no further action. There had been little point, in Harry's view: the mouse plot seemed to have been foiled, Graham was dead, and Quinton was in custody. The operation was over, case closed. Why had Huxley said nothing about her whereabouts or his visits?

It had been Harry's decision, too, not to tell Margaret that he had seen Sir Robert leaving Thames House the previous night. That was the only part of the plan he did feel guilty about but telling her would serve no useful purpose.

The meeting with his team went better than Harry had hoped. All of them, including Andrew and Thomas, the two junior analysts, were grateful that Harry was sharing the information. None of them believed Harry could be involved in Kilsdale's death. There was some speculation as to why Harry had been targeted, which Harry warned against, pointing out that it was a matter for the Thames House investigators to determine. The point of the meeting, he told them, was to make them aware and to put them on their guard. Whatever was going on, he told them, it was likely targeted at only his good self, quite likely an opportunistic building on

174

the events at Blackheath. Tragic though that death was, the police were no longer treating it as suspicious.

The only tricky moment was when Huxley pointed out that Harry had been summoned to Thames House at short notice several times in the past week and asked why that was. Much to Harry's surprise, it was Ben who responded:

'Oh, come on, Hux. Some serious allegations have been made against Hamilton. Of course, Thames House are going to ask questions, and they're not going to make appointments in advance, either. Not just Harry, but probably all of us, especially you. And afterwards, do you think they're going to say, "Oh, it's fine. If anyone asks, feel free to tell them everything we've discussed"?'

Huxley looked a bit sheepish and didn't push for any more information. It was, as far as Harry could tell, Huxley just being Huxley and wanting to know everything rather than some malevolent fishing for information.

Harry was content but apprehensive as he walked past Parliament, heading for the embankment and New Scotland Yard. The meeting with the Tufton Street team had gone well, particularly the support that Ben had given so unexpectedly, though it still seemed rather odd to him that the Met had asked to speak with him on his own. His unease grew as he entered New Scotland Yard to find that DCI Salisbury was waiting for him. Harry had never met her before, but she was quite confident in recognising him.

'Brigadier Newcomb phoned to say you were on your way,' she advised him, seeming to sense his surprise and unease. It took Harry a second or two to register that she was referring to Nicholas. They walked in silence as she led Harry through into the building and then down the stairs.

She walked briskly, two steps ahead of Harry, giving him no chance to strike up a conversation, and into a part of the building that looked rather utilitarian. As she opened a door off the drab corridor, she stood to one side.

'Your car's waiting for you.'

Harry looked from DCI Salisbury to the underground car park and back again. She just smiled at him.

'Ours is not to reason why,' she quipped, an enigmatic smile on her lips that reminded Harry of Nicholas, whilst gesturing for him to go through the door where an unmarked, black car was waiting, engine running, with the chauffeur standing by the open rear door.

The chauffeur was as silent as the detective chief inspector had been as he headed north along the embankment, only to turn left across the front of the MOD building, then south along Whitehall and along the north bank of the river. The driver seemed to be taking a rather indirect route to anywhere Harry could think of, and Harry wondered if it was to avoid traffic or make it difficult to be followed. As they turned left onto Vauxhall Bridge Road, Harry was completely perplexed as to where they were heading.

* * *

About three hundred yards away, Veronica was sitting in the café of the Tate Gallery, a newspaper on the table in front of her. She was panic-stricken as she stared at the article about a body being found in school grounds in Pimlico. The police were treating the death as suspicious and had released the victim's name. They were looking for anybody who could help them with the whereabouts of a Matthew Kilsdale over the previous weekend. If only she could talk to somebody, but she was too frightened.

Chapter 22

Day ten: Wednesday

Harry looked out across the Thames. To his right, Millbank Tower stood tall, announcing its dominance over the landscape. Closer to him, he fancied he could see the top of the Tate Gallery's portico entrance. To his left, he searched for the brick façade of the Dolphin Square buildings, home to Quinton Bickley-Morris and adjacent to the site where Kilsdale's body had been found.

If Harry had been surprised when the car had turned left immediately after crossing Vauxhall Bridge and into Vauxhall Cross, home to MI6, he was completely bewildered when the door to the room opened and Sir Robert Hamilton strolled in.

'Bob?'

'Harry.' Sir Robert greeted him sheepishly. 'I guess you're wondering what's going on. Oh dear, where to start?'

'Slowik?' Harry suggested, recalling Ben's insistence that Anna Slowik was somehow the key link between the events of the last ten days. Had it really been only ten days? 'And perhaps our friend Quinton?' he added as an afterthought.

'Just a small group of players, that's for sure, Harry, but more than one drama being acted out, I suspect. The question is, who is in which play? And who is starring in more than one?' Sir Robert's thoughts echoed what Margaret had wondered the previous week.

Harry said nothing, waiting for Sir Robert to organise his

thoughts.

'We have to protect Slowik. She has been useful to us, very loyal too, saved a fair few British lives. A few weeks ago, my colleagues in Berlin sent us a warning. Thankfully, we were prepared, and Anna's debriefing was coming to an end anyway.'

'And have you protected her?'

'Yes, but it was all rather rushed in the end.' Sir Robert pointed to the metal-framed, black leather seats around a small table with matching legs and a grey oak top.

'Let's sit.'

Harry sat with his back to the window, opposite his friend and colleague, who was gazing across the room at the view. The look on Sir Robert's face told Harry that he was still organising his thoughts. Sir Robert sighed.

'Actually, not just rushed, but complicated by some… Well, what would you call the events of the past week? Bizarre? Unexpected?'

'What is unexpected,' Harry pointed out to Sir Robert, 'is that you're here now, not to mention you were at Thames House yesterday, yet everyone's searching for you. At least, supposedly. After all, there have been some serious allegations. Oh, and let's not forget my supposed meeting at New Scotland Yard this morning.'

Harry was beginning to sound fractious, though in truth, his guard had slipped, and the emotions he had been bottling up for the past week were beginning to surface. Sir Robert knew Harry well enough to recognise the apparent frustration for what it was.

'Let me continue with Anna Slowik, then we'll get onto other matters. There have been some – what shall we call

179

them? – eventualities we had neither planned nor foreseen. And you, Harry, you have a role to play, and I'm not sure if those who oppose us have realised that. You need to understand, Harry. That's why we're having this meeting and why we want to keep it confidential.'

Sir Robert reminded Harry that he had already told him that Slowik was in danger. She always had been since the fall of the Berlin Wall. There were those who would prefer to ensure her silence, "people who may have realised…" Harry was intrigued by this last unfinished remark but held back from saying anything. A number of things were beginning to come together in his mind, but he needed to hear Sir Robert out.

A couple of weeks ago, information that had increased the concerns about Slowik to a critical level had come from Berlin. There was a notorious former Stasi officer by the name of Tobias Tschesche who had disappeared several years ago. Sir Robert described him as "little more than an assassin". It was believed that he had worked for Abteilung A X, the so-called "Active Measures" section of the HVA, East Germany's foreign intelligence service. It was part of the same group as Slowik's counter-intelligence group Abteilung A IX, and Tschesche would have been familiar with both Slowik and her unit. His name had surfaced again, and the German authorities had told the UK's Berlin embassy that they believed that Tschesche was now in the UK, possibly using the alias David Fredericks.

'If he's taken the risk of becoming active again, there must be a reason, an important one, one that outweighs that risk. No prizes for guessing what that might be.' Sir Robert looked at Harry as if expecting an answer. Harry obliged.

'Slowik?'

'We have reason to believe so.'

'But that means you're suggesting that the Stasi are still organised and active. After six or seven years?'

Sir Robert shared Harry's scepticism. 'No, not the Stasi, but residual elements.'

Sir Robert explained further, reminding Harry that small networks were easier to manage, easier to disband, and were more difficult to detect. "Less likely to leak", for want of a better phrase. People like Quinton, agents placed within British government departments, were few and far between. Characteristically, the Stasi would make use of informal collaborators, middlemen, rather than flood the streets with professional agents. When East Germany was swallowed up in the reunification, however, those core networks had nowhere to go. They were likely still in place, redundant but bound together by the need for self-preservation. A residual hardcore cabal of former Stasi loyalists, seeking to preserve their own anonymity in the new German state, could reactivate such a redundant network, giving those people still in place the choice between collaboration and exposure. Crimes committed in the past were still crimes.

Slowik's debriefing had led to the belief that the flow of information between government agencies had, in the past, been compromised. There was a concern that this was happening again, in the wake of Slowik's request for sanctuary, and evidence had been building that it was information flowing between departments, via the Joint Intelligence Committee, that was at risk.

In light of Sir Robert's remark that he had a role to play, Harry now recognised that his new position to act as a focus for JIC communications was not the matter of convenience that the Director General had suggested.

'Bob, I can understand what you're saying, but with all that going on, it's hardly the time to stage some kind of, I don't know, theatrical disappearance? Especially with that damned dossier appearing. I'm confused. Why make yourself seem guilty? The fact that you're here now says the allegations are not true, so why not just prove that the dossier is a work of fiction?'

'Because it isn't. All the facts in that dossier are true. They came from my own records from when I was in Berlin.'

Harry struggled to make sense of what Sir Robert had just admitted.

'True? Then why are you here now? If you were under arrest, we wouldn't be having this conversation.'

'Facts are one thing, Harry. Interpretation is another matter entirely.'

Sir Robert explained. They believed Slowik's whereabouts had been compromised some weeks earlier and, with the possibility of Tschesche in the country, they could take no chances. The residual UK network, they believed, was quite small, probably only four or five people, perhaps six if you included Quinton. Finding Slowik again would stretch them, especially if they could be distracted. The dossier had been the distraction.

'Just a moment,' Harry cut in, 'are you telling me the dossier came from within the Service? From you?'

'Let's just call it a collaboration, but yes. More or less. Or rather more, in the sense that distraction was just one objective.'

Although the final dossier seemed to have been

182

embellished a little, essentially, the core material had been uploaded into the Joint Intelligence Committee portal. It had been a document fed into the same system that they believed had led to Slowik's location being compromised. The report accompanying the dossier had been written to suggest that there was an attempted whitewash; his crimes had been revealed, but in order to avoid a scandal or embarrassment, Hamilton would be quietly retired. If there was an organised but unofficial group of former East German agents in the UK, exposing Hamilton, the man who had chased them down and unmasked Quinton Bickley-Morris, would be hard to resist, even though verifying the facts with Berlin would be impossible now that the Stasi were formally disbanded. In some ways, it was a sophisticated double bluff. With her protector under investigation and the agencies themselves distracted, the shield around Slowik would be weakened. The combination of bringing down Hamilton in public and the chance to eliminate Slowik would be too good an opportunity to miss.

'Oh, my goodness.' Harry's words come out slowly and with a certainty that caught Sir Robert off guard. It was not a response he had been expecting. Harry stood and held up both his hands. 'Let me think.'

He turned and walked to the window. Although he was looking out over the London skyline, his mind was not registering the view. It was digesting the information that Sir Robert had been revealing. He turned to his right and, not looking at his colleague, slowly walked the width of the room and back. Still crossing the room with measured steps and not looking directly at Sir Robert, he articulated his thoughts.

'What you're telling me, Bob, is Slowik is one of ours – has been for some time. Since you knew her in Berlin, perhaps? Explains why she's here seeking refuge, co-operating in her debriefing. It's why we're protecting her. Why her former fellow officers are seeking her out.'

Sir Robert didn't interrupt Harry, letting him continue to think out loud.

'She sought you out. Why? You knew her in Berlin, what, thirty years ago? But she seeks you out, and somehow you're very much involved, the man responsible for her safety.' Harry stopped his slow pacing and turned to face Sir Robert. 'The man responsible for her?'

Several unrelated facts slotted into place. Despite being a respected and senior figure, Sir Robert had never been fully integrated within the Security Service. His office, in the Curzon Street registry rather than Gower Street headquarters, for example. The Tufton Street operation genuinely providing a valuable service, but at arm's length. Was it also providing Sir Robert with a valuable cover, just like supplying the names of low-grade Stasi operatives, not worth the bother of prosecuting, whom Slowik could then be seen to save? Sir Robert had always enjoyed a high degree of independence and flexibility, including his stint at the Ministry of Defence whilst seeking out Quinton. Was he being supplied with information directly from the Berlin embassy? Then, there was the fact that this conversation was taking place in Vauxhall Cross. Sir Robert seemingly having free access; there was no chaperone. Just the previous year, there had been no difficulty in Sir Robert putting someone in place in Greece to monitor Quinton's movements. Then Harry's own short-notice travel to Greece with Sir Robert and Huxley. All that assistance, almost certainly facilitated by Secret Intelligence Service officers provided without question. Perhaps the deepest mystery of all: what were the services that had led to Sir Robert's knighthood? Could he have been Slowik's controller? The last place you would look for an MI6 coordinator would be within MI5. Still facing Sir Robert, he asked a more direct question.

'Who do you work for, Bob?'

'You know I can't tell you that, Harry.'

Sir Robert's reply confirmed Harry's suspicion. There was no issue at all with a fellow Security Service officer confirming he worked for MI5, and Sir Robert would not wish to lie to a close comrade. Harry nodded to acknowledge Sir Robert's admission that he was an MI6 officer.

'Is this the right time to remind you that you have signed the Act?' Sir Robert was referring to the Official Secrets Act that bound them all together, but the smile on his lips and sparkle in his eye was simply further confirmation to Harry that there was substance to his unspoken hypothesis.

The gravity returned to Sir Robert's voice.

'We seem to have become a little sidetracked. We still have serious business to discuss. Things took us by surprise last week, and they seemed somehow connected to Mrs Blakeridge. I'm afraid she's back under the finger of suspicion. Graham was dead before the dossier was prepared – he couldn't have had a copy.'

It wasn't what Harry wanted to hear, he had tried to give Veronica the benefit of the doubt, though it was getting more difficult to justify doing so. It was a crestfallen Harry who tried to keep his hope alive.

'If the material originally came from your Berlin files, is it possible that security could have been compromised at some time in the past?'

'It's a possibility we thought about, too,' but no. The garden fire was a little suspicious, so we asked the embassy to do some checking with the Aegina police force. Graham's house looks untouched. Small garden, no sign of any fire recently. There wouldn't be, though. Our friend Captain Miltiades tells us the summer fire ban is still in place.'

Harry felt as though a cloud had descended over him. It wasn't just the suspicion about Veronica, but there was the effect it was bound to have on Huxley. He had no choice but to advise Sir Robert about his own concerns: the supposedly delayed flight, stories that didn't quite match, how unlikely it was that Veronica could have legally inherited Graham's house. Much to his surprise, however, the news seemed to brighten Sir Robert's mood.

'Well, if she went somewhere she hasn't mentioned, presumably to collect the dossier, then she can identify at least one of the people involved.'

'Are you going to pick her up?'

Harry was surprised when Sir Robert answered, 'No, not yet. She mustn't know what we suspect.'

As Sir Robert continued, it seemed to Harry that his colleague was perplexed about some aspects of the case. Although the police were discounting Huxley's claim of another person in the house, he was not. That person could have been Tschesche, and if so, he would almost certainly have known that Veronica was due home that afternoon. Did he also know that Kilsdale was on his way? It seemed a bizarre scenario, but as Sir Robert explained to Harry, a double murder, the dossier found in a search of the premises – the finger would be pointing directly at the Security Service.

At Harry and Sir Robert in particular. It would fit with the crude attempt to link Harry to Kilsdale's death, but Kilsdale had implicated Quinton in the business at Blackheath. That just did not fit.

Harry, still standing and feeling self-conscious, was relieved when Sir Robert asked him to sit, saying he needed to explain something. The mystery of Blackheath and Kilsdale's murder was not his highest priority. Soon, it would be time for Harry to upload the monthly Security Service update reports to the JIC portal, and Nicholas would give him an additional file to add to the bundle. A special file that was part of a new security system they were testing, whereby physical copies of the file were not circulated. A single copy would sit on the mainframe computer and could only be read when there was a live connection. This particular file had been amended. Sir Robert didn't understand how, and when it had been explained to him, he had been none the wiser. He wasn't sure he had heard the jargon correctly, but it had sounded to him like it contained a "tracking pixie", something which had amused him. Whenever the file was opened, a covert record would be made, logging the date and time of access, which computer account and terminal were being used, and if there was any attempt to make a copy. The accompanying overview file would identify the main file as the Security Service assessment of the authenticity of the Hamilton dossier. The major JIC players would not find it of particular importance a placeholder rather than a need for action; the investigation being no more than an internal matter for the Security Service unless something significant was found. If the original dossier material had been leaked through access to the JIC portal, however, it would certainly be of interest to those concerned, and covert copying would identify the potential suspects.

Sir Robert Hamilton glanced at his watch.

'We have much more to discuss, Harry, but we need to get you back. If you're too long at Scotland Yard, people will begin to wonder.'

'Shall we meet again?' As Harry spoke, he realised his words were an allusion, albeit imperfect, to Shakespeare's Scottish play. A premonition of tragedy, perhaps? Reassuring though the meeting had been in some ways, if anything, Harry felt even more isolated, very much on his own in dealing with developments. If the last ten days were anything to go by, developments tended to be unpredictable and chaotic, and Harry knew it was unlikely that he would be fully briefed about Sir Robert's activities and motives. Trust can leave you very alone and exposed.

Sir Robert leant back in his chair and tried to lighten the mood by jokingly reminding Harry that he was still a potential suspect in a murder investigation. The police would almost certainly need to interview him again.

'In the meantime, keep the Brigadier informed.' Sir Robert never called Nicholas anything other than "the Brigadier", and a curtain of seriousness fell on both his tone and countenance.

As he stood up, Harry paused and looked Sir Robert directly in the eye.

'Before I go, there's one thing you can help me with, something that's been troubling me, that doesn't really fit anywhere. It may point us in the right direction, or it could just be a red herring, but Francis Buckingham hauling me into Thames House, saying Tufton Street is to be closed.

What was that about?'

'Mea Culpa, I'm afraid, Harry.' Sir Robert had a sheepish look on his face as he explained it had been a rather hurried and crude attempt to check if Harry could keep a secret. Unnecessary in Sir Robert's view, but something his colleagues who didn't know Harry so well had insisted on. Harry assumed that when Sir Robert had used the term "colleagues", he was referring to the Secret Intelligence Service rather than his own organisation on the north bank of the Thames. Harry smiled.

'Explains why I couldn't trace him in the Security Service directory.'

As Harry opened the door, Sir Robert stopped him.

'Harry. Don't forget. Be careful. We haven't released the details of Kilsdale's death, but let's just say it's not inconsistent with *Herr* Tschesche's work.'

Chapter 23

Day ten: Wednesday

On his way back to Tufton Street, having been returned to New Scotland Yard, a troubling thought came into Harry's mind. The third person in Veronica's home in Blackheath: could it have been Tschesche, as Sir Robert had suggested? If it was, then it was clear that Veronica could have been, and perhaps still was, in danger. Harry was uneasy about the thought that he should just stand aside. Yet it was clear from the discussion that he should not warn her. Nor was she to be detained, not even for her own safety. If his fears were real and something did happen, something undoubtedly fatal, could he live with it on his conscience? Even if Veronica was a traitor?

* * *

Not far away, Veronica Blakeridge was also on Reid's mind. The plan had been that, once delivery of the dossier was confirmed, she was to be given a signal to return to the bookshop, where she would pick up a new passport and a ticket for an onward flight from Athens airport. To all intents and purposes, she would have returned to Greece and disappeared. If Bickley-Morris had stayed his hand, waited as he had been told, then she would be untraceable by now. His cock-up in Blackheath had brought her to the attention of the police, and fleeing the country would have been seen as an admission of guilt. Not that Reid was bothered by any police investigation; that, to him, was irrelevant. As was Veronica's fate. Things had changed; she would have to take her chances. What worried him was that the Security Service, especially Nevile, even in the absence of Hamilton, would follow things up. They would need to establish whether Veronica had been living a double life, passing on information for the past few years. Reid had no idea how much she could be trusted, and right now, he had no idea where she was or if she would respond to a signal to return to the bookshop. Even if she did, he would have to be prepared, whatever course of action he decided to take.

Reid's problem was that he no longer had either the people or the funds to collect the information he needed. And he needed to find Veronica. Even with his limited resources, he knew she had not returned to her house in Blackheath. At some point, she would, even if it was just a short visit, but there was no way he could keep a constant watch on the house. He did have an informant in Thames House – a man who would swap information for cash. Not a senior figure, somebody much more useful. Every large organisation had one: the man who seemed to walk around all day with a piece of paper in his hand, seemingly trying to avoid any real work. A man whom most people in Thames House treated as a joke, but a man who could pick up quite a lot of information. Few questions would be asked, even when he wandered outside of his own department's offices. The problem was the isolation of Tufton Street. Reid wondered how many people knew of its existence, let alone what went on there.

One thing Reid needed to decide was whether he should

activate part two of his plan. Part one had gone reasonably well. It was clear from his man in Thames House that the existence of another copy of the dossier had worried the Security Service. When he had first come across the document, he knew that, if he blew the whistle on the cover-up, tracing the leak back to his office would not be difficult. He had needed a plan to divert attention away from himself, and that's when the idea of using Rod Graham's legacy to his benefit had arisen. Graham had been a crooked policeman, that much was known, as were his dealings with Quinton Bickley-Morris. Despite the outcome of the trial, Bickley-Morris was known to have been in the service of East Germany, so there was a direct link: Berlin to Bickley-Morris to Graham. The original document, which Reid had seen, contained information that could only have come from MI6, the Secret Intelligence Service, so it was quite feasible that the primary source had been Berlin. Where else could the information about Hamilton aiding the East Germans have come from?

Part two of the plan was to leak the information to the press. That gave him another reason to need Veronica out of the way. Whatever happened inside the Security Service or the Secret Intelligence Service, Reid feared there would be another cover-up to avoid a scandal. He had let Tobias believe that leaking the document to MI5 had been simply to divert their attention, but Reid wanted more. He wanted Hamilton's head. Enough time had elapsed since preparing his plan to provide evidence that there was a cover-up, now was the time to execute it. He couldn't, however, leak the original memo that had accompanied the information in the dossier; it was too risky, too easily traced back to his office.

The journalists could put two and two together. If, however, they knew that the original dossier had been found and brought to the UK by a former security services officer, yet no action had been taken, there could be little doubt that there was a cover-up. But Reid did not want the journalists to get hold of Veronica too easily. One careless word could upset everything, and he did not know her well enough to have absolute confidence about her ability to lie.

If Hamilton had truly disappeared, that could add a little spice to the story. An insider tipping him off, perhaps? A wider conspiracy? Reid could not get away from the thought that it was out of character for Sir Robert. If his nefarious dealings had been exposed, he would co-operate with the cover-up, be gently sidelined. From what Reid's contact had been able to discover, and there was precious little evidence to support it, Sir Robert's absence had caught his colleagues unawares; he had not been quietly ushered out of the back door.

The timing of Sir Robert's disappearance was something else that caused a headache for Reid, partly because he had insufficient information to be certain about the course of events. It was quite possible that Sir Robert had gone missing before the Security Service had been made aware of the existence of the damning file, but that hardly mattered. Not only was fleeing out of character, but if that had been his intent, why wait until now? His exposure and any agreement to co-operate would have happened by now, almost certainly before the information was shared on the JIC portal. The fact that Anna Slowik seemed to have been spirited away at much the same time was something else that disturbed Reid. Could there be a link? That, too, made no sense, but it was too much of a coincidence to be ignored. It was clear from the memo that Reid had intercepted that the intelligence services had, for some time, accepted that the allegations against Sir Robert were true. If that was the case, then there was no way that Sir Robert Hamilton would have been party to what Reid suspected was Slowik's reincarnation. Hamilton may have been allowed to continue, temporarily, whatever role he was playing in her debriefing, just to avoid raising his suspicions. Once his guilt was established, however, that would have ceased, and he would have been kept in ignorance of any further actions taken to ensure her security. What was it, Reid wondered, that he was missing?

Reid knew what he was really missing. Independence. Not only that, but his anonymity was also at risk. When the Berlin Wall had fallen and all seemed lost, Reid had not panicked. Keep the network together, look out for each other, and trust that the people in Berlin who had run agents in European countries would look out for themselves. There were too many files in the Stasi's Lichtenberg HQ for all to be destroyed, but there would be some order of priority. Citizens who informed on their fellow citizens would be left to their fate, but the senior people would eradicate evidence against themselves. Evidence that may not even have been kept in such an obvious location. Play the long game, keep your cover, let natural attrition disband the network, had been Reid's course of action.

All had been going well until earlier in the year, the seventh year since the fall of the Wall. Reid had been getting comfortable. There were no suspicions. He had independence and anonymity. That was when Tobias had appeared on the scene, and it became abundantly clear there was a residual core still active in unified Germany. No doubt funded by, and reporting to, their former puppet masters in Moscow. One job, one focus, do as we ask or be exposed. Find Slowik.

Reid had heard of Slowik, but he knew her background and reputation less well than that of Tobias Tschesche, the man who was now making demands. Demands that Reid struggled to fulfil. His residual network was now more informal than operational; people as reluctant to re-engage and take new risks as Reid himself had been when Tobias' appearance had shattered his growing sense of security. It may sound mundane and uninspiring, but the Stasi did not pay a pension; the Civil Service did.

Then there was the question of Bickley-Morris. In common with many people in government service, Reid despised him and his kind. Men who owed their success to privilege and connections, men who would have no place in the new order. In Reid's view, Bickley-Morris was a man who was so totally devoid of the smallest vestige of integrity or modesty that his mere presence was an act of aggression. His every action, an act of dominance, a statement that said, "I am the most important person here. I am the one in charge". How Bickley-Morris had evaded detection for so long was a conundrum. Perhaps his behaviour, his bullying and toadying, was so extreme that no one could believe that somebody so incautious, so overbearing, could have anything to hide. Reid himself was the complete opposite. If he had become a musician, he would have been a second violin, blending in, unnoticed, invisible. Every aspect of Reid's behaviour and appearance conformed to expectation. He wore the uniform of uniformity. It was a cloak that conferred invisibility.

Reid had hoped that Kilsdale's death in Blackheath would have backfired on Bickley-Morris. A former MI5 officer brings evidence of serious misconduct about a very senior figure, then returns to Greece. That senior figure, along with Nevile, had investigated Kilsdale's role in the mouse droppings plot and his involvement in Bickley-Morris' money laundering, yet no charges had ever been brought. Kilsdale's death in Veronica's house would not fail to raise suspicion. Without Hamilton, however, Nevile would be like a rabbit caught in the headlights, not knowing which way to turn, but he was quite aware of the historical connection between Kilsdale and Bickley-Morris. At the very least, it should cause the latter some disquiet and discomfort. Reid had even hoped that there was a chance that Bickley-Morris would be incriminated by his trademark blundering. This time, there would be no Reid, no network to save him.

As it was, it had been Reid who had been caused the problems by Bickley-Morris' blundering. Bickley-Morris who hadn't listened, who hadn't waited and who had put the whole plan in jeopardy. It had been a close call: deal with Kilsdale, mainly to prevent a second blundering mess by Bickley-Morris, or deal with Bickley-Morris himself? Not both. Another body in addition to the woman in Blackheath was risky enough, but two more would be crass stupidity, drawing unnecessary attention. With Berlin no longer there to protect Bickley-Morris, he could be dealt with. Reid, however, had changed his mind, agreeing with Tobias as to which of the two presented the greater risk. By meeting with Nevile, Kilsdale had sealed his own fate.

Reid felt as though he was firefighting. Chaos and uncertainty threatened him. In the past, he had run a tightly controlled organisation, not huge, but an efficient, if covert, extension of the East German embassy. If extra resources were needed, Berlin would provide for them. Now everything was different. Tobias, who was controlled by the post-Berlin rump, was making increasing demands, demands that not only was Reid unable to fulfil with his own reduced operational abilities, but demands that put his own residual group at risk. In the past, he had assumed that Berlin would look out for him when it was time to leave, but that assumption had disappeared along with the Federal Republic. They couldn't, or wouldn't, provide for him now, let alone secure his future. Had Tobias not appeared on the scene, he would have started to put his retirement plans into action, but now things were different. It wasn't loyalty that bound him to help Tobias, it was the certain knowledge that if he abandoned the task before it was complete, he would not be forgiven. He was also beginning to think that if they failed to find Slowik, Tobias would make him a scapegoat, and his safety would be very much at risk. His hopes had risen in recent weeks, and his worries had decreased, but now that bastard Hamilton had wrecked everything. Reid had no hard evidence, but his gut instinct was still telling him Hamilton was somehow involved with Slowik slipping off the radar. Even though it didn't make any kind of sense, Hamilton's career ought to be over, regardless of any actions Reid himself might now take.

* * *

Harry's walk back to Tufton Street had taken him just under fifteen minutes. Little had been said by Nicholas on Harry's arrival, but the deliberate nod of the head had told Harry all he needed to know. Harry was just about to call the lift when he hesitated, turned and crossed the vestibule back to Nicholas' front desk. Harry wasn't sure why he spoke so softly; it just seemed appropriate.

'Tell me, Nicholas,' Harry almost whispered, 'if you had to choose a number between four and seven, what would you choose?'

Nicholas' knowing smile confirmed Harry's suspicion, though his answer wasn't quite what Harry was expecting.

'Five and a half, sir.'

CHAPTER 24

Day eleven: Thursday, morning

Quinton's bulk sank into the oxblood-coloured leather of his high-backed Chesterfield armchair. The morning sun was catching the wall of the flats opposite as he looked over the central gardens of Dolphin Square. He had deliberately chosen his flat because it caught the evening light. Morning sunshine had been of little interest to a man who had spent the latter part of his working life inside the neoclassical Portland stone edifice that housed the Ministry of Defence.

There was very little that he missed about his life in Greece. The island of Agistri may have offered him anonymity, may have appealed to holidaymakers seeking the simplest of Greek lifestyles, but for Quinton it lacked what he considered the essential sophistication necessary to sustain a gentleman. He did miss the warmth and the sunshine, although in the winter the island was cold, deserted and much too isolated for him to feel comfortable.

The letter sat in his lap. Quinton picked it up to read it again. It was typewritten, apart from the signature: Vera Beamann, a name that meant nothing to him. In the letter, she explained that she was a journalist who had picked up on the transcript of his trial. That much seemed plausible as she had contacted him through his legal team: Quinton did his best to keep his address out of public records. She had no interest, the letter stated, in his innocence or his guilt, but she had been monitoring what she called SOD litigation: stifling of dissent. Quinton deplored the growing trend to reduce everything to an acronym, but this one amused him, not that it stopped him thinking, *Typical of a grubby hack.*

The main aim of SOD litigation, Miss Beamann's letter revealed, was not so much to secure a favourable verdict as to legitimise terminating somebody's employment, and to so tarnish their reputation, on the basis of there being no smoke without fire, that it would cause them difficulty in pursuing their career elsewhere. More crudely put, it was a case of "Mud sticks". She claimed to have noticed a growing trend of SOD litigation in the public sector, but none having a high enough profile to attract media attention. Quinton's case was different. It had all the characteristics of a SOD case, and she was keen to know more about the background. In the first instance, she proposed a meeting, somewhere public, lunch perhaps. If they both agreed to take the investigation further, she promised anonymity to Quinton. Her hope was to produce a television documentary, something which should attract more attention than a written article. In the event that she succeeded, Quinton's face would not be shown, and his voice would be dubbed over with that of an actor.

Quinton was in two minds. Despite her assurances of anonymity, if high-profile cases were rare, it would not be too difficult to guess his identity. On the other hand, he had little to lose. Even though he should tell his story himself, part of him would enjoy weaving a tale of persecution at Hamilton's expense. Although he had never been included in the discussions, he knew that Reid was planning to discredit Sir Robert Hamilton, and the link was close enough that when Reid's plan emerged, it could give added momentum to Miss Beamann's hoped-for exposure.

At the back of Quinton's mind was the thought that Reid's plan may involve "evidence", or, more precisely, documents somehow connected to the late Rod Graham and Nevile's little workmaid, Veronica Blakeridge. Reid had suggested the house in Blackheath and the cover story that Graham had stolen some documents from Quinton. He didn't trust Reid – one of the reasons he had taken action on his own timescale and not Reid's. He couldn't explain why there was a body in the house when his triggerman had turned up, and he didn't even know whether to believe the story his man had told him. Nor could he explain Reid's anger over the incident, but it was clear it had compromised Reid's plans in some way.

Quinton was concerned about Reid's recent behaviour. Reid was a man who stayed in the background. A man who wore his anonymity like the embroidered initials on his shirt cuffs. Exposed enough to be noticed but restrained enough for people to discount him. A combination of being considered indispensable and not being high-profile enough to draw any attention to himself.

Although there had never been any love lost between Quinton and Reid, Reid had undoubtedly been useful, especially in facilitating Quinton's escape from the Cambridge business a few years ago, not to mention his more recent trial. Reid had let it be known to Quinton that the withdrawal of Slowik as a witness had been no happy accident. Not that there was much in the way of gratitude from Quinton. Slowik's testimony, as revealed in the pretrial disclosures, had not caused him any undue concern. Her name wasn't even disclosed, just her former position and rank. Slowik may have been a senior figure in the East German Intelligence

201

Service, but she had not held a position that would have made her privy to the identity of the Stasi's UK sources. If that were so, she would have denounced Reid by now. Although it was true that Slowik and Quinton had met fifty years ago, in post-war Germany, Quinton would deny it; without access to Stasi files, she would have no evidence. Almost seven years since the fall of the Wall, seven years in hiding, the chance that she had access to Stasi files, currently, was negligible.

Reid had never let Quinton know the full truth about Slowik's withdrawal as a witness, nor had he been forthcoming about Tschesche's presence in the UK. Reid had intercepted and passed on information about Slowik's forthcoming role in Quinton's trial, and, as a result, Tschesche had been sent to the UK. Security would be so tight that it would be difficult for Tschesche to put a reliable plan in place in relation to Slowik's court appearance. Instead, a rather more subtle plan had been devised. Shortly before the trial was due to start, knowledge of Tschesche's presence in the UK was leaked to the British embassy in Berlin. With little time to gather further intelligence, the security services would, in effect, have to choose between ensuring Slowik's safety or convicting Quinton. If the trial went ahead with Slowik, Tschesche would still have a chance, but the hope was that she would be withdrawn. That would cause some fallout, ripples in the pond, which Reid used to locate Slowik, but it had come at a price. With limited resources, Reid had been forced to stretch himself, to step outside of his normal persona and put himself at risk of exposure.

Despite his ungracious bravado about facing Slowik, Quinton had been relieved when she was withdrawn. There was something, something that had happened half a century ago, that meant Slowik would never have forgotten Quinton, a reason why she might have tracked his career. It was not revealed in the pretrial disclosure, and Quinton doubted it was something she would willingly reveal. More likely that she would have had to bury it deep in her psyche in order to survive in the chaos that was post-war East Germany. In any case, it was a double-edged sword. She may convince a jury that it gave her reason not to forget Quinton, but it also gave her a reason to seek revenge. Revenge by fair means or foul, a reason why she might be willing to perjure herself. For Quinton, his response would be denial. Yet another accusation without evidence, his word against hers. Just another part of the conspiracy that had caused him to flee the country back in 1991.

But there was one thing – a detail he had not given any thought to at the time, a detail that, given the circumstances, Slowik may not have noticed: his birthmark. If she had, revealing her knowledge of it would identify Quinton unequivocally.

Accusations by Slowik were no longer something that caused Quinton any concern. His outlook was not to worry about what might have gone wrong, not to worry about what may go wrong, but just to focus on the here and now. Right now, it was Reid's behaviour that was troubling him. The ranting over the telephone last week, berating him. That was unlike Reid. Reid was calm and confident, chillingly so if there were people who needed bringing back into line or punishing. Quinton didn't think Reid was out of control; it was more that he was no longer *in* control. How could that be? The organisation was all but disbanded. Running a tight ship was understandable. Stay safe, stay afloat, but the waters were calm now. The change in Reid's behaviour had started earlier that year, not long before Quinton's trial date. Not out of control, but not *in* control. It disturbed Quinton. The question was, if Reid was not in control, who was?

Quinton realised his mind was wandering and brought his attention back to the letter sitting in his lap. Picking it up, he turned it over – not that there was anything written on the back – it was just a reflex. Leave nothing to chance. There was nothing special about the paper, standard A4 white paper, typical of the kind you could buy in any supermarket to feed the growing home computer market. It was the printing that caught his attention. Not the common dot matrix typeface, this was either laser or inkjet printing, technologies which had yet to make an impact on the home market. If nothing else, Miss Beamann did at least appear to be professional.

If he co-operated, here was an opportunity to strike at the annoyingly persistent Sir Robert Hamilton and his damned underling Harry Nevile. Reid, who had warned him against getting in the way when it came to dealing with Hamilton, would not be happy, but Reid himself had hardly been playing by the rules of late. In the last couple of days, Quinton had been interviewed twice by the police in connection with his association with Matthew Kilsdale. Thankfully, he had an alibi, or at least a partial one, for Monday evening; he had dined at his club and could name several well-respected witnesses to that fact. The estimated time of death was hardly precise to the minute, but even so, Quinton could not have met with Kilsdale and been seen having dinner at the same time. The police had argued that Quinton could have had a meeting with Kilsdale on another day, as a result of which Kilsdale had sought him out on Monday evening, perhaps accosting him on his return home. After all, the body had been found close to Dolphin Square. Unfortunately for Quinton, confirmation of his whereabouts after 9:30 p.m. depended on a taxi driver, inevitably anonymous and unlikely to be found, and even if he was, Quinton had no further alibi for that night. He had protested that the police would be better off directing their attention towards Harry Nevile – it was his business card after all. He had thought of suggesting that perhaps Nevile had lured Kilsdale to Pimlico on the pretext of a meeting with himself, but realised that would raise awkward questions as to why Kilsdale might want to meet with him.

Quinton fully intended to continue his belligerence in his further dealings with the police. Ultimately, there was no evidence that linked him to Kilsdale's death, though, if any came to light, Quinton was quite prepared to claim yet another falsification in an ongoing MI5 plot to discredit him. In such circumstances, it was a line he felt he could pursue with Miss Beamann. The more he thought about it, the more Quinton was inclined to respond positively to the letter. Reid, who had crossed a line, the former linchpin who could no longer be trusted or relied upon. If Reid had a plan to discredit the Tufton Street team, it had to be a plan he intended to execute imminently. Why else had he suggested killing Kilsdale in that house in Blackheath?

It would take some time for Miss Beamann to prepare her story and to sell it to the television producers. If, in the meantime, Reid brought down Hamilton, Beamann's storyline would not garner a lot of interest, and Quinton's own efforts would not come to Reid's attention. If Reid failed, then Quinton saw no reason for holding back, whether Reid liked it or not. There seemed to be no harm in meeting the lady; even better if it came with a free lunch. He was free the next morning, and giving Miss Beamann short notice would put her on the back foot, something that appealed to Quinton. The letter contained a number to call if he wished to discuss the matter further. He reached for the telephone.

CHAPTER 25

Day eleven: Thursday, morning

As Veronica stepped into Villiers Street from the side entrance to Charing Cross station, she paused as if deciding which way to go. A quick glance to her left told her there was no black cable tie around the short, pillar-mounted handrail at the bottom of the station entrance, just before the Evening Standard newspaper stand. No signal that she could pick up the package, no signal that she could be on her way. She had been waiting a week. It was supposed to have been a quick operation – deliver the documents, tell her story, then disappear. At least that was what she thought had been the plan.

It wasn't just that something had gone wrong; she was genuinely afraid. She hadn't been sure at first, but now she was convinced that Huxley really had seen somebody else hiding inside her house the afternoon she arrived back in London. Somebody, she was not quite certain who, but *somebody* had been waiting for her. Whatever had happened that afternoon didn't matter. There were only three people in the UK, other than Huxley, who had known she was coming home. Her neighbour and her cleaner were two, and her cleaner was now dead. The other was the man who had organised her return and had passed on the documents to her. That day had been the first time they had ever met. Why, after all these years, take the risk of meeting her in person?

There was one obvious solution to that puzzle: it wouldn't matter if she was dead.

The news from Huxley, just two days ago, about the existence of a second copy had been what had convinced her. Had there ever been any intention of supplying her with a new passport and a ticket to a new life? Any intention of setting up a bank account in her new name? She had become disposable. There was only one explanation for that second dossier. She could see it now. An anonymous call brings the police to her house. They find her body. It would not have mattered if there had been two bodies; what was important was that the dossier was found. Except it hadn't been. Huxley, the lovesick imbecile, had saved her life. She gave him that, but what was she supposed to do? She wasn't going to spend the rest of her life with him, saying thank you. How long had it been, she wondered, before it was realised she had not been the victim? Long enough to trigger a response, to have another copy of the dossier delivered to Thames House, of that she had little doubt.

Yesterday, she had considered her options. There were no good options, but there was one that might just guarantee her safety and exact revenge on her behalf. Harry Nevile, the man who would always put his duty first and always ask the question, "What is the greater good?" He would be interested in the bastard behind it all, the bastard who had planned to kill her, and she had seen him. She didn't know who he was or where he lived, but she knew a lot about him. Enough to know he was somehow connected to Quinton Bickley-Morris.

That was how their paths had crossed. He had known she was supplying information to Rod Graham, and he wanted her to supply him with information about Graham and Quinton Bickley-Morris. He wasn't police; he wasn't in the security services, that much was clear, and that didn't leave many options. None of them were legal or above board. When she had learned about the connection between Bickley-Morris and East Germany, things began to slot into place. An organisation built on distrust would not trust its own people.

At first, she had tried to resist: Graham was abusive and violent; what would he do if he found out she was passing on information about him? She failed. The truth was that she had been given no options. "Do as we ask or be exposed for giving away secrets and, if that's not bad enough, risk the wrath of Graham as well as jail. Accept our offer, and if Graham finds out, he will be dealt with." In the end, he hadn't found out, but he had become a risk and had been dealt with. She had played her part, and it had come with an additional bonus – she was out of Tufton Street, which had been becoming more and more stifling.

It hadn't all been plain sailing. After Graham's death, her plan had never been to stay in Aegina one moment more than was necessary. Surely Bickley-Morris had a choice: stay, and risk a fate similar to Graham's, or disappear. It didn't matter where he went; there was no point in her staying when there was no one left to monitor. She had not foreseen the detention of Bickley-Morris. That had put everything on hold. The day that inane bore Huxley had turned up in Perdika, her first thought had been to flee, but passing on the information about Bickley-Morris' detention wasn't rewarded – it seemed to lock her in further. That was when she began to have doubts about the people she was working with. Be patient, get any information you can out of Tufton Street, and use Huxley. "Quinton will say nothing", they had said. She didn't believe them. Loyalty! They were being loyal to a crook. Her opinion of Quinton Bickley-Morris was that he was a man who would say anything to save his own skin. But she was trapped.

She regretted having tried to seduce Huxley that day he turned up in Perdika, suggesting he stay the night. The thought of compromising the trust that Nevile had in him had amused her. Whatever story he might have told Harry, she doubted he would have given her away. Even if he did tell, Nevile couldn't touch her in Greece; she had done nothing illegal. Walking out on your job was no crime, and she would maintain it had been done out of fear of Rod Graham. But Huxley, the wimp, had backed out. He was just like the rest of the Tufton Street team: latter-day daydreamers who thought they could put the world to rights. Naive idiots who deserved to be exploited, more like.

The problem was that the fool really did seem besotted, thought she really did care for him, and saw himself as some sort of knight in shining armour who could save her. If only he knew that he had – by turning up at Blackheath the previous week. Even before saving her life, albeit unwittingly, he had been useful. He had bought her story, the story written on the computer disk that Huxley had sent to Harry, clandestinely. Huxley had also provided a refuge for her this past week or so. His usefulness had, however, come at a price. His secret visits to Perdika had been something to endure. Even as a lover, he had been as naive and gauche as he was in every other aspect of his life. He hadn't even proved to be a useful source of information. She had come to realise that he wasn't being the high-minded good servant of the Crown; he simply did not know. Veronica had grown as tired of Huxley as she had of her relatives who had given her a home in Perdika.

Veronica's thoughts returned to the man who had deceived her. She had never for one minute thought that Reid was his real name, and the initials embroidered on his shirt cuffs had confirmed her suspicions. It was another clue that would help Nevile track him down, as was the address of the esoteric bookshop where he had sent her to pick up the dossier. It was time for Mr Reid to learn that if you didn't pay the piper, you didn't get to call the tune. It was time not only for Reid to dance to her tune, but Harry Nevile too. He had never looked out for her, even when Graham was at his most dangerous. Nevile was so focused on his front-office team, the tiresome Huxley and the righteous-minded Margaret Millard, that he took his back-office people for granted. Gave them the dull and tedious work, saving the glory for himself and his two acolytes. Veronica wouldn't be surprised if there was some history between Millard and Nevile, some sordid secret that bound him to her.

Last year, Harry had started to include Ben in the core team; Nevile's quadrumvirate, if there was such a word. Ben the deserter, looking after himself, abandoning his back-office colleagues at the first opportunity. It wasn't surprising. He had never given her a second glance, never noticed her affection for him. If only she could find a way to bring Tufton Street down, teach them that they had been ignoring her at their own peril. Even Huxley, the sop, for all his obsequious fawning, had never recognised her for her professional ability. If bringing Hamilton down brought them down, it was no more than they deserved. For now, though, she needed Harry Nevile, but she had no intention of throwing herself on his mercy. He would accept her deal. He wouldn't like it, but loyal Service lapdog Harry Nevile would choose the greater good. Especially as it came with information that could allow him to step into Sir Robert Hamilton's soon-to-be-vacated shoes. Not even Harry Nevile was so honest and virtuous that he would turn down an opportunity like that just because he didn't like the terms it came with.

Veronica wasn't making the decision lightly; she had given Reid the time and opportunity, but he had let her down. Worse than that, she couldn't take the risk that he would come after her. There had been more than enough uncertainty and doubt over the past week. Yesterday, she had thought everything over, and over and over again. Today, she needed to act and to do so quickly. Would it have made any difference if there had been a cable tie around the handrail? No, the chance that she would have walked into a trap was too great. *Stick to the plan*, she told herself, and the plan was to find a Post Office, buy a phone card, then find an inconspicuous phone box and make the call.

* * *

Telephone calls to Tufton Street were not a common event. Few people knew of its existence and even fewer knew any direct dial numbers. Extraneous phone calls went through to Nicholas' switchboard and, in general, went no further. When Harry picked up the receiver, he was not surprised to hear Nicholas' voice and expected some routine housekeeping reminder. Even when Nicholas announced that Veronica wished to talk to him, Harry assumed she had forgotten his direct number and was not expecting anything ominous when he asked Nicholas to put her through.

'I'm afraid, sir, I can't do that. The young lady is insistent that you take the call in private, in the meeting room. For your ears only, she says.'

When Harry expressed his surprise, Nicholas ventured, 'Mr Huxley, perhaps?'

Harry was intrigued and a little apprehensive. Whatever the call was about, he knew he would have to come up with some excuse; neither Huxley nor Margaret would miss the fact that he had taken a brief phone call in private. He went into the meeting room, closed the door and picked up the phone.

Veronica got straight to the point.

'That dossier, the Hamilton files. Didn't come from Graham's house.'

The surprise in Harry's voice was genuine. Not because Veronica had revealed something he didn't know, but because she was admitting to her deception. He tried to remain calm, dispassionate, but her plan to grab his attention had been entirely successful.

'That's not what you told us,' he said cautiously.

'Never mind what I told you last week, Harry. Listen to what I'm telling you now.'

Harry tried to take his mind off the other fact he was aware of: that the documents had been put together by Sir Robert himself.

'Are you saying the content is bogus? Some kind of a hoax?'

'No, Harry, they're real enough. I just didn't get them from Graham's house.'

Harry had to decide how he was going to play this, and opted for playing the innocent.

'Veronica, Ron, I don't understand. What are you trying to tell me? You found them somewhere else?'

'I didn't find them, Harry, I was given them.'

'By whom? Why?'

It seemed Veronica had her game plan well-rehearsed.

'Who, Harry? Someone very unpleasant. Why? I don't know. Maybe Hamilton double-crossed him. I don't know, I don't care. Look, Harry, I'm in danger. I need your help. That man, the one Huxley saw in my house. He was sent to get me. I was set up – I was the target. They're going to kill me, Harry. Unless you help me.'

Harry knew she was wrong about the man Huxley had seen. Kilsdale had clarified that the man was waiting for him, that he was the target. It still didn't all make sense, but Kilsdale was now dead, murdered. That was a powerful argument in favour of Kilsdale's hypothesis. It didn't mean that Veronica was not in danger; she may well have got herself tangled up in some extremely distasteful business, and with people who regarded their enemies as disposable. The most likely explanation that Harry could see was that the documents that Veronica had handed over could only have come from the people who had intercepted the material when it had been uploaded to the JIC portal. Sir Robert had speculated that Veronica may have met with one of those people, seen him and could possibly identify him. It seemed to Harry that Veronica was confirming that speculation. He had to keep her engaged, keep her onside. Veronica was quite unaware of what Harry already knew as she played what she thought would be her trump cards to get Harry's attention.

'These people, they're somehow involved with Bickley-Morris and his spying. They're dangerous, Harry. They killed Graham, and they want to kill me too. I'm not going back to Huxley's tonight, Harry, I'm not putting him in danger too.'

Harry would fall for that. Veronica was sure her feigned concern for Harry's "favoured son" and the link to Quinton would prove irresistible. She didn't know for certain who had killed Graham, but she was ninety-nine percent certain that Reid and his organisation had been behind it. Not that it mattered; Rod Graham, too, was dead. She could use that to her advantage, proof of how dangerous these people could be. Harry Nevile would agree to her proposals.

Harry hadn't considered that Graham's death could have been linked to Quinton's activities and the people in a larger organisation, but he realised it was quite possible. Sir Robert had never felt that Quinton had chosen the Saronic Gulf at random for his base after he fled the UK. Agistri was just a short sea crossing from Aegina. If there was an active ex-Stasi group in the Athens area, they could have made the arrangements for Quinton and kept an eye on his activities into the bargain.

Harry's response to Veronica's plan was predictable.

'Does Huxley know?'

'No, and you're not to tell him. Otherwise, I won't help you.'

'Help me, what?' Harry sensed Veronica was about to tell him what she was after. There was no question he would co-operate. For the time being, at least.

Veronica laid out her demands. In return for information that would lead Harry to the people responsible, the people who wanted Robert Hamilton disgraced, she wanted protection now. A safe place to stay, secrecy about her involvement and whereabouts, and, in the near future, a new identity, a new life.

There was something cold and calculating about the way she outlined her proposal that made Harry uncomfortable. He wondered if there was a part of her personality, a better part, that he could appeal to and, once again, he asked her about Huxley. Veronica's reply was short, sharp and brutal.

'I don't give a toss about Huxley. He's not my problem. Time he grew up.'

Realising that he was risking antagonising her, Harry tried a more conciliatory approach.

'OK, we need to talk about this. Let me know where you are.'

'Where I am is none of your business. Meet me in the National Portrait Gallery cafeteria in half an hour.'

'Look, I can't just drop everything I—'

'Can't risk them finding me, Harry. National Portrait Gallery. Cafeteria. Half an hour.' She put the phone down, knowing she was taking a risk. If Harry Nevile didn't take the bait, she was on her own. She couldn't go back to Blackheath; she wasn't going back to Huxley's, and if she went back to Aegina, they would soon find her if her suspicions were true. All of those options would leave her looking over her shoulder for the rest of her life. Harry would come. He had to come. She knew it took about twenty-five minutes to walk from Tufton Street to the National Portrait Gallery – she had rehearsed the route yesterday. Half an hour did not give Harry any time to do what a good civil servant would do: alert his masters, arrange for her to be arrested. All he could do was walk. Not even getting a taxi would help him. All she had to do was wait. The phone box on Saint Martin's Place, opposite the gallery entrance, would provide her with cover. She wouldn't be in the cafeteria waiting, like a sitting duck. If Harry turned up in person, alone, she would follow him.

Harry knew his options were limited. Veronica had never intended to stay after delivering the files; her return ticket had been for Sunday last. If she had a plan in place to leave the country, he couldn't risk her activating it if he failed to turn up, or if he turned up late. He opened the meeting room door and stepped into the office.

'Damned police.' Margaret and Huxley looked at him. 'The Kilsdale case, they're making a pig's ear of it, want more information. It's going to be quicker to go down there and sort it out now.' It was all he could think of and, picking up his coat, he headed for the lift.

Nicholas looked surprised to see Harry step out of the lift, looking ready to go outside. Harry didn't give him a chance to say anything, quickly crossing the foyer to his desk.

'Veronica, Mrs Blakeridge. Tell Sir Robert. He was right – the dossier wasn't at Graham's. Says she's in danger, wants to tell us who's behind this. National Portrait Gallery cafeteria. If I'm not there in half an hour, she'll disappear. No one upstairs knows.'

He had decided to play for time, give Sir Robert at least a fighting chance of arranging some kind of response, though what that might be he had no idea. All that he could do was to play along. Walk there, take the half hour, and talk to her as long as possible. Go along with whatever she proposed. If she truly believed she was in danger, she would come over sooner rather than later.

With that, he left. The narrow strip of sky visible between the confines of Tufton Street's narrow roadway and tall buildings looked forebodingly grey. Harry hoped it wouldn't rain. He hadn't brought his umbrella with him today.

CHAPTER 26

Day eleven: Thursday, late morning

Once inside the gallery, Harry followed the sign down into the basement and to the cafeteria. It wasn't large, and it was quite busy – lunchtime was approaching. He couldn't see Veronica. He did a circuit of the room. To all intents and purposes, just somebody else looking to join his friends for lunch, but she wasn't there. Perhaps she had been delayed. He would have to wait. Joining the queue, he bought two coffees. With tables filling up, sitting alone with one coffee risked somebody joining him at the table, someone who spotted a man with only a coffee and no food, a man who wouldn't be staying that long. A second coffee said this seat is already taken. Harry picked up the two coffees, turned around looking for the empty tables he had spotted earlier and saw her sitting at one of them. She had taken the small bench facing the room, leaving Harry the chair opposite.

There was no greeting from her. Harry held her gaze as he put the two coffees on the table, then sat down.

'Well?'

'Well?' Veronica had a hard look in her eye and paused before continuing. 'Have you come to help me or not?'

'Veronica, naturally, I'm concerned that you might be in danger, but why me? Why not go to the police?'

Veronica sat up straight in her seat, putting her hands on the table as if about to stand up.

'Don't treat me like an idiot, Harry.' Veronica kept her voice low so that she couldn't be overheard by the people at nearby tables, but there was an unmistakable note of disdain in the way she spoke. 'I may as well just leave now.'

Harry motioned for her to remain seated.

'I just need to know what's going on. Huxley isn't all that sure that there was somebody else in your house.' Harry wasn't letting on about everything he knew and was hoping that if Veronica knew more, he could draw it out of her.

'Oh, for Christ's sake, are you being deliberately fucking stupid?'

For a moment, Veronica wondered if Harry was part of the plot, after all. He had always been close to Sir Robert Hamilton. Too close, maybe? Although the thought troubled her, she tried to be rational; she *had* to be rational. As far as she could see, Harry was her only way out. She had worked for him for years now, and if she had learned one thing, it was that Harry played by the rules. Always. Harry was somebody you could trust. If Robert Hamilton could fool the Security Service all these years, he would have no qualms about stringing Harry along too. If Harry had a fault, it was that he was too trusting of his colleagues, and right now, she needed him to trust her. Her life might depend on it.

'Look, I'm sorry. I'm just worried. Somebody died at my house, remember.' Mentally, Veronica took a deep breath and pushed her emotions to the back of her mind. She asked Harry if he really thought it was a coincidence that somebody just happened to die in her house on the same day that she was given a dossier to deliver, evidence that a senior member of the Security Service was a traitor. Surely she deserved the benefit of the doubt about somebody else being there, or was there something she didn't know?

The implication was quite clear to Harry: maybe this was being swept under the carpet on the instructions of the Security Service, something they didn't want to come to light. Maybe it was the Security Service itself, or a senior officer, perhaps, who had wanted her dead.

'Why else has he disappeared, Harry? If he is innocent?'

Harry was about to ask who she thought had disappeared, but thought better of it. It was a question that could only antagonise her further as Huxley had almost certainly found out that Sir Robert had taken a leave of absence and passed on the information. Besides, Harry was quite certain there had been somebody else in her house that afternoon, even though he was sure that Veronica had not been the target. Nevertheless, it was good enough reason for her to be worried, and he could use that worry. They needed to know who had intercepted the inculpatory information that Sir Robert had uploaded to the JIC document repository. Tomorrow was the last Friday of the month, the day he himself was due to upload his first set of files to the portal, and he was expecting Nicholas to give him an additional file; the file that was more than it would seem to be. If Veronica's testimony backed up whatever the tracking of that file revealed, there could be little doubt about culpability.

'You do realise, don't you, that there are going to be serious questions asked about why you were the chosen envoy? But first, I do need to know who? Who gave it to you?'

'Nice try. I'll tell you what I know when I'm somewhere safe.'

'What you're asking, I can't conjure up out of nowhere. I need to involve other people. I need some evidence. Give

221

me something I can use to help you.' Harry knew that this would not come as a surprise to Veronica. She already knew this; she must have something prepared, something to make him take the bait.

'Three bodies – Graham, my cleaner, and now Kilsdale. Isn't that enough?'

Harry chose not to reply; he just held her gaze, waiting for her to fill the silence. If she were genuinely concerned for her own safety, she would come across with something.

'Somebody who knew Graham, who knows Bickley-Morris, someone who shits in the same toilet as all the other double-dealing Judases. Dare say he knew quite a lot about Kilsdale too.'

'And how does he know you?' Harry wasn't sure that Veronica would answer, but the vitriol in her description suggested she was close to breaking.

'As I said, he knew Graham, knew he was blackmailing me. Only he didn't trust Graham, recognised him for the snake he was. Graham wanted information, and somebody wanted information on Graham. So I obliged. Call it paying him back for threatening my mother, for threatening me. And worse.'

Harry had little doubt that "paying him back" came with a payment of its own, but if she could identify other people in the same network as Quinton, he was prepared to listen.

'Come back to Tufton Street with me now. We can look after you. Whilst I sort things out.'

Veronica gave a half-choked snort.

'Another night at Margaret's? Whilst she pumps me for information, goes through my things? Not to mention Huxley. No thanks, Harry.'

'I'll have to say something to Huxley. If you're not going back to his, he'll worry.'

'No. You say nothing to Huxley. Not if you want me to talk.'

Harry was shocked by the hard edge to her voice and her clear indifference to Huxley's distress. He had assumed that Huxley's feelings for Veronica had been reciprocated. 'But—' Veronica cut him short; she was clearly in no mood to negotiate.

'Don't we all have to suffer a little for the greater good? It might even help him to grow up.' Veronica picked up her shoulder bag from the bench beside her and stood up. 'I'm going now. You have until tomorrow. I'll call to say where and when. Don't try and follow me, and let's hope there's no one outside waiting to pick me up because if there is, the deal is off.'

The truth was, Veronica wasn't concerned if Harry had managed to arrange for her to be detained. If he had, she would be safe. It would give her a bargaining chip when she was interrogated. Nor was she concerned if Harry set a trap for her the next day – it was the same outcome – she would be safe from Reid and his cohort. Her only worry was whether Reid or his people knew where she was now. She doubted it; she had been careful. In any case, if they were going to abduct her, or worse, they would do it at Huxley's flat, and she wasn't going back there. She had her journey planned. Leicester Square underground station, a detour on the Tube before going to Charing Cross, then a local train to Dartford before picking up the mainline from Victoria to Whitstable. She had a guest house booked for the night, and there was a restaurant. She had visited both with her husband before he

223

was killed in the accident. Whatever happened, this evening was likely to be her last night of freedom for some time. She would relive something that had made her happy.

Harry didn't try to follow her. He gave her ten minutes before leaving. As he stepped out onto St Martin's Place, a smartly dressed gentleman stepped forward.

'Mr Nevile. Your appointment at Vauxhall Cross. I have a car.' The gentleman who spoke, casually but smartly dressed, held out his arm, gesturing towards Orange Street. Harry had little doubt Sir Robert had sent him.

'Mrs Blakeridge?' Harry queried, wondering if anybody had been sent to intercept or follow her.

'Wouldn't know, sir. I was sent to pick you up. I am not aware of any other colleagues present.'

Harry nodded as he was guided towards a black cab parked in a bay on Orange Street. He noted there was already a driver in the cab and wondered what his new companion would do. He was a little apprehensive. Had he been too trusting? Harry breathed a sigh of relief as the gentleman opened and closed the cab door for him before walking off and disappearing amongst the people crowding Charing Cross Road. A second thought occurred to Harry: he wasn't sure if he had enough change to pay for a cab, then realised that this was not a public taxi; the driver hadn't set the meter running.

Harry was deep in thought, wondering how to deal with Huxley and his inevitable upset, when a squall of rain hit the windscreen. Harry looked up. They had just passed the Palace of Westminster, and he realised the driver was pulling into the middle of the road, about to turn right into Dean Stanley Street. A wave of unease swept through his body.

'This isn't the way…'

'Yes, sir. Nobel House, Smith Square.'

Harry was both relieved and confused. Nobel House, he was quite certain, was a government building, but he wasn't sure which department was based there. And he wasn't sure the driver was telling him the truth. Harry relaxed when, a minute later, the driver pulled into the corner of Smith Square.

'Wear your lanyard, sir. Ask for room six-one-seven. You are expected.'

Harry looked up at the carved stone face adorning the keystone of the portico's arch, underneath what he considered the slightly pretentious, carved Latinised building name 'NOBEL HOVSE'. The face wasn't quite smiling at him as he went up the steps, thankful to be out of the drizzle that had started. The receptionist looked carefully at his Security Service ID badge, now hanging around his neck, before telling him he was expected. Harry refrained from saying that he already knew that and thanked the lady.

Room six-one-seven overlooked a rather shabby internal courtyard at the back of what Harry knew to be the former Imperial Chemical House. Judging by the architecture, Nobel House had been part of the complex at some point in the past. Sir Robert was waiting for him.

'Sorry for any confusion, Harry, but I can't stay in one place too long. Risk of being recognised, not ideal for a body officially on a leave of absence, or indeed one who is unofficially, but officially, missing but wanted.' In response to Harry's bemused expression, Sir Robert explained that the "Min of Ag, Fish and Food", as he called them, were in a state of flux, reorganising which departments were in which

225

building, so a new, unknown face was taken for granted at Nobel House. 'Officially, I'm a security consultant for a junior minister's new office, which means they suspect I'm MI5 but don't like to ask too many questions.'

Sir Robert was clearly amused about the subterfuge, but taking on a more serious aspect, he gestured towards a small table with a coffee pot and cups and invited Harry to sit.

'Mrs Blakeridge. It seems we've underestimated her. What's her story?'

Harry repeated what Veronica had told him, adding that if she had been passing information on about Rod Graham, it could explain why she followed him to Aegina. It was something that had puzzled Harry, who hadn't fully bought her "hiding under his nose" explanation and suspected that somehow she had been involved in Graham's death. Quite possibly seeking some form of revenge whilst reporting on his activities, and no doubt those of Quinton Bickley-Morris too.

'It was rather a coincidence that Graham, Bickley-Morris and Mrs Blakeridge ended up in such close proximity,' Sir Robert mused. 'Not our concern, of course, once we had our man. Case closed. Perhaps we were naive, Harry, and should have looked beyond Bickley-Morris. But we did have other things to worry about. There was a clear intent to infect the government with that wretched mouse virus. We may have rumbled the possibility of an attack at the party conference, but who was to say they wouldn't try something else?'

Harry and Sir Robert both agreed that there could be little doubt that whoever had given her the copy of the dossier had to be close, very close, to whoever had been accessing JIC documents.

'The timing is awkward,' Sir Robert remarked, 'but we have little choice other than to hear her out.'

'Awkward?' Harry wasn't sure what Sir Robert was referring to. 'Oh,' he added. 'The files.' Tomorrow was the day that he was due to upload the Security Service's monthly reports to the JIC portal, including the special file that Nicholas was due to give him. 'It's certainly going to be an interesting day.'

Sir Robert smiled in acknowledgement.

'The way I see it,' Sir Robert confided, 'is that we're looking at a win-win situation.' He explained his thoughts. If whoever had given a copy of the dossier to Veronica was not the man who had intercepted it, then it would give them more information about any network that existed. If it were the same suspect, then that would strengthen their case against him. Veronica had asked for protection, and they would provide it. They would bring her into protective custody the next day.

Harry thought that "custody" was rather a foreboding term, but Sir Robert reminded him that, whether Veronica was aware of it or not, she had been circulating restricted access documents. Nor could they simply ignore the fact that she had admitted passing information to Graham. It may have been done under duress, but it was still illegal, and agreeing to pass on the dossier, not to mention informing on Graham, might constitute collusion with the agents of an unfriendly power, albeit a former one.

'Mrs Blakeridge does indeed have much to explain,' Sir Robert noted, 'and as to her future, that does rather depend on the value of what she has to tell us.'

Although it sounded harsh to Harry, he knew there was no

alternative, and he knew that Veronica would be quite aware of what she was risking.

At the back of Harry's mind was the thought that she might be playing some sort of devious game. Amongst the other questions that still hung over her disappearance last year was why, exactly, had she forewarned Rod Graham about his imminent arrest? There were two nagging doubts that had been troubling Harry. The first was whether she had been a more willing informant than she was prepared to admit. The second was worse. It had been something she had said to him after her outburst at Sir Robert last year: "There's only one way to stop Rod Graham". Had she been part of a conspiracy to murder Graham? A conspiracy orchestrated by the people she now thought were turning their attention to her? If either doubt turned out to be true, Veronica had been a cuckoo in the nest at Tufton Street. To put it more plainly: a traitor.

Sir Robert pulled Harry's attention back to the matter in hand.

'Something's worrying you, Harry, I can see it in your face. What is it?'

It wasn't the thought of Veronica that was disturbing Harry; it was the certain knowledge that he would be sitting in the same office as Huxley for the rest of the day, unable to say anything. And later that evening, there would be the inevitable phone call from a devastated young man.

Chapter 27
Day eleven: Thursday, late afternoon

Ich verstehe.
Herzliche Grüße,
JT

Tobias sent the fax acknowledging the update to the plan yesterday evening. "JT" was a code to verify the date rather than the sender; the fax machine in the upstairs room of the bookshop sent its own signature. Not that the coded message updating his instructions had arrived via the same piece of equipment. Send and receive by different routes was standard procedure.

For the first time in several weeks, Tobias felt a sense of relief. He liked neither Reid nor the ill-conceived plans he had put into action. There was no doubting his own overriding objective: Anna Slowik. It was as simple as that. Reid had his instructions, yet the man who had a reputation for not taking unnecessary risks seemed to have lost all sense of purpose. It wasn't just the stupid vendetta against Sir Robert Hamilton. To Tobias' way of thinking, if a man had posed that much of a threat, he would have taken him out several years ago. Even so, when the dossier came to light, Reid should have just exposed it; there was no need to bring in a third party – and an ex-MI5 officer at that.

The list went on. This was no way to run a covert operation. If the untrustworthy and uncontrollable Bickley-Morris wanted to exact revenge on one of his former associates, let him. Let him take the risk. Don't get involved, and certainly don't set him up to kill somebody in a house owned by the ex-MI5 woman you have been using for a number of years and have just involved in your pointless vendetta. Why turn her from a retired asset into a loose end?

If Reid had shown poor judgement about influencing the Bickley-Morris trial, the unauthorised plan he had put into action had ultimately sealed his fate. A fate that may have been delayed whilst the need to find Slowik was paramount, but would soon catch up with him now that he was no longer of use. When Reid's source in Thames House discovered that there were growing reservations about Slowik testifying at Bickley-Morris' trial, he should have let things take their course. There were reasons enough to withdraw her; no need to interfere. It would have caused enough division within the intelligence services – division between those who wanted Bickley-Morris jailed and those who wanted to keep Slowik's defection secret. Trying to influence opinion in Whitehall was risky enough. Trying to panic the Security Service by leaking information about Tobias' presence in the UK to the British embassy in Berlin had been madness. What could it achieve other than putting the Security Service on alert and limiting the time and opportunity Tobias had to fulfil his task? In a sense, Tobias had been proven right: it would seem that that particular piece of intelligence had not been passed on in a timely fashion, and Slowik had still been withdrawn from the case. Tobias was fairly sure that the information had now been passed on, and that was what had triggered Slowik's disappearance just as her location had been found.

In the meantime, that damned dossier had appeared and

taken over Reid's attention. If anything should have been leaked to the embassy in Berlin, it was that dossier, and there were still people in Berlin who could have done so and imparted it with a greater aura of authenticity.

There was one thing Tobias would have liked to know the answer to, and that was why Slowik's defection seemed to be being handled by Thames House and not Vauxhall Cross. Surely she had more to tell about activities in Berlin than about any internal threat to the UK. It was too late now; the chances of finding Slowik again were low, and the Security Service was on alert about Tobias' presence in the UK. Whatever Slowik had to tell the UK authorities, she had probably already done so, but Tobias' task had been as much to send a message as to prevent her talking, or since they were not sure quite how long she had been in the UK, talking further.

Tobias would return home, but first, he had Reid and his loose end of an ex-MI5 courier to deal with. There would be no fuss, no high-profile assassinations; they would simply disappear. There had been little doubt in his mind that his former Stasi associates would be in agreement. True, they had made a few minor changes, by and large, a reminder that if things went wrong, they would no longer have the assets to help him. Take out the kingpin and the structure collapses; Tobias knew that. He was no fool and had spent the last few days making careful preparations. Soon, he would be just another anonymous German tourist heading back to Europe. He picked up the black cable tie, put it in his pocket and left the bookshop with nothing more than a curt nod to the proprietor, who watched him walk eastwards along Cecil Court.

* * *

As the light faded in his room, Harry waited with increasing anxiety for the phone to ring. When it did, even as he picked it up, he had no idea what he was going to say. He had no idea how he could avoid misleading Huxley. The one thing he couldn't do was to tell the truth.

'Harry Nevile.'

'Harry, it's Margaret.'

'Margaret?'

'Sorry, Harry, are you expecting a call from somebody else. You sound... Well, on edge.'

'No, I'm fine, but is there a problem?'.

'It's Huxley – he's in a state. Veronica's gone.'

Those last two words, delivered with an almost matter-of-fact intonation, summed up what Harry had been dreading having to say to Huxley.

'Oh.' Harry paused whilst he tried to get a grip on the conversation. 'Poor Huxley, better tell me all.'

Huxley had phoned Margaret to ask if Veronica was at her house – the only place he could think she might be. He had been out of the office that afternoon, doing some research at the British Library and had left for home reasonably early. When he arrived, he hadn't been too surprised that Veronica wasn't there. Yet there was something about the emptiness of the flat, almost as though a void had opened up in the place. He had taken a look around and realised that all her belongings were gone – a clear indication that she had not been abducted, but he didn't want to believe it. His only thought was to find her, and he had taken a taxi to Blackheath,

232

but her house was as sickeningly silent as his own flat. In his distressed state, he had wondered if something had happened and she had been taken into hiding; they just hadn't let him know. Yet. The last place she had stayed, to keep her safe, was Margaret's. He would call her. He didn't want to listen to his sensible head that was telling him that if something had happened, officially, Veronica would have been taken somewhere more secure. Harry had been out of the office, too, so it had made sense to Huxley to call Margaret. She had been in the office; she would know. More importantly, she would tell him.

Margaret had been unable to help. She too recognised that the absence of Veronica's belongings screamed that her leaving had been planned: it had been no spur-of-the-moment panic, nor an abduction. She had asked Huxley if he had contacted the police, given the events of last week, but Huxley's rather curt reply had pointed out that she was an adult; she could do what she wanted. The police wouldn't treat her disappearance as suspicious for several days, if at all. Given her status as a former Security Service officer, they may not want to get involved until officially invited.

'Her clothes have gone. All her belongings. What's…?' Huxley hadn't finished the sentence. It was his admission that she had left of her own free will and chosen not to tell him. An admission that had left him bereft. His future, which had seemed so bright a few hours ago, was now a dark abyss, swallowing his hopes and dreams.

'I'll get a flight to Greece. I can be there by morning.'

Margaret knew it was his desperation speaking. Rather than dissuade him directly, she had realised he needed someone to talk to.

233

'Come to mine, Huxley. Don't be on your own. I've got a spare room. I'll ring Harry.'

That was what she had done, but she hadn't expected Harry's reaction. Huxley was on his way to her house; she didn't have time to avoid what she felt was a central issue.

'Harry, you know something, I can tell. And I'm guessing it's important, but you can't tell me. Don't bugger me about, Harry, and don't bugger Huxley about. I know we have doubts about her story, but is she safe?'

There were times when Margaret demanded straight talking, and this was one of them. Harry's hesitancy to respond not only confirmed Margaret's suspicions but provoked a more insistent demand.

'Harry. Is she safe?'

'Not until tomorrow. Her choice, Margaret, her terms.'

Margaret understood that Harry was being more honest than he should be, but he would not lie to her. Might he have to lie to Huxley?

'Do you want me to come round, Margaret? Talk to him?'

'No, Harry. At the moment, you would be about as much use as a chocolate fireguard.'

It wasn't intended as an insult or a considered opinion of Harry's interpersonal skills; it was said with a laugh. It was a recognition that, because of the constraints on what he could say, it was unlikely that Harry could be helpful. Better to say nothing than create doubt. Or false hope.

'What will you do? You know… when he arrives?'

'Feed him and very probably get him drunk. Well, just enough to help him sleep. I can't rule out that we'll be a little late in the morning, though. You, Harry, are going to have to tell the rest of the team before we get in.'

CHAPTER 28

Day twelve: Friday, morning

The day began with telephone calls.

Veronica had phoned Nicholas shortly before leaving Whitstable. It wasn't that she didn't care to talk to Harry, but Nicholas was dependable; Nicholas would be at his desk. Harry, on the other hand, given the time of day, was likely to be on his walk to work, and Veronica didn't want to change her schedule – she had a train to catch. Waiting until she arrived back in London before phoning Harry would be a risk, giving him less time to put his plans into action, plans that Harry would have started to make yesterday after their meeting. She was certain of that and did not want anything to go wrong. Veronica was also certain that Nicholas would trace the call, though an anonymous payphone on the Kent coast would tell him very little.

* * *

Harry had only just finished his breakfast when Sir Robert called him on the phone. Everything was in place to take Veronica into protective custody. It only needed Harry to advise the time and place of the meeting, and for him to make a preliminary judgement as to whether Veronica really did know anything of value. It wasn't that she wouldn't be given protection; it was to be an indication of the level of security that would need to be put in place. If he thought it unlikely that she had enough information to identify the person who had passed her the dossier, he was to leave the meeting place on his own. Sir Robert's team would then move in and escort Veronica to Nobel House, where Sir Robert would interrogate her further to establish just how useful her information was. Otherwise, Harry was to leave with Veronica. They would be picked up and taken to a secure location where Sir Robert would join them.

A potential impending dilemma occurred to Harry. If Veronica had the information she claimed to have, he would not be returning to Tufton Street later that day, the day when Huxley would need him most. It was unfortunate, but the situation had not been of Harry's making or choosing. He also hoped that the timing of his meeting with Veronica would not affect his uploading of the JIC files, especially the additional file which Nicholas was going to provide. His duties in that direction, he realised with more than a twinge of guilt, would be an additional restriction of the time he would have available to support Huxley in his hour of need. *It's not my fault*, he told himself. *It's Veronica's.* Harry realised that he no longer thought of her as "Ron", the member of the team he had had such high hopes for. She had been replaced by "Veronica", the cold, calculating and unsympathetic woman he had met yesterday. What had happened?

Harry's heart grew heavier with each step he took towards Tufton Street. The truth was, he was weary. It was less than two weeks since he had met with Sir Robert in Victoria Square, yet so much had happened that Harry was having trouble keeping track of everything. He had woken that morning thinking about Quinton, and he was still puzzled as to where the man fitted in with recent events. If what had worried Kilsdale was true, and Quinton had meant to harm him, then it was difficult to believe Quinton was entirely innocent in respect of Kilsdale's subsequent murder. If Quinton had planned the execution, it was unlikely that he would leave the body on his own doorstep. Could that and the business card be some form of elaborate bluff? Or was it, as Harry had suspected, some kind of warning?

There was no logical reason why Quinton would have tried to lure Kilsdale to Veronica's house, but it did suggest he knew that the house was empty. Kilsdale had mentioned some files that Graham had stolen. Could he have been referring to the Hamilton dossier? It may have seemed obvious, but whoever had given Veronica the dossier almost certainly knew about the story of the files being found in Graham's house and also knew that Veronica was out of the country. Was that what had given Quinton the idea? Blundering about, following his own agenda with no regard for anybody else, was hardly out of character for the man. Nor was it out of character for him to try and stage his own show, and a dossier with evidence against Sir Robert Hamilton would be something Quinton could use to his own advantage. The dossier had been leaked only to the Security Service, suggesting the intent was entirely to discredit and harm Hamilton. Leaking to a wider audience, to the press, could taint the whole of the Security Service. That would appeal to Quinton.

Harry knew it wasn't a full explanation. If Quinton had indeed caused problems by running roughshod over someone else's plans, why kill Kilsdale? Why just a warning? Why not take out the man responsible directly? His hypotheses may not be entirely true, but Harry's instinct told him that

237

he had grasped some elements of the truth. There had to be a connection between Veronica's mysterious contact and Quinton Bickley-Morris. If nothing else, Veronica had also seemed convinced of the connection. Harry knew that this wasn't a novel; this was real life. In the less-than-clear waters of the intelligence services, you didn't have the luxury of dotting all the i's and crossing all the t's; you did the best you could with the parts you could connect.

The matter was unresolved when Harry arrived at Tufton Street. Most mornings when he stepped through the blue door, he felt a sense of solidity, of safety, almost like returning home as a child, but not this morning. He couldn't avoid Huxley and wanted to avoid misleading him, though he didn't know if that would be possible. Much depended on Huxley's frame of mind.

'Good morning, sir,' Nicholas greeted him. 'A busy day, I suspect. In response to Harry's questioning look, Nicholas added, 'Miss Millard is already here.'

Harry was caught off guard. 'Margaret? Already?' His stomach began to sink. 'And Mr Huxley?'

'At this time of the morning, sir? I am afraid not.'

Harry sensed that Nicholas knew more than he was letting on, but was trying to make light of the situation. He wasn't sure how to reply, but Nicholas pre-empted him.

'I have a message, sir, from Mrs Blakeridge. St John's, Smith Square. 11:45. The north side, sir. I suspect the lady has done her homework.'

Harry looked bemused, but Nicholas explained the building was rather symmetrical, with similar steps on opposite sides of the building. 'They say it was modelled on an upturned footstool. Queen Anne's, I believe.'

Inwardly, Harry breathed a sigh of relief, though it struck him as a curious place to arrange a meeting. Nevertheless, the message meant she was safe, at least for the moment. Then he steeled himself. Despite his personal concern for Veronica, he still had to deal with her. She had, after all, been misleading them as to the origin of the dossier. What else had she been misleading them about? Was her claim that Graham had blackmailed and coerced her as truthful as it had first seemed? One thing Harry was sure of was that Veronica wasn't planning a long meeting, at least not on the concert hall steps. He doubted she had chosen the location because of its proximity to Tufton Street. It would be unlikely that she would want to come back to the office and risk coming face to face with Huxley. It was equally unlikely that she would know that Sir Robert was housed, temporarily, just a few yards away. Harry's best guess was that she was hoping to be picked up quickly and taken to a place of safety. Firstly, however, she would need to give him something of substance.

'Is everyone aware? The location, I mean.' Harry wasn't sure why he didn't want to mention Sir Robert by name, but there was little doubt that Nicholas would understand who he meant.

'Yes, sir. Suitable arrangements will be in place.'

There was no need to say any more. Harry was quite sure that Nicholas would be briefed fully by Sir Robert and would pass on any relevant information. Harry thanked Nicholas, and as he turned towards the lift, Nicholas stopped him.

'I believe you're expecting this, sir.' Nicholas held out a three-and-a-half-inch floppy disk, undistinguished by its light grey plastic case. Taking the disk, Harry nodded his thanks to the concierge but, eager to find out more about Huxley, mumbled an apologetic, 'Best get on, then.'

Upstairs, Harry didn't have to ask; Margaret responded to his look.

'I've sent him home. If nothing else, he needs a change of clothes.'

Inwardly, Harry breathed a sigh of relief but knew his reprieve may only be temporary.

'And later?'

Seeming to sense Harry's relief, Margaret smiled.

'I've told him not to come in. Suggested he might spend the weekend at his parents', on the coast. Don't worry, Harry. He'll be OK.'

'OK? Are you sure?'

'He will be, Harry. He will be. He's not a child.'

The irony of Veronica saying it was time for Huxley to "grow up" and Margaret's view that "He's not a child" was not lost on Harry.

'No, but he's bound to be distraught. You know, all things considered.'

'All things considered, Harry? What "things" do I need to consider? Tell me what you can.'

Harry looked around, even though he knew they were alone in the office.

'Sir Robert is no traitor. I can vouch for that, but someone has been intercepting information, possibly the same person who gave Veronica that file on him.' Harry picked up on Margaret's puzzled look and explained. 'Veronica's missing hours? Last Monday? I think she met someone who gave her that copy of the dossier. If not the same person who has been intercepting government documents, then someone very close. Veronica says she can identify him.'

'But why run? And why in such a heartless way? If Veronica wanted to come clean, why didn't she just come into Tufton Street and ask for help?'

'I'm not sure. She's frightened, I have no doubt about that. Still thinks she was the intended victim at her own house. She doesn't know the full story – at least I don't think so. Not sure any of us do, or indeed how much store we can set by Kilsdale's claims about Quinton luring him there. Look, I have something important to do right now, but I'm meeting Veronica later. Whatever happens, she'll be taken somewhere safe, even if it's only temporary.'

Margaret furrowed her brows at Harry's use of the word "temporary". Harry responded to the look.

'There's only so much *I* can guarantee. The rest depends on what she knows and what she's prepared to tell us.'

'Not to mention what she's been up to.' Margaret's tone of voice confirmed that she, too, was beginning to wonder where Veronica's loyalties lay. Doubt has a habit of contaminating anything it can touch, and Margaret voiced the question that had to be asked. 'And Huxley? Could he be involved?'

Harry was quite sure on that point. 'No, not involved. Though he may well have been used. I don't know what's happened between them, but she's adamant that nothing is to be said to him.' He waited a few moments before adding, 'Her terms, not mine.'

They were both distracted by the sound of the lift beginning its journey down to the ground floor. Not knowing who would be next in the office, Andrew or Thomas most likely, Harry realised he didn't have the luxury of explaining more.

'Tell the others Huxley won't be in today. Better to play

241

it down, no great speech from me. Get Ben up to speed on everything, discreetly. I'll know more later.' Harry had no more time as the lift doors opened and the two Disciples, Andrew and Thomas, arrived.

* * *

Veronica had one last thing she wanted to do before meeting up with Harry. It was about nostalgia, and recognition that she had left her former life behind. As a child, a favourite treat had been to take the riverboat from Embankment Pier to Bankside Pier and then walk back into the city along the south bank. If the tide was right, she would sometimes be allowed onto Thames Beach to look for treasure.

Veronica had deposited her suitcase at the left luggage company in Victoria station. She would give the ticket to Harry. She was neither sure nor concerned whether it would be picked up. Leaving Embankment underground station, she headed up Villiers Street away from the Thames. There was something she needed to do to satisfy her curiosity before heading back towards the river. As she approached the side entrance to Charing Cross station, she could see something around the handrail. Veronica was oblivious to the curses of the passersby who almost knocked her off her feet as she stopped abruptly in front of the station steps. She had not expected to see a black cable tie, but it was there. Her mind immediately brought up doubts; she was certain that it had not been there yesterday, nor any other day since she had picked up the dossier from the bookshop in Cecil Court. Had Reid made good on his promise? Had she misjudged both the man and his intentions? Could there be a reasonable explanation for the delay in activating her exit strategy? Her doubt lasted only that brief moment. The cable tie was a signal: return to the bookshop; your new passport, travel documents and payment are ready. It was a risk she dared not take. The more she had thought about it, the more convinced she had become that the exit strategy Reid had planned for her was deadly. Huxley had seen somebody in her house, the house in which somebody else had died, and Veronica didn't share the lack of interest shown by the police. Had it not been for Huxley turning up at her house, she could have been a victim too. The dossier would have been found, Hamilton would have been exposed, and nothing would have been traceable to Reid.

When Veronica had first become involved with Reid, it had been in the hope that she might wreak some kind of revenge on Rod Graham. Informing on the man who had bullied and blackmailed her into informing on her colleagues seemed appropriate. The two acts somehow cancelling each other out, leaving her not with a feeling of innocence, yet somehow guiltless. The truth was, nobody associated with Rod Graham could be trusted. Veronica felt she was meting out justice of a kind, as enshrined in the proverb "As you sow, so shall you reap".

It wasn't the lack of trust that was worrying Veronica so much as the rising body count: Graham himself, Veronica's cleaner and Matthew Kilsdale, who had been bound up in that unsavoury business in Pitsea involving both Graham and the odious Quinton Bickley-Morris. There had also been the attack on Margaret and the so-called "accident" that had hospitalised one of the workers at Kilsdale's Pitsea-based diagnostic company. It did not take a lot of imagination to suspect both could have been attempted murder. Veronica felt she had been lucky not to have walked into a trap in her own home; she wasn't going to walk into one in a bookshop in Cecil Court. The existence of Cecil Court was something else to give up to Harry, adding weight to her testimony, and if Harry was able to bring down more of Reid's organisation, that would make her own future that little bit more secure.

CHAPTER 29
Day twelve: Friday, morning

Uploading the files to the JIC portal hadn't been as onerous a task as Harry had feared. He wasn't incompetent or hesitant when it came to using modern technology, though he was uncomfortable with reading text displayed on a screen rather than printed on paper. He put that down to years of training at school and university. He absorbed information through his eyes and ears, processed it in his brain and passed it out through his fingers, immortalising it with a pen on paper. Using a keyboard didn't trouble him – he had been using a typewriter for twenty years or more – he just found it difficult to absorb information when it was presented to him on a screen and not on a sheet of paper. Worse than that, because it was difficult to absorb, he found himself scrolling up and down, struggling to rediscover something he had read moments before. It was so much easier to flick back and forth through a sheaf of papers, scanning whole pages at a time rather than the small segment displayed on his monitor.

Although the process for uploading the files was simple enough, it was a task that was tedious. Only the current "Pope" was allowed to transfer files to the JIC portal on behalf of the Security Service. Harry had been told it was for reasons of security, though he suspected it was simply a continuation of the historic system in which one person had been responsible for collating all the files to be shared. Files that were printed on paper and photocopied for distribution. Restricting access for security reasons had made sense then, but those days had passed. The "Pope" had his own computer account, to which the various departments sent their reports, the titles of which identified the subject and the status. Harry's job was to transfer the individual files to the JIC account and fill out a simple spreadsheet, which provided a digest of current concerns. Harry liked spreadsheets; they were one aspect of computerisation that he actually felt was a genuine advance in information handling.

Adding Sir Robert's counterfeit file proved to be as simple as the instruction suggested, much to Harry's relief. A typed label on the disk casing advised: "1. Log into Vatican Account. 2. Insert disk. 3. File will autoload". And that was exactly what had happened. Harry had been equally concerned and impressed when, at the end of the transfer process, a pop-up box on his screen indicated that the disk contents were being erased. When he carried out the confirmatory check, to all intents and purposes, the file had been loaded as if it had come, originally, from the Director General's office. All that Harry needed to do was update the spreadsheet with "Robert Hamilton Status Update" and mark the priority as level one. Even as "Pope" Harry did not have the necessary permissions to access the file. He knew it wasn't the contents that were of interest, but the fact that embedded somewhere in the file was something called a Trojan Horse Virus, which would be activated if the file was copied.

Harry had finished his papal duties before 10:00, leaving him with almost two hours to fill before he was due to meet Veronica. This particular morning, that was not too much of a problem for him. So much had happened in the last two weeks that he had a backlog of administration and housekeeping that needed tackling. Margaret, who was keeping a watchful eye over him, recognised that he was trying to keep himself occupied, partly as a distraction and partly to avoid the attention of his colleagues. It was just something he did when he was troubled, and although he wasn't saying anything, she suspected it was Huxley, rather than his forthcoming meeting with Veronica, that was the cause of his concern. Harry had no children of his own, and the age difference between him and Huxley was similar to that of father and son. Although he could never be accused of favouring Huxley over the rest of the team, there was no doubting that Harry took a certain pride in Huxley's successes. She caught Harry's eye shortly after 11:00 and mouthed 'Veronica?' Not that she thought the meeting would have slipped his mind, she was just surprised he had yet to leave.

'Shortly,' Harry mouthed back, nodding that he understood her concern, and regretting that he hadn't briefed her more fully. Part of the reason for that was that he felt there had been far too many meetings lately with just himself, Margaret and Ben. The term "papal enclave" had crossed his mind. Working in the intelligence services, often on a need-to-know basis, it was inevitable that there would be exclusive meetings, but Harry tried to keep them to a minimum. There were only six of them in the Tufton Street office since Veronica had left, and Harry wanted to keep them working together as a team, united. He knew the back-office group jokingly referred to Margaret, Huxley and himself as "The Triumvirate", but that was related more to the focus of their activities than any suggestion of favouritism. He wanted to keep it that way. Pleased though he was that he had been able to include Ben more fully of late, Harry was all too aware that he was excluding Huxley, even though there had been no option. *Heaven forbid,* he thought, *that "The Triumvirate" should be replaced with a new "Holy Trinity".* He smiled to himself at the unintended joke.

Even though it was only about a three- or four-minute walk to Smith Square, Harry left the office shortly before 11:30. The anxious looks on Ben's and Margaret's faces told him that Ben had been brought up to speed on what was happening. Harry handed over the erased diskette to Nicholas, a confirmation that the file had been uploaded.

'Thank you. Your lunchtime meeting at Nobel House, sir. The lady is expected.' Nicholas' message conveyed a slight change of plan. The easiest option, whatever the value of Veronica's information, would be to take her to Sir Robert's current office. It was only a few hundred yards away from the entrance to Saint John's.

If the National Portrait Gallery meeting was anything to go by, Harry was certain that Veronica would be watching to double-check he was on his own, even though she must know arrangements would have been made to pick her up after the meeting. He had no intention of catching her unawares, but the sooner he was there, the sooner she would feel reassured enough to join him.

It was a pleasant enough day, but the north-facing entrance to Saint John's was in shadow, and Harry felt a chill that warned winter would be here all too soon. There were a few tourists sitting on the steps outside the entrance, but none in the small alcoves on each side. Harry chose the eastern alcove where, sitting on the low wall, he would be seen easily, and it would afford a small degree of privacy for their discussion. As he waited, he noticed that a smartly dressed elderly lady, heading for the entrance, was looking at him. She didn't quite hesitate on her way up the steps, but her look was more than a casual glance, and there was an expression of uncertainty on her face. Harry felt that he had seen her before. Perhaps she was part of Sir Robert's plan to take Veronica into custody. It would make sense; a woman would seem less threatening than another man. A movement on the far side of the entrance distracted Harry's gaze. Veronica had arrived.

'Do you have a name?' Harry was deliberately cold and direct. Yesterday, Veronica had put up a wall even before Harry had sat at the table. She had been there to do business, not to swap pleasantries.

'He calls himself Reid, but that's not his real name.'

'Which is?'

'I don't know.'

This wasn't the answer that Harry wanted or needed. It wasn't going to get her the protection she had demanded. He needed to explain how things were going to work.

'Veronica. Ron. We need to identify this man. It isn't me you have to convince, it's others, and without his identity, they can't assess how much of a threat he is to you. If they don't see a threat, they won't help you.'

'He's left-handed.'

Harry was about to say there were probably half a million left-handed men in London, but the look on Veronica's face stopped him. It was a look of despair. He bit his tongue and said nothing, hoping that the silence would draw out some more information.

'There's a bookshop he uses. That's where he sent me to

pick up the dossier. He gave me a receipt so I could collect it. That's how I know he's left-handed. His real name, his initials anyway, are GG.'

'GG? How would you know that?' Harry was genuinely puzzled. Had it been something on the receipt, something far from definite?

'They're on his shirt cuffs. Embroidered. I saw them when he gave me the receipt.'

Everything clicked into place for Harry. A left-handed man, with the initials GG. Giles Gifford, the man he had met only a few days ago. Mister Nondescript, apart from his embroidered shirt cuffs. Perfectly placed to intercept JIC communications.

'Ron, we have a place close by, where we can talk more fully. We'll look after you.' Harry held out his arm, as if to guide her.

As Veronica turned towards the steps, there was a commotion by the main door. A man was pushing his way through a line of Japanese tourists waiting patiently to be allowed inside. Her head snapped back to face Harry.

'Bastard! I was wrong about you. You're all in this together!'

Harry caught sight of the man just as he disappeared through the door. It was Quinton Bickley-Morris. In the second or two it took Harry to grasp what was happening, Veronica had raced down the steps, barged through the line of tourists, knocking one of them to the ground, and was away. Harry tried to follow, but the orderly line of tourists was now more of a melee, floundering around, trying to help the lady who had been knocked over, trying to make sense of what had just happened. By the time Harry had skirted around them, Veronica had disappeared.

* * *

Veronica was confused and more frightened than before. She had got it all wrong. They were in this together, Hamilton, Harry, Bickley-Morris. Traitors, all of them. Probably Huxley too; that was how they had known she would be back at her own house. They weren't just after her; they wanted the dossier. Clearly, something had gone wrong, and Huxley calling the police was their way of covering up what had really happened.

Bickley-Morris' escape from the Cambridge hospital a few years ago. Orchestrated by Hamilton? Just like his detention on Aegina. A ploy. They must have thought whoever had killed Rod Graham had Bickley-Morris in their sights, too. Where better to keep him safe than in the custody of Her Majesty's armed forces and intelligence services? It explained why his trial was such a sham. Arranged at the earliest opportunity, there never had been any intention of putting him in jail.

Reid had only been trying to do what he had *said* he was trying to do: exposing Hamilton for what he was. Veronica had always been wary of Reid, never fully understanding his motives, but it didn't matter. In the words of the old proverb, "The enemy of my enemy is my friend". Whatever the reason, Reid was certainly the enemy of Hamilton and his nest of vipers.

There was only one place she could go.

CHAPTER 30

Day twelve: Friday, late afternoon

'Mr Huxley. Please explain to me, once again, what you were doing at Smith Square.'

Sir Robert Hamilton was at Tufton Street. A visit he hadn't planned, but one he deemed necessary when he learnt that Huxley had become involved.

The events of the past few hours had played out in a way nobody had expected. Events that had started with Harry bursting into his Nobel House office without Mrs Blakeridge.

'She's gone. Ran. Spooked by Quinton. But I know who it is. It's Gifford,' Harry had exclaimed.

Sir Robert had tried to take it in. What had been planned as a simple pick-up operation, a two-minute walk from St John's to Nobel House, had turned into something altogether unexpected. And how the hell had Quinton become involved?

'Slowly, Harry. Slowly. Take a seat. Tell me all.'

Harry had taken one of the two armchairs to the side of the desk, taken a deep breath, and let his training kick in. He explained everything that had happened in his few minutes with Veronica, concisely, factually and in strict chronological order.

'Quinton, you say?' Sir Robert had been as confounded as Harry. 'I'll get someone round there.'

Much to Harry's surprise, Sir Robert had phoned Nicholas.

'Brigadier, I need someone at St John's, Smith Square.

Strictly obs only. Our friend Bickley-Morris. Soon as.'

'Now, Harry, tell me about Mr Gifford, again. Did she actually name him?'

Sir Robert had listened to Harry recount his conversation with Veronica. She hadn't named Gifford. Even if they had Veronica as a witness, it would be difficult to build a case on a her-word-against-his basis, but at least they would have reasonable cause to detain him. As it was, they didn't even have that – just supposition on Harry's part.

It was a waiting game. Even with Veronica as a witness, they would still wait. The uploaded file deception had never been intended as an end in itself but as a means to help identify whoever was intercepting information flowing between government departments. Linking them to the dossier conspiracy may put an effective end to their activities, but it would not be enough to bring them to trial. A claim that the dossier had been received from an anonymous source by someone trying to act in the best interests of the country may be of dubious veracity, but it would be hard to disprove. Even more difficult would be linking the suspect to the murder of Matthew Kilsdale.

Although Sir Robert had agreed that Gifford should be investigated, he was reluctant to put him under surveillance immediately. If Gifford was at the centre of the interception, Sir Robert wanted to give him enough rope to hang himself. Any slip-up in monitoring Gifford's day-to-day activities could make him go to ground, and the opportunity would be lost. Besides, Sir Robert had argued, if the file were to be copied, it would likely be in the next day or so, sooner than an effective surveillance operation could be put in place.

There was little that Harry could do at Nobel House, and

by 1:30, he had returned to Tufton Street. Margaret had looked expectantly at him as he stepped out of the lift, but Harry had just shaken his head slowly.

'What's gone wrong?' Margaret had been able to tell from Harry's expression alone that all was not well. 'Is she safe?'

Harry had given the only honest answer that he could: 'I don't know.'

'Did she not show?'

'Yes, we met, but… Quinton turned up. Spooked her. She ran.'

'Quinton?' Margaret's astonishment had been evident. 'Can you explain?' It had been clear to Margaret from earlier that morning that Harry hadn't been at liberty to be open about the circumstances of his planned meeting with Veronica, but she couldn't help him if he didn't explain what exactly was going on.

Harry had pointed to the meeting room. 'I'll get Ben. There's more to this than the dossier.' Harry was losing track of how much he had told Margaret and Ben about recent developments, but if they were to work as a team, he had to trust them.

Harry had recapped the doubts they had concerning Veronica's possession of the dossier and her movements on the day of her arrival from Greece less than two weeks ago. He told them there had been a phone call from Veronica yesterday and that they had met. Veronica had admitted the Hamilton dossier was given to her in London, and she would identify who had given it to her in exchange for a guarantee of protection. It had been the reason she had arranged to meet him that morning, and the plan had been to take her into custody. Harry didn't like the word "custody" with its implication of wrongdoing, but there was no sugar coating the pill. It might be protective custody, but it was still custody. He had explained that Veronica had given him enough information to identify the person who had been the source of the dossier, but she hadn't given a name. That's when she had noticed Quinton and had taken fright. Harry had repeated Veronica's words: "Bastard! I was wrong about you. You're all in this together!"

Even before he was asked, Harry had admitted that he did not have any idea what Quinton was doing at Smith Square. The obvious conclusion was that Veronica had thought there was some kind of plot, and he, most likely Sir Robert too, was involved and meant her harm.

Ben had voiced his concern. 'Could she be in danger? You know, if Quinton had planned to kill Kilsdale at her house?'

Harry had admitted that he didn't know, but he could not see any way that Quinton would know the time and the place of the meeting this morning. 'Even *I* didn't know until I arrived here this morning. The only people who knew were me, Sir Robert and Nicholas. Veronica, too, so we can't rule out the possibility that she had told somebody else.'

'What about the pick-up team? How much did they know?' Margaret had been as sharp as ever, but Harry thought that even if they had been told the name of the target, it was very unlikely that they would know of any connection to Quinton.

'You know, Harry, you may not like it, but coincidences do happen.' It wasn't the first time that week that Margaret had said that to Harry. His reply had echoed what the others were thinking.

'There have been rather too many of them in the last few weeks.'

Harry had then explained that Sir Robert had organised some discreet surveillance of Quinton and that they might discover that Quinton had an innocent motive for being there if it was a true coincidence. If it wasn't, the implications were rather disturbing.

In a change of tack, Harry had revealed more. 'Look, there is something you don't know, something important. This isn't about Sir Robert. Someone is leaking, or rather intercepting, government information.'

'A mole?' Ben had stated the obvious. "Mole" was a term that Harry didn't like.

'Well, that's what popular spy fiction would call him.'

'Him?' Margaret had pounced on Harry's assumption. 'You're sure it's a him?'

Harry had nodded. 'Yes, I am this time, but you need bringing up to speed.'

As concisely as he could, he'd explained that documents were being intercepted, particularly those relating to Anna Slowik. Though he didn't know all the details, it had become clear that Slowik was in danger, and the dossier had been part of a plan to distract attention from her. The fact was that the dossier had been leaked by Sir Robert himself, and it had some basis in fact. There had been clandestine, but nonetheless sanctioned, co-operation with East Germany in the uncertain world of a divided, post-Cold War Berlin. Sir Robert's "disappearance" being a ploy to give credibility to the accusations. It was thought that the people threatening Slowik, intercepting the documents and using Veronica as envoy were all part of the same group. Not a large organisation, just a small but significant remnant of East Germany's overseas intelligence network.

That was when Huxley had burst out of the lift and into the office. Harry. Margaret and Ben had still been staring as he had barged open the meeting room door. 'I know where she is! I know where to find her!'

* * *

Huxley had seen Veronica fleeing from Harry in Smith Square. A sixth sense had told him there was something suspicious about her behaviour, and he had followed her. Even from a distance, he could tell she was in some distress, but it was inconceivable that Harry posed a threat to her. Unless...

Huxley didn't want to think about it. Had Harry discovered something sinister about Veronica's involvement with the dossier? Certainly, whenever the matter of the dossier had come up in their conversations, Ron had changed the subject. Had she been trying to hide something? That could explain why she had abandoned him without a word of explanation. Even if that were the case, why would she be meeting Harry in Smith Square? Despite it taking place in public, Huxley had no doubt it was also a covert meeting. It had to be, otherwise it would have been held in Tufton Street. Unaware that Huxley was following, Veronica had made her way to a bookshop in Cecil Court.

Huxley had stayed outside, watching, perplexed. If you were running away from somebody, buying a book would be the last thing on your mind. This had to be some kind of meeting place. Huxley had waited for the best part of an hour, but Veronica had not reappeared. Whatever she was doing, she was not buying a book. Huxley knew it was a risk, but wanting to be certain, he had gone into the shop. An antiquated shop specialising in rare and collectable books, and one in which there was no trace of Veronica. Could there be a rear exit? Huxley wasn't sure – this was theatre land – there was likely to be a maze of courtyards and alleyways, but did they connect? Even if they did, why would Veronica use a rear exit? If she knew she was being followed, she was hardly likely to bring her pursuer to a place that was connected to her deceitful activities. This was not a puzzle that Huxley could solve on his own. He couldn't search the rest of the building; he had to tell Harry. Frustrated to find he had neither small change nor a phone card, Huxley couldn't make a direct call to Harry's line. He was reluctant to use the Service's free access code; Tufton Street wasn't on the main network, and his call would go through to a communications centre, probably not even in London. It would take time and would alert Thames House. If Harry was meeting Ron covertly, as the location had suggested, involving Thames House might just complicate matters and waste more time. Huxley felt he had no option other than to return to Tufton Street, all too aware that Veronica could leave the bookshop unobserved. If she had some dark secret, however, and this bookshop was somehow associated with that, it was useful intelligence that Harry would be pleased to know.

* * *

Huxley's return to Tufton Street had been the first of two surprises for Harry. Huxley had been at Smith Square and had followed Veronica. It was information he had had to pass on to Sir Robert. It had to be the same bookshop that Veronica had said was used by Reid. The second surprise was that, on hearing the news, Sir Robert had decided to come to Tufton Street. 'Time we all lay our cards on the table and see if we can figure out this game,' had been his rationale.

Within half an hour, Sir Robert Hamilton arrived at Tufton Street. He was still struggling to grasp everything that Harry had told him over the phone following Huxley's dramatic appearance.

As the lift door opened and Sir Robert stepped into the Tufton Street office, Huxley was completely taken aback. 'What the fuck…?' He had assumed Harry had phoned a senior officer at Thames House with the news about Veronica.

'I take it Mr Huxley is not aware of the fuller situation.' Sir Robert addressed his remark to Harry, who replied with a simple, 'No'.

'Then join us in the meeting room, Mr Huxley. Miss Millard, too. Harry, would you be so kind as to bring Mr Chowdhury?'

Sir Robert sat at the head of the table, if indeed a small table could be described as having a head. He explained to Huxley what Margaret and Ben had been told earlier. Government documents were being leaked, and there was an operation ongoing to identify the source. It was hoped that success would come in the next day or two. The likelihood of that success could not be compromised.

'I compiled that dossier, the one that accused me of being a traitor, Mr Huxley. It was part of the operation, and it was one of the documents that was leaked.' Sir Robert ignored the look of surprise on Huxley's face and went on to explain that there was no doubt that there was a direct link between

259

the felon responsible and the person who supplied the dossier to Mrs Blakeridge. Possibly it was the same person.

'Is she a traitor?' The thought had hit Huxley like a sledgehammer, and the question left his lips before he realised he had asked it. Sir Robert was honest: he wasn't sure. It was quite possible Mrs Blakeridge had been acting in good faith, believing the document to be authentic, duped by the people responsible. It was equally possible that she had been acting out of fear, or under duress.

'But first, Mr Huxley, would you be so kind as to tell me what you have told Harry?'

Huxley had already told his story to Harry, Margaret and Ben, and he now repeated it to Sir Robert. Just like Harry, Sir Robert seemed to be somebody who liked people to repeat what they had told him. Repetition could jog the memory and bring out small details otherwise forgotten.

'Mr Huxley, thank you, but please indulge me. I'd like you to run through it once again, starting with what you were doing at Smith Square?'

Telling it for a third time did not ease the awkwardness that Huxley felt about explaining his behaviour that morning. He told them what they already knew: that he was upset, and recognising this, Margaret had suggested he take the day off. What he didn't tell them was that with the events of the past two weeks – Veronica's reappearance; the revelations about Sir Robert, now sitting opposite him; the death in Blackheath; the concern that Ron had been killed; his own arrest and detention; the second copy of the dossier; Kilsdale's murder; concern for Ron's safety and her sudden, unexplained departure, when he thought they might have a future together – things were getting too much. He needed some time off.

Yet, even though he knew Harry had sidelined him, using the Iraqi bioweapons intelligence to keep him away from what was undoubtedly Tufton Street's main concern, he knew this wasn't the time to walk away.

Instead, he repeated his story. He had just needed to talk to Harry. Coming in late, he had taken his usual shortcut through Dean's Yard, and as he emerged into Tufton Street, he had seen Harry leaving the office. He assumed Harry was off to a meeting and thought it would be easier to catch Harry as he came out of his meeting, later, and have a talk in private. When it was obvious that Harry was waiting on the steps of St John's, he doubted it was a business meeting, more like meeting someone for lunch. If that was the case, Harry might be none too pleased to learn Huxley had followed him, seen it as an intrusion into his personal life, so Huxley had wondered if he should wait until Harry returned to Tufton Street. That was when he had seen Ron walking up the steps. Huxley had stayed out of sight, debating what to do, when he had heard a commotion. A tourist had been knocked to the ground, and Ron was running away. On the spur of the moment, he had decided to follow her.

Huxley had no idea, until Harry told him, that Quinton had turned up, and that it had been the sight of him that had caused Ron to flee. It crossed Huxley's mind that Quinton might have posed a threat to her, and she had gone to Cecil Court as a place of safety. It was a theory based more on concern than confidence, and it was no surprise to Huxley that although his colleagues thought it quite possible, they felt it was further evidence of something more sinister.

'It would seem, Mr Huxley, that Quinton was just having lunch. There's a small restaurant in the crypt. Much as Harry doesn't like these things, his presence does seem to have been an unfortunate coincidence.'

The watcher who had been sent to Smith Square had reported back. Quinton had met someone for lunch before leaving by taxi. It hadn't been possible to follow him, but subsequently, it had been established that Quinton had returned home to his flat.

Thanks to Harry's short briefing whilst waiting for Sir Robert to join them, Huxley was now aware that Ron had admitted she had lied about the origin of the dossier and had agreed to co-operate in exchange for protection. If she wanted protection, Huxley argued, then she must be in danger and, despite all the unknowns, she was a former colleague, and it was their duty to protect her.

'From whom?' was Sir Robert's response, pointing out that whatever the reason she had gone to the bookshop in Cecil Court, she had gone of her own volition. Although Sir Robert had arranged for the bookshop to be kept under surveillance, he pointed out that Mrs Blakeridge may have left before that was in place, and there was little point in taking any more action.

Huxley reiterated his belief that they had a duty to protect Veronica and that they should not delay in raiding the bookshop. Sir Robert had held firm. He would not jeopardise the success of the operation. He intended to catch the people responsible, not warn them off by alerting them to the fact that the bookshop was known about.

'It's not a decision that I take lightly, Mr Huxley, but we can hardly describe your former colleague as innocent. At least not in the full sense of the word.'

Before Huxley could continue the argument, Sir Robert's

pager sounded, and he excused himself from the room, closing the door behind him. 'An important phone call to make,' had been his reasoning. All eyes were on Sir Robert as he made the call from the phone on Harry's desk. It was a brief call. Sir Robert nodded, and a smile spread across his face. Looking up, he turned towards Harry, then lifting his forearm, he tugged at his shirt cuff. Harry seemed to understand the mysterious gesture.

The grin was still on Sir Robert's face as he opened the meeting room door.

'It's your lucky day, Mr Huxley. We may be visiting the bookshop after all. The file was copied, we have our man.'

'Who?' All three of them had spoken at once, but it was Harry who answered them.

'A certain Mr Reid, I'm sure. Though known more formally as Mr Giles Martin Linthorpe Gifford.'

CHAPTER 31

Day twelve: Friday, evening

The five of them were back in the meeting room in Tufton Street by 7:00 p.m. Sir Robert had left immediately after the phone call, asking them not to leave until they had heard from him. 'We need to discuss Mrs Blakeridge. Her evidence could be crucial. If she's prepared to co-operate.'

It had been an anxious wait. Margaret, Huxley and Ben had pressed Harry for more information on Giles Gifford and what Sir Robert had meant when he had said "The file was copied". Without going into full details, Harry had explained about the monthly digest of government departmental concerns that was collected for the Joint Intelligence Committee's attention. Gifford was a linchpin in the system, collating all the files for the committee. The file in question, like many JIC files, was "eyes-only", no copying. Except this file was a trap, somehow reporting back if it was copied. It was Ben who had said, "Oh, a Trojan," and had then had to explain that the file was the computer equivalent of a Trojan horse, which instead of containing soldiers contained computer code.

Huxley had listened to what Harry was saying, but as soon as he felt he had grasped the essential points, he had grown increasingly restless.

'You don't get it, do you?' Huxley had interjected, slapping his hand on the tabletop as he spoke. 'She's in danger – we've got to help her! Hamilton off chasing spies won't stop Quinton getting to her!'

Ben had reached across and put his hand on Huxley's forearm. 'Hux, did you hear what Sir Robert said? She went to that shop of her own free will. I don't know why she ran, but if she was worried, then she went there for protection.'

'Or she went there to warn somebody.' Margaret's remark had stopped her colleagues in their tracks, their stunned expressions inviting an answer that Margaret didn't have. 'I don't know. I don't know who or why. And I don't think Ron knows what she wants or who's on her side.' Margaret had then added an afterthought before anybody else had spoken. 'Whatever side that is.'

At that point, Harry had called a halt to the conversation, telling his colleagues that there was little point in speculating and reminding them that Sir Robert had suggested that a visit would be made to the bookshop. If Veronica were there, they would find her. He had made a joke that his time for tea was long overdue and mentioned that it was Friday afternoon, and he was sure they all had things to tidy up before the weekend. Recognising that Huxley wasn't feeling at all social, but that it would not be a good idea to leave him on his own, Ben had stepped in. 'Come on, Hux, I'll make you a coffee. There's this great new computer game I want to tell you about. All action – a lady who's searching for an ancient artefact in old tombs.'

For all of them, it felt like an interminable wait until Sir Robert reappeared. Veronica was on all their minds. Whichever way they looked at her behaviour, it made no sense. There was no logical thread connecting her actions. Ben did a sterling job of keeping Huxley distracted, though

Harry was quite certain what they were doing had little to do with business. Ben seemed to have produced a small hand-held minicomputer, and judging by the noises Harry heard whenever the door to the back office was opened, they were playing some kind of game. Huxley's sixth sense, however, was on high alert, and he was out of the back office before Harry realised that someone was coming up in the lift.

'Did you find her? Did you go to the shop?' Huxley was halfway across the front office before Sir Robert had even stepped out of the lift.

'Whoa, Mr Huxley! A moment, please.' Sir Robert held up both his hands as if to put a barrier between himself and Huxley. 'We have been to the bookshop, yes, and she wasn't there.'

Huxley's face fell, and Sir Robert doubted that Huxley had registered him saying he did need to talk to him, but first, he needed to update the whole team. Sir Robert indicated the meeting room, and Huxley furrowed his brows and gave Sir Robert a look of disdain. Why use the meeting room? There were only the five of them in the office; Andrew and Thomas had left a while ago.

Mr Gifford, Sir Robert informed the group, was currently in the custody of the Metropolitan Police, languishing in an interview room at Charing Cross Police Station. He had been arrested on suspicion of a breach of the Official Secrets Act. Gifford was not being co-operative, protesting his innocence of anything untoward, whilst refusing to answer any questions until his solicitor was present. He would be allowed access to his solicitor; they could not deny him that right, but they would not interview him formally until the morning. A night in the cells would focus his mind, Sir Robert commented, adding that there was the additional bonus of having time to check the background of the solicitor. Sir Robert intended to conduct the interview himself. Hopefully, his unexpected reappearance would disturb Gifford's composure.

'Yes, but what about the bookshop? What about Ron?' Huxley's composure was disturbed.

Sir Robert sat back in his chair, and taking a deep breath, turned to face Huxley sombrely.

'Mr Huxley.' Sir Robert paused, gathering his thoughts. 'Based upon your account of this afternoon's events, I went out on a limb to arrange a, what shall we say, an official but covert visit to that bookshop. There wasn't time to arrange a search warrant, so we were reliant upon the goodwill of the owner. He was none too happy at first when our people turned up late in the afternoon, but he was pleasant enough and shut the shop to show them around the premises. Even so, we did rather stretch that goodwill. To little benefit, unfortunately. Other than the testimony of Mrs Blakeridge, I have no evidence or legitimate reason to suspect the proprietor of any offence. Likewise, our evidence against Mr Gifford is somewhat thin. We would like to link him to the recent killings, and much more besides. He may, *just may*, be part of a residual covert East German cell. As such, we would like to link him to Mr Bickley-Morris, but more importantly, to a plot to assassinate Miss Slowik. I take it you are all aware of who Miss Slowik is?'

The nods around the table confirmed that Sir Robert's supposition was correct. Until that afternoon, no one other than Harry had known of the plot to silence Slowik, and when he thought about it, for reasons he couldn't fathom, something stirred in Harry's mind. What it was, he couldn't put his finger on. Sir Robert continued.

'Given that Mr Gifford has been caught illegally copying an Intelligence Committee report, it's likely he has intercepted other documents, including the dossier that, well, appeared to damn me.' Sir Robert couldn't resist a little chuckle. 'Mrs Blakeridge can identify the man who gave her the dossier, and she has already told Harry that she believes he's linked to Mr Bickley-Morris and his nefarious affairs. She is a key witness who needs to be found. Now, Mr Huxley, where the hell is she likely to be?'

All eyes were on Huxley, but even when prompted by questions, he was unable to help. All of the Tufton Street team realised how little they did know about their former colleague, other than the sad fact that her husband and father had been killed in the same road accident. More recently, they had learned that although Veronica had always maintained she was an only child, she did have a half-sister in Greece, Eliana, born before Veronica's mother had married her father. Beyond that, they knew remarkably little. Huxley recalled that when he had been looking into her family history after her disappearance last year, Rod Graham had been the only relative he had traced. Veronica had never talked about family, or friends come to that; they had all accepted her as a very private person.

Sir Robert pursued Huxley: 'Surely, she must have mentioned some friends?'

But, much to his embarrassment, Huxley realised Veronica had never mentioned anybody outside her sister's family in Greece. Sir Robert acknowledged there was little they could do other than put out an "All Ports" alert. As a long shot, they could check if the people who had adopted Eliana and subsequently returned to Aegina had any other relatives in London. It was all they had to go on.

'Did they not find anything at that bookshop?'

Margaret tried to steer the discussion away from the blank wall they were facing. As far as Sir Robert had ascertained, the bookshop leased only part of the building, which was still owned by the Cecil family after whom the street had been named three hundred years ago. The bookshop owners sublet a couple of rooms in that part of the building they had access to, and the police had been able to search those rooms. There was a link that they were investigating: the tenants were an import-export company that appeared to deal only with a company in Germany, a small company just outside Munich. Apparently, the company used the offices only sporadically, but Sir Robert said they couldn't ignore the link to Germany.

'Do we know the name of the company?'

Harry asked the question more to keep the conversation alive than with any hope it might give them a clue.

'Rather dull, I'm afraid. Planegg Partners Shipping Limited, with the "Shipping" enclosed in brackets.'

'Holy shit.' Ben had everybody's attention, though their stares disconcerted him. Almost by way of an apology, he added, 'It's a curious name, Planegg. One you don't forget, especially when it's near an airport that has a name that sounds like Over Faffing.' They were still staring at him. 'Give me a minute to double-check,' he said, before dashing out to the back office. He was only gone a few minutes, though it seemed much longer to those left in the meeting room. Ben came back with a grin on his face.

'Last year, when we were checking the accounts of Kilsdale's company in Pitsea, they had bogus dealings with a company in Planegg. So did that Greek company Quinton was involved with, Lysander Corporate Partnering. Different names but the same address, one that sticks in your mind. Einsteinstrasse. I bet when you check them out, they're not in Planegg itself, but a nearby village, a so-called "Science Suburb", Martinsried.'

Now they were all looking at Ben in surprise. How did he remember these things?

'Say that again.' There was a little more than surprise in Margaret's voice.

'Not in Planegg, but in a suburb called Martinsried.'

'Oh, my goodness, so blatant that nobody notices.' The blank looks, now directed at her, told Margaret nobody else in the room had noticed.

'Martinsried.' She repeated it more slowly. 'Martinsried, different spelling but the same pronunciation. Martin's Reid,' she repeated, with a slightly different emphasis. 'One of Gifford's middle names. Martin. Martin's Reid. Martin apostrophe s Reid. Martin *is* Reid.'

The penny dropped.

'Well, well.' Sir Robert congratulated Ben and Margaret. 'We'll certainly chase that company up.' He looked at his watch. 'Tomorrow,' he added. 'Though it does mean you all coming in on a Saturday, but no time to lose. And I'll arrange lunch.' Sir Robert turned to Huxley, a serious look in his eye once more. 'I have not forgotten Mrs Blakeridge. That can't wait until tomorrow; I already have a team working on finding her.'

Harry had remained seated as the others filed out of the meeting room. There was something new on his mind, something quite perplexing. Quinton's name coming up

270

again had taken him back to the events of that morning. The lady he had seen – the lady who had gone into St John's shortly before Quinton had arrived. Her hairstyle was certainly different, a different colour too; she could have been wearing a wig. She may have been wearing a jacket and skirt that was quintessentially English country lady, but he had realised who she was. Harry had little doubt that the lady he had seen was none other than Anna Slowik. Harry could accept that Quinton turning up at Smith Square may have been a coincidence, but Slowik too? Just who had Quinton met for lunch today? It was a question that troubled Harry, like the last obscure clue preventing him from completing a crossword.

'Sir Robert – Bob – a moment. There's something else.'

CHAPTER 32
Day thirteen: Saturday

As each member of the team arrived on Saturday morning, they were surprised to find that the Tufton Street office had been turned into a makeshift operations room. A second telephone, a desktop computer and what looked like a radio transmitter and receiver had been installed in the meeting room, which was now serving as Sir Robert's office. The makeover of the office was not the first thing they noticed, though. As they stepped out of the lift, they were greeted by the aroma of fresh coffee and croissants. A table had been set out along one wall, and the cutlery and crockery suggested that Sir Robert would be honouring his promise of lunch.

'Don't get used to it,' Harry had repeated as each of them arrived, though, in truth, it was as much a surprise and delight to him as to the rest of the group. Huxley didn't look as though he had slept much, but in response to Harry's concerned look, he whispered, 'It's OK – I'm fine.' Harry wasn't so sure, but it was clear that Huxley didn't want to talk about it. No doubt the distraction of the morning's activities would be a welcome diversion for him, if indeed something so serious could be called a diversion.

'Harry, a word. Before we start.' Sir Robert gestured towards the meeting room and, to Harry's surprise, closed the door behind them.

'Miss Slowik. I tried to get in touch yesterday evening,

but she wasn't there.' Sir Robert's words put Harry on alert, but noticing his look of concern, Sir Robert continued. 'I don't doubt what you saw yesterday, but officially, Miss Slowik is on a spiritual break in the Cotswolds.'

Harry's concern turned to puzzlement. 'Rather odd, isn't it? I mean, I know she was working with us, but spiritual? Not a word I would associate with a senior Stasi officer.'

'That's harsh, Harry. She's dying. A year, if the treatment works, possibly less.'

'Oh.' Harry was lost for words, wishing he could take back what he had said. After a moment or two, he asked, 'Is that why...? You know, she came across?'

The answer to Harry's question was 'No', her condition had only been diagnosed since she had been in the UK. 'Concern for her own safety, Harry. That's why we were – still are – concerned about Tschesche.'

'Is it wise? Going away?

'She's not a prisoner, Harry. But we will check her whereabouts. You're probably the two people I trust most in this world, yet I'm not sure I'm going to like what I find.'

'I could be wrong.'

'You could be, Harry. But you believe what you saw. Come, the others will start wondering what we're keeping from them if I don't start this briefing. In any case, the lady is due back tomorrow evening.'

Sir Robert called the group together and ran through what they knew and what they needed to find out. A civil servant was in custody and would be charged with the illegal copying of a restricted file. He would be appearing in court on Monday morning, and although bail would be opposed on the grounds of national security, the charge itself was

273

relatively minor and may not be enough to sway the court to deny the man his right to bail. It was believed that other files had been copied in the past but knowing it and proving it were entirely different propositions. Intelligence received suggested these files related mainly, but not entirely, to the defection and debriefing of Anna Slowik, a former senior officer in the East German Stasi. Quite independently, it was believed that there were still residual active members of what had been quite a significant, if officially denied, East German intelligence community in London.

'Huh, and we all know who worked for them.' Huxley's interjection needed no further explanation; they all knew he was referring to Quinton Bickley-Morris, a former PPS to the secretary of state for defence. Sir Robert reminded the group that the court had found Quinton innocent of the charges brought against him, and however galling they found that decision, it was one they had to respect.

The material that was in the dossier, which Veronica – or Mrs Blakeridge, as Sir Robert referred to her – presented, could only have come from another document that had been illegally accessed and copied. Mrs Blakeridge had met with a mysterious Mr Reid, who had directed her to the bookshop where she had picked up the dossier. It was difficult to avoid the suspicion that this was the same bookshop that she had visited yesterday. It was also difficult to avoid the suspicion that, like it or not, Mrs Blakeridge was somehow connected to the death of Kilsdale. Looking in Huxley's direction, he re-emphasised "somehow". Sensing another interjection from Huxley, he held out his hand, gesturing to him to stay silent. Kilsdale had claimed he had been lured to Veronica's house on the pretext of recovering a stolen document. Had there been any intent to do him harm? His subsequent murder, a couple of days later, testified that there had. Quinton had claimed a document had been stolen by Graham, and Veronica's initial story had been that she had found the dossier in Graham's house. There was a known link between Quinton and Graham, and between Veronica and Graham, but how much of a link was there between Veronica and Quinton? They had both fled to small Greek islands less than five miles apart, and if Kilsdale had been telling the truth, Quinton knew about Veronica's house in Blackheath. Quinton was also connected to Kilsdale via the bogus activities of DCM Diagnostics in Essex, as was Rod Graham. Yesterday, they had unearthed a connection between DCM Diagnostics, Quinton and a company near Munich, which just happened to lease some rooms from the bookshop Veronica had visited.

'A tangled web indeed, and Mrs Blakeridge holds the key to understanding it. We need to find her, if for no other reason than to link Mr Gifford to the bookshop and the dossier, thus ensuring he remains in custody.'

'So you want to find her on the off chance that Mr Gifford and Mr Reid are one and the same person.' Huxley's tone, at first sceptical, turned to cynical anger. 'You don't give a toss about her safety. Oh, so a couple of people have died – how very unfortunate, but no need to worry.'

'Mr Huxley.' There was no hint of anything but calm control in Sir Robert's voice. 'I am more concerned about her personal safety than you can possibly appreciate. Mr Kilsdale's murder, the MO was reminiscent of a gentleman by the name of Tobias Tschesche.'

'Who?' Several voices spoke almost in unison.

'Mr Tschesche, *Herr* Tschesche to be exact, is, in fact, no gentleman. *"Kein Ehrenmann"*, as I believe they would say where he comes from. He is, for want of a better description, a Stasi hitman. We believe him to be in the UK, and we believe his target is Anna Slowik.'

'He's killed Kilsdale? And he might kill Veronica? Is that what you're saying?' Margaret's voice conveyed genuine concern.

'It is a possibility, Miss Millard, but let's not pretend otherwise; the weight of evidence is beginning to point to her being, shall we say, a willing participant? Perhaps even a team member.' It was a thought that had crossed all their minds, though none had wanted to articulate it.

Huxley slumped in his seat. He couldn't deny that the possibility had occurred to him, but hearing somebody say it crushed him. Ben automatically reached across and put his arm around Huxley's shoulders in an attempt to comfort him, but something stirred in Huxley's mind. Pushing Ben away and seemingly fighting back tears, Huxley made a stand.

'If she is one of them, why did she run from Quinton?' He didn't wait for anyone to respond, supplying the answer himself. 'Because she decided to do the right thing. She met Harry to name names, to spill the beans. Harry's said so himself – she wanted protection.'

'Then why go to the bookshop?' Sir Robert asked Huxley the question he had asked himself many times since yesterday afternoon. Not waiting for anybody else to answer, he admitted his own lack of understanding. 'I don't know, Mr Huxley, but we have to work with the information we have. And we *are* looking for her, have been since yesterday evening. On the face of it, she thought Harry and Quinton were working together and saw that as a threat. There could be only two possibilities – the bookshop offered some kind of protection, or she had gone there to warn somebody.'

Sir Robert chose not to say more on the matter or to speculate.

'Speculating will get us nowhere,' he reminded the team, before outlining his plans for the morning.

He had secured a warrant to search the bookshop and would take Harry and Huxley with him. They would be looking for any evidence that linked Veronica to the bookshop. Sir Robert himself would remain outside. If the owner was party to the dossier plot, he may well recognise Sir Robert, which would not be helpful. Margaret and Ben were to remain at Tufton Street to find out as much about Planegg Partners as they could. Sir Robert admitted to being sceptical about how much information they could glean from the government's own computerised records, or from the rapidly growing World Wide Web. It was, after all, Saturday, and departments were closed – and time was of the essence. If anybody could unearth what records there were, it would be Ben. Gifford was currently being interviewed by Special Branch, and Sir Robert would call in at Charing Cross Police Station for an update on his way back from the bookshop. The group would reconvene at 2:00 p.m.

The Tufton Street group were met at Cecil Court by a uniformed police sergeant and a woman in plain clothes. Sir Robert introduced Fiona Renner as a forensic computer analyst from the intelligence services. On the visit to the premises the day before, a desktop computer had been noted in Planegg's offices. Removing it for analysis would have taken time; it was quicker to bring the expert to the computer.

277

Sir Robert's man had noted that the computer was connected to a telephone line, and the plan was simple: Miss Renner had prepared a disk that, on loading, would override the computer's own initialisation routine and instruct the machine to copy the entire contents of the hard drive to a secure server via the phone line. The Service's software would interrogate the hard drive far more efficiently than Miss Renner could, sitting at the keyboard. At the end of the download, which would run in the background and be undetectable even if somebody logged on to inspect the computer, the programme would erase all records of the subterfuge.

Nobody had expected the bookshop owner to be at all pleased to have a second visit, especially when faced with four people – twice as many as the day before – but Harry was struck by his agitated manner. The previous day, the owner's behaviour, despite his initial resistance, had been reported as pleasant and co-operative, but his manner now was distinctly belligerent.

'Another incident, officer?' was the response that greeted the four of them on entering. Sergeant Winter had been fairly brusque, striding in, declaring he had a warrant to search the premises, with no preliminary pleasantries. Harry got the impression that the owner had been expecting the visit. His sarcastic reference to "another incident" had been a nod to the police's excuse for yesterday's visit: their claim there had been an "incident" on Charing Cross Road, and a witness had reported seeing the suspect enter the bookshop.

The owner, Mr Jeremy Mathis, insisted on reading the warrant in full, taking more time than Harry felt was necessary. He stared hard at the three people not in uniform but didn't ask who they were, something which confirmed

Harry's suspicion that this second visit was not unexpected. Handing back the warrant, Mathis sighed, muttering, 'Help yourselves,' and gesturing towards the shelves that filled the room. When Sergeant Winter asked for the key to Planegg's offices, Mathis resisted, claiming they were not part of his shop. They all picked up on an edginess in the man's voice. Winter insisted, pointing out that the warrant referred to the entire building, not just the bookshop itself. As Huxley and the intelligence officer headed upstairs, Harry caught a smirk on Mathis' face, as though he were thinking, 'You won't find what you're looking for up there'.

Harry's job was to interview Mathis, starting by elaborating on the incident of the previous day. There had been a snatch and run theft of some valuable coins being taken to a numismatist's shop on Charing Cross Road. The thief had been apprehended but had not been in possession of the coins. He had either passed them to an accomplice or hidden them for a later pick up, and it had been reported that he visited the bookshop. No one had expected the story to be believed, but the blatant and provocative cynicism of Mathis was unexpected.

'Of course, I could be his accomplice. That is what you're insinuating after all. If I were, do you honestly think I'd be stupid enough to keep the spoils on the premises after yesterday's visit?'

'I'm just doing my job, sir.' Harry, struck by the banality of his own response, decided to play the role of the simpleton police officer. 'You're not his accomplice, are you?'

Mathis just snorted and shook his head in response. Harry's attempts at further questioning were partly frustrated by Mathis' apparent indifference. Rather than engaging with

Harry, Mathis busied himself with changing his window display, repeatedly turning his back to Harry.

Whilst Sergeant Winter made a decent pretext of searching the bookshelves downstairs, Huxley and Miss Renner spent most of their time searching for anything that might link Planegg to Giles Gifford or Veronica.

The bookshop was a small set of premises – the shop and a small office downstairs, with two offices, sublet to Planegg, upstairs. The visit to the Cecil Court bookshop had taken little more than an hour, meeting the low expectation of finding anything incriminating. The brief visit yesterday had unearthed little by way of evidence that suggested Planegg was an active, let alone thriving, business. The same conclusion was drawn by Huxley and Renner, suggesting the offices served mainly as a meeting room and a post box.

At 2:00 p.m., the team reassembled in the Tufton Street office. There had been mixed results that morning. When Harry and Huxley had arrived back, Ben and Margaret had looked at them expectantly, but Huxley had just shaken his head and then confirmed that there had been no sign that Veronica had ever been to the bookshop. They had, however, found a rear exit, a courtyard behind the book shop which was accessed by a door from the shop itself and a fire escape from the upper floors. The courtyard appeared to wrap around three sides of the Duke of York's Theatre. On questioning, Mathis had admitted that there was a narrow passage along the southern face of the theatre leading to an exit onto St Martin's Lane. A locked metal gate guarded the exit. There was a key in a glass-fronted case on the courtyard side of the gate, but each property accessing the courtyard had a key for emergency use. Huxley and Harry had double-checked, and there was a locked gate on St Martin's Lane, just to the south side of the theatre. Veronica could have left the bookshop undetected.

'Assuming she didn't leave between Huxley leaving and the obs team arriving,' Harry reminded them.

It was clear from his comment that he believed Huxley's assertion that Veronica had gone to the bookshop. Mathis, however, had been rather vague when questioned about possible suspects entering his shop the day before. He claimed he couldn't keep track of all his customers, but he believed a young lady had come in about that time, though she may well have left whilst his attention was elsewhere. Although he had said nothing at the time, Harry had been sceptical. The bookshop could hardly be described as having been thronged with customers, and as many of the books were quite valuable, he doubted Mathis would take his eye off a stranger browsing his stock.

Mathis had also claimed that there had been nobody at the Planegg offices for the last week, something that, he said, was not unusual. If Veronica had called at the Planegg offices rather than the bookshop, Mathis was clearly covering for her. When asked for contact details for the people who rented the offices, Mathis had volunteered only the details of a firm of solicitors. His descriptions of the people who used the offices were so generic as to be of no value.

In the few hours since the visit, Fiona Renner had made an initial assessment of the Planegg computer and sent brief details to Tufton Street. The copied contents of the hard drive were telling a different story. Somebody had been in the Planegg offices the day before. In the time available, a full examination had not been possible, but there had been a partition on the hard drive, and that had been deleted the previous afternoon. She wasn't sure how much of the erased data she could recover, although fragments remained. What was clear was that the computer had been used as a fax machine. The telephone number was the same as the handset in the office, and the line would be put under surveillance. What she had been able to recover was part of a fax received two days ago. It was in German and read, *"Schließen Sie alle Türen, bevor Sie gehen."* Harry remembered enough of the language from his time in Heidelberg to be able to translate. "Close all the doors before leaving."

Sir Robert's visit to Charing Cross Police Station had been brief and disappointing. Gifford wasn't co-operating. He had insisted on his own solicitor being present, which had delayed the interview, and his responses had been a consistent "No comment". The solicitor was from the same firm that Mathis had named in relation to the Planegg offices. Harry was not the only one to doubt that it was a coincidence.

Ben and Margaret's investigation of Planegg Partners (Shipping) Limited had been equally unilluminating. From the reports filed with Companies House, and Planegg's tax returns, the company appeared to do little in the way of trading and ran at a small loss. Although he wasn't sure, Ben had the feeling that the accounts were, to a certain extent, bogus and guessed that the reported running expenses were rather too closely matched by income. Ben suspected payments from an undeclared parent company. Prior to 1990, the company had been much healthier and, as far as he could tell, had been trading mainly with a company or companies in Germany. He would need access to the company's bank statements to be more certain.

'Well, it would fit with the decline of East Germany,' Sir Robert noted, before asking if Ben had been able to find any details of recent activity. The only thing that had caught his attention was the replacement of one of the directors. A Lucas Cranach had resigned about a year ago, and earlier this year, a Caspar Friedrich had been appointed. Sir Robert lifted his head quite sharply.

'Middle name David, by any chance?'

Ben was taken aback. 'Yes, do you know him?'

'Hardly.' Sir Robert was smiling as he answered, 'He died about a hundred and fifty years ago.'

Everyone was staring at Sir Robert, who explained that Caspar David Friedrich had been a German artist, as had Lucas Cranach. 'Known, I think, as Cranach the Elder. Probably been dead for four hundred years or so.'

They all agreed that it was possible that somebody could have the name Caspar Friedrich, but having two German artists listed as being, or having been, a director, ruled out the possibility of coincidence. 'And we know how much Harry hates coincidences,' quipped Huxley. Harry was pleased to see Huxley returning to his former persona.

The only address that Ben had for Mr Friedrich was the company's registered address, which was that of a firm of accountants. It was agreed that he should search to see if he could find any trace of Mr Friedrich in other records, but it wasn't seen as a matter of urgency. It was unlikely that Mr Friedrich used the name in any context that could lead to his address being discovered.

'Are you putting Mathis under surveillance?' Margaret asked. 'He might lead us to Friedrich, that's all.'

Unfortunately, that wasn't happening, Sir Robert informed

them. With no link having been found between Mathis and Gifford, nor Mathis and Veronica, and nothing to link Mathis to Friedrich, other than Friedrich's company leasing two rooms, he doubted he could present sufficient justification. Resources were scarce, and it was the weekend. He was, he said, expecting some censure over yesterday's covert search of the bookshop, 'May not have gone through all the appropriate channels. Don't want to rock the boat too much, just yet.'

It had not been the most productive of days, their best hope being that Miss Renner could recover more information from the copy of the hard drive. Sir Robert thanked them for their efforts and for coming in on a Saturday at short notice, and even though they all knew that their terms of service gave them no other option, they were grateful that he expressed his gratitude. There was little he could see that they could achieve by any more weekend work, and pointing to the meeting room that he had taken over as an office, he made a joke saying he hoped they could bear more of his company on Monday morning. Ben wondered if the meeting room office was a convenience or if Sir Robert was operating off-grid. Was there some truth behind the dossier? He quickly put the thought out of his head; Sir Robert could be unorthodox, but it was always because he prioritised urgency above bureaucracy.

Sir Robert turned to Huxley and surprised him by saying, 'Mr Huxley, I really would recommend you take Miss Millard's advice and visit your parents. I need you back here on Monday morning with an uncluttered mind.'

'Some hope of that,' Ben joked. 'He wouldn't be Hux unless there were three zillion ideas rushing round his head.

It's the way he plucks out the most relevant one that amazes me.'

'OK, I want the normal Mr Huxley, warts and all, back here on Monday,' Sir Robert replied in jest. Then, turning serious, he reminded the whole team, 'The formal rationale for this operation may be to serve justice on Mr Gifford and his like, but my immediate goal is finding Mrs Blakeridge, if only for her own safety.' The last phrase sent a chill down the spines of the entire team. Sir Robert told the team that he had people, other people, trying to access her bank and credit card details. Sensing Huxley might be about to object, Sir Robert pointed out that there was very little she could do without access to her own money. 'Unless I'm completely wrong about her motives.' Harry took that to mean, despite the evidence and her lies about the dossier, whatever role she had been playing in the mayhem that had engulfed them in the last two weeks, Sir Robert believed there had been no malicious intent.

Harry was not so sure. *You weren't at the National Portrait Gallery to hear the malevolence in her voice,* he thought. *Nor her contempt for Huxley.*

CHAPTER 33

Day fourteen: Sunday

Harry was doing housework on Sunday morning. He couldn't settle, the recent events running around his head. The housework was an attempt to distract, and when the phone rang, he hoped it was with news of a development that would give him an excuse to go into Tufton Street. It was more than that. Much more.

'Harry, how's your spoken German these days?'

'Bob? Rusty but passable. Why?'

'Can't explain on the phone. Car's on its way. Mathis is dead, Gifford is singing like a canary.'

With that, Sir Robert ended the call, leaving Harry with much to contemplate, though he had little time to think as a car pulled up outside his window a few moments later. Whatever Sir Robert needed him to do, it was urgent.

Harry had assumed Sir Robert was at Tufton Street, but when the car failed to turn right at Parliament Square and, instead, headed towards the embankment, he gave voice to his surprise.

'Where...?'

'Scotland Yard, sir,' the driver said as he turned left just before Westminster Bridge.

A few minutes later, Harry was ushered into a room where Sir Robert and Detective Chief Inspector Clare Salisbury were waiting for him. Harry hesitated for a moment, feeling a little underdressed in his casual clothes. Both Sir Robert and DCI Salisbury were wearing suits. DCI Salisbury put him at his ease.

'Take a seat, Mr Nevile. Glad you could come at such short notice. Coffee is on its way, no biscuits though, I'm afraid.'

Over the course of the next twenty minutes, Harry took in the full story of what had been a very eventful morning. Mathis' body had been found in Brompton Cemetery by a member of the public taking his dog for an early morning walk. Mathis had been shot: two shots to the body, intended to disable, not to kill, and a single shot to the head, all at close range as the powder burns testified. Tschesche's trademark execution style. The death was thought to have occurred on Saturday evening.

'Brompton Cemetery? It's a Royal Park, isn't it?' Something had stirred in Harry's memory.

A drawn out cautious 'Yes' from DCI Salisbury confirmed that Harry was correct.

'Yesterday, when I interviewed him at the bookshop, he changed the window display, or at least part of it. One of the books he put there was an *Official Guide to the Royal Parks of London*. It seemed odd to me. An early edition, yes, but hardly antiquarian. A signal to meet? Not the strongest of links, but a plausible connection between the bookshop and Tschesche?'

'Well spotted, Harry, but we do have something stronger.' Sir Robert continued to expound on the next set of that morning's events. With three deaths in less than two weeks since the dossier had surfaced, and with time running out to link Gifford to something more serious than copying a file,

287

pressure was growing to achieve a breakthrough. Renner had been able to reconstruct most of the German fax. It had been sent from the Munich district and addressed to David Fredericks. Sir Robert had remembered the name as a possible alias for Tobias Tschesche. Could Tschesche, Fredericks and Caspar Friedrich be the same person? It put a chilling interpretation on the cryptic message to "Close all the doors before leaving", especially as two of the deaths had been carried out by a method associated with Tschesche. "Close all the doors" could be a covert signal to kill all the witnesses. At that point, Harry interrupted Sir Robert, asking if they should warn Quinton. Fear for his own safety might be enough for him to come clean.

'That was the line of reasoning we took with Gifford,' DCI Salisbury explained, 'and it worked. We have an address for Fredericks, which is where you come in. Trust me, we shall deal with Quinton in good time, but no point risking him warning Fredericks.'

DCI Salisbury and Sir Robert had gone to Charing Cross Police Station, where Gifford was being held in an interview room, complaining loudly that his solicitor was not present. He had stopped dead when Sir Robert walked through the door, an involuntary 'What the...' leaving his lips before he had recovered himself.

'Good morning, Mr Gifford. Or is it Mr Reid?'

Gifford had sat stiffly, his elbows on the table, staring belligerently at Sir Robert.

'I don't need to introduce myself, do I? Besides, this isn't a formal interview.'

'I want my solicitor.' Gifford's words had been spoken quietly but determinedly.

'No need, Mr Gifford. As I say, this is not an interview. In fact, I'm inclined to let you go.'

It had been clear from the look on Gifford's face that he was expecting a sting in the tail, and Sir Robert had obliged. 'Just one or two things to show you before I do.'

Putting a photograph of Matthew Kilsdale's body on the table, Sir Robert had said, without further elaboration, 'Matthew Kilsdale. Two to the body, one to the head. All close range.'

He had followed up with a photograph of Jeremy Mathis' body, repeating, 'Two to the body, one to the head. All close range.'

Gifford had leant forward, gripping the edge of the table with his hands, scrutinising the second photograph. On recognising the victim, he had blanched, the shock written clearly for all to see. Sir Robert had continued in his calm, precise manner.

'Mr Jeremy Mathis. Runs, sorry – ran – a bookshop in Cecil Court. We are still looking for the body of Mrs Veronica Blakeridge, last seen entering the same bookshop.'

Although he had no evidence that Veronica was dead, he knew Gifford's first thought would be that she had been killed in the same manner. Sir Robert had also stretched the limits of what he actually knew with his final gambit. He had put a copy of the reconstructed fax on the table.

'A fax. In German, but I doubt that will bother you. From Martinsried to Mr Mathis' bookshop. Or rather, the offices rented out to Planegg Partners. Addressed to a Mr Fredericks. Or should that be Friedrichs?'

Gifford had remained silent, and Sir Robert had studied him, only for about thirty seconds, though he had no doubt it would seem an eternity to the suspect. Sir Robert had then stood, saying, 'I'll leave you now.' Then he had pushed the photographs of the two bodies closer to Gifford before adding his final twist. 'I shall leave the door open. It seems *Herr* Tschesche is the one closing all the doors.'

With that, Sir Robert had turned his back on Gifford and walked out the door. He had remained out of sight in the corridor, waiting. DCI Salisbury had played her last card. She had formally charged Gifford, under the 1989 Official Secrets Act, on the basis of being a Crown servant who had without lawful authority made a damaging disclosure, as defined by the Act, adding that he was to present himself at the City of London Magistrates Court, Queen Victoria Street at 9:00 a.m. the following morning. Written notification would be given to him, she had explained, and Sir Robert noted that at no point, as the officer in charge, had she suggested he was free to go. Sir Robert had heard her chair scrape on the floor as she stood, preparing to leave, before Gifford's nerve had broken.

'Wait,' he had said, 'There's more.'

As the car sped westwards out of the City, Harry, feeling uncomfortable dressed as a uniformed police sergeant, was still trying to digest what had been happening that morning. Gifford had admitted that Tschesche had, as he put it, "taken care" of Kilsdale, but he knew nothing about the death of Mathis. When asked about the incident at Veronica's house, he had replied, "You'll have to ask Bickley-Morris about that". On being told, Harry had asked if Quinton was being detained.

'All in good time, Harry, but not now.' Sir Robert had then explained his reasoning. Gifford had confirmed some of their suspicions, but other than his testimony, they still had no real evidence. Tschesche was the priority target, and there were the risks that he would kill again or flee the country. 'Close the doors before leaving,' Sir Robert had reminded Harry. 'Tschesche is planning to leave.'

'So why haven't you arrested him, and what has any of this got to do with my being able to speak German?'

Once again, the problem was a lack of evidence to corroborate Gifford's word. Tschesche may have been known to employ a particularly cruel method of execution: two shots to the body with no intention to kill, the fatal shot delayed to ensure that the victim was all too aware of what would happen, but the "Mozambique Drill" was not exclusive to Tschesche. They also only had Gifford's word that Tschesche was living in Ham, a district of Richmond, under the alias of David Fredericks. To what extent they could trust Gifford's assertions was not clear; they would only have one chance to catch Tschesche, and they couldn't risk Gifford sending them on a wild goose chase to alert him.

'That's where your language skills come in, Harry.'

They couldn't detain Fredericks without any further evidence, and it was unlikely he would be willing to co-operate, but if they could prove the reasonable suspicion that Fredericks was Tschesche, they could detain him under an existing Interpol Red Notice. Tschesche's fingerprints were on file courtesy of the ruthless efficiency of the Stasi's own archives, commandeered by the German authorities.

In the case of David Fredericks, what records there were, according to Gifford, described the character as an employee of Planegg's parent company in Germany. A local man from the Munich area. 'I need to hear Fredericks' accent,' Sir

Robert had said, and pointed out that irrespective of whether or not Fredericks was Tschesche, it was likely he had been involved in the dossier business and would recognise Sir Robert. It had to be someone else, and at short notice, Harry was the obvious choice. Tschesche was from Berlin, and Sir Robert had lived in Berlin for a couple of years; he knew the accent. It was as distinctive as Geordie, and no one who had lived in Newcastle would ever confuse the Geordie accent and dialect with Cockney.

'You'll be wired,' Sir Robert had advised Harry, and taking a look at his colleague's casual dress had added, 'It may be Sunday, but no on-duty policeman would dress like that.'

Time was of the essence. It would take the best part of an hour to drive to Richmond – there just wasn't time for Harry to go home and change. The sergeant's uniform had not only been conveniently at hand, but it had the advantage that there was no need to hide the transmitter: a sergeant would be expected to be carrying a radio.

Just before Harry knocked on the door, something prompted him to check the time. 1:13 p.m.. Just over two hours since the phone call from Sir Robert had set his day in an entirely unexpected direction. As the door opened, DCI Salisbury stepped forward.

'Good afternoon, Mr err...?'

The man who had opened the door obliged by introducing himself as Mr Fredericks. Although it wasn't strong, even with the few words that had been spoken, Harry recognised the accent as German. Salisbury, pointing to a wooded area to the northwest of the house, explained that they were investigating an incident which had occurred the previous evening and asked if they could come in. Fredericks was hesitant to allow them, claiming he had been out for the day but had not seen or heard anything unusual on his return.

'No, Mr Fredericks, you wouldn't have,' DCI Salisbury countered, 'but it's not the first incident in this area, and we believe that there's a risk of further attacks, especially against older people. It will only take a few minutes. May we?' Rather reluctantly, Fredericks allowed them in. In what he hoped would be seen simply as a pleasantry, Harry took his opportunity.

'I don't suppose you're from Germany, are you, Mr Fredericks?' The look he received in reply warned Harry that Fredericks was on his guard. 'It's just the accent. I lived in Germany for a couple of years.'

Fredericks relaxed a little. 'Yes, I lived with my grandparents when I was a child. In Germany.'

'Oh, *wo hast Sie gelebt?*' Harry asked, in German.

DCI Salisbury, who had been posted in Germany briefly whilst serving with Nicholas, couldn't follow the conversation entirely, but she knew the tack that Harry would take. If Fredericks stuck to the story of being from the Munich area, Harry would mention a holiday he had taken in Bavaria, touring the castles. Salisbury was able to pick out the words "Linderhof" and "Neuschwanstein", confirming that Fredericks had taken the bait.

Both Harry and Salisbury had pagers in their trouser pockets, and a silent vibration told them that Sir Robert had heard enough of the conversation. Feigning irritation, Salisbury interrupted the conversation, saying she did not want to detain Mr Fredericks for too long as they had other people to see. She questioned him about his whereabouts on two specific dates, giving a window of time for each. Fredericks claimed not to have been at home at either of the times, in one instance claiming he was on his way home from working late, and on Saturday evening was on his way home, having had a day out cycling up the river to Windsor. DCI Salisbury didn't ask him for an alibi – he wasn't a suspect – at least not in the bogus case she had described, and she had no wish to raise his suspicions.

Another silent vibration from the pagers alerted them that Sir Robert was happy for them to leave. Would there be another pager signal in about thirty seconds? The second signal came: Sir Robert was prepared, and the game was on.

DCI Salisbury thanked Fredericks for his time, saying they had to press on; they still had his neighbours to question. Although Harry knew what was going to happen, he was still startled when it did. As Fredericks turned the door handle to see them out, and with the door only open a few inches, Harry caught sight of a swift movement as someone stepped out from the cover of the side of the house. The door was shoved open brutally, catching Fredericks by surprise and wrenching the door handle from his grasp. Fredericks had no time to respond before he found himself looking at the business end of a Heckler and Koch submachine gun and a darkly clad, fully kitted out firearms officer blocking the doorway. A second armed officer stepped into view from the other side of the door. His gun, too, was aimed at Fredericks. Harry doubted it had taken as much as three seconds. DCI Salisbury stepped forward.

'David Fredericks, I am arresting you on suspicion of the murder of Matthew Kilsdale.'

CHAPTER 34

Day fourteen: Sunday, late afternoon.

Harry and Sir Robert returned to Tufton Street via New Scotland Yard, where Harry changed back into his own clothes. Laid out in the first-floor office was a small buffet that the ever-present Nicholas had somehow procured to make up for the lunch they had missed.

Tschesche had been taken to Paddington Green Police Station in order to avoid any accidental encounter with Gifford. He would be detained and questioned regarding the death of Jeremy Mathis, though that was mainly a pretext to take his fingerprints. On the journey back from Richmond, Sir Robert had been of the opinion that they were no more likely to find solid evidence of Tschesche's involvement in either Mathis' or Kilsdale's murder than to elicit a confession from Tschesche. Once his identity was confirmed, however, he would be extradited to Germany to face several equally serious charges there. The evidence used to justify the Interpol Red Notice was more than sufficient to secure a conviction.

On their arrival at Tufton Street, they had asked Nicholas if there was any update regarding Giles Gifford. In particular, they were interested to hear if he had given any indication of Veronica's whereabouts. Despite the misgivings about her behaviour, her safety was still a priority.

'I'm afraid not, gentleman,' Nicholas had responded.

Although Gifford had corroborated Veronica's story about picking up the dossier in the bookshop, he maintained that there had been no contact since.

'Mr Gifford would have us believe he is a victim, blackmailed for a former indiscretion. Even had the temerity to suggest he went along with the dossier plan in the national interest, exposing a cover-up of the nefarious activities of a certain Sir Robert Hamilton.'

Both Harry and Sir Robert had to suppress a grin as Nicholas went on to explain that, once Sir Robert and DCI Salisbury had left, Gifford had protested vigorously about Sir Robert's participation in the investigation.

'Would have us believe the real villains of the piece are *Herr* Tschesche and our old friend Mr Bickley-Morris,' Nicholas continued. 'The feeling is that Mr Gifford is being somewhat modest about his involvement with former agents of the Federal Republic of Germany.'

'Should we bring in Quinton?' Harry ventured, still arguing that if he thought his own skin was in danger, he might well give something up that would help in the case against Gifford. Sir Robert was not in favour of the idea. It was unlikely that Quinton could say much that wouldn't incriminate himself, and thus, he was unlikely to be co-operative.

'Not to mention the threat of retribution,' Sir Robert added, reminding them of the possible sinister interpretation of the fax found on the Planegg computer.

'Perhaps all the more reason,' Harry had persisted. 'Protect his own hide if he thinks he could be on Tschesche's list.'

Sir Robert was uncharacteristically unfeeling, replying that Quinton would just have to take his chances in that direction. He also pointed out that Quinton had been complaining bitterly about police harassment after he was interviewed concerning Kilsdale's death. Questioning him again would only add fuel to the flames.

'He still knows people in high places,' Sir Robert reminded Harry, 'Besides, I want to get to the bottom of why he and Slowik were both at St John's last Friday.'

'Do you think there is something going on? Something we should know about?'

'No, Harry, I do not. As I said earlier, I trust her. I know you don't like them, but coincidences do happen. In any case, an afternoon in Oxford will do you good, take your mind off everything that has been happening.'

Harry shot him a quizzical look.

'It's where Miss Slowik's alter ego now lives. She'll be home tomorrow.'

There was little they could do at Tufton Street and, after having made a couple of brief telephone calls, Sir Robert left, intending to check on progress at both Paddington Green and Charing Cross police stations. With the day already disrupted, Harry decided to stay and write his report on the events in Richmond before heading home. It was difficult to keep either Veronica or Huxley out of his mind. Huxley, he hoped, had taken the advice he had been given and gone to visit his parents on the Kent coast. Veronica troubled him still, even though he knew there were still people looking for her. He argued to himself that the only logical explanation for her disappearance was that she had left the bookshop via the rear courtyard and its emergency access to St Martin's Lane. Irrespective of what may have happened since, that suggested either she had prior knowledge of the bookshop and the escape route, or she had gone willingly with somebody who did know. Both suggested that she was more involved with the people operating out of Cecil Court than she had admitted. Difficult as it was to accept that Veronica may have been duping them all for quite some time, Harry could find no other explanation. It caused him considerable unease. If she had left with Tobias Tschesche, even if she knew him only as David Fredericks, the death of Jeremy Mathis did not bode well for the chances of finding her alive. *Unless…* he asked himself, *could she have been more involved in the deaths of Kilsdale and Mathis?* The circumstances surrounding the death of Rod Graham were still somewhat uncertain, but there was no getting away from the fact that Veronica had followed him to the Greek island of Aegina. Could there be a connection? Quinton's supposed plan to kill Kilsdale had been enacted at Veronica's house on the day she had returned from Greece. That did suggest a connection. He tried to remember Veronica's whereabouts on the night Kilsdale had been killed. *No, this is unthinkable.* He re-focused on his report.

It was approaching 6:00 p.m. Harry was clearing up to go home when he heard the lift ascending. *Could this be Sir Robert returning?* He wasn't expecting a rather sombre-looking Nicholas to step out of the lift. Harry had a sick feeling in his stomach – Nicholas rarely came into the office; something serious must have happened.

'Veronica?' There was trepidation in his voice; he wasn't sure that he wanted to hear the answer.

'No, sir. Not Mrs Blakeridge. Mr Bickley-Morris.'

'Oh, good heavens, what has he been up to now?'

'*He* hasn't been up to anything, sir. He was shot this

298

morning.'

'Is he…?'

'Dead? Yes.'

* * *

Daylight had almost faded when Harry met Sir Robert in the gardens at Dolphin Square.

'Tschesche?' Harry was as much seeking confirmation as he was asking a question. Sir Robert's reply was unexpected.

'That was my first thought, too, but I suspect not. Time of death yet to be confirmed, but most likely this morning. There was a bit of a delay in getting Tschesche's house under observation, and it's just about possible that he could have returned to Richmond before the team got there, but not his style, Harry. From what I've been told, a single shot from close range, yes, but not *Herr* Tschesche's trademark.'

At first, the police constable controlling the ground floor entrance was reluctant to let them enter. He had never seen an MI5 warrant card before and was unsure that such things existed or what they might look like if they did. A brief radio call to the forensic team in Quinton's flat confirmed what Sir Robert had told him. Two Security Service officers were to search for any documents in the flat that might be of relevance. Their familiarity with Quinton Bickley-Morris and his activities over the past few years might help identify evidence that could otherwise be overlooked.

Harry made for the lift, but Sir Robert cleared his throat and pointed to the stairs. Harry's heart sank.

'Bob, it's on the eighth floor.'

Sir Robert relented, on the understanding that they would

use the stairs on leaving. Once their identities had been checked again, and they had donned clean Tyvek suits and disposable gloves to avoid contaminating the crime scene, the officer guarding the flat let them in.

Sir Robert's first question to the team inside was, 'Have you checked the stairwell?' The forensic team lead gave Sir Robert a look that could only be interpreted as "I do know how to do my job", and Harry kicked himself mentally. It had been a long day in a long two weeks. He should have been more on the ball. If he had just shot somebody, he would not wait around for a lift to come, especially not up to the eighth floor.

The team leader pointed to a door on the north side of the room. 'There's an office through there.'

As Harry and Sir Robert made their way around the perimeter of the room, they could not quell a morbid interest in the layout. Although Quinton's body had been removed, there was no mistaking the scene of the crime. Quinton had been sitting in a high-backed Chesterfield armchair opposite the window when he had been shot.

Were it not for the oversized desk and expensive swivel chair that seemed to dominate the room, the office would have been unremarkable. The desktop was tidy: a telephone to one side and a large leatherbound blotter in the centre. Sitting square on top of the blotter was a laptop computer, the lid closed, but the logo marking it as an IBM ThinkPad. Next to the computer was a small brown leather-bound Filofax and a DL-sized envelope, standard stationery for any office. The envelope, its contents still inside, had been opened, and the handwritten address indicated it had been sent to Quinton care of some legal chambers in Lincoln's Inn Fields.

Sir Robert carefully opened the drawers on each side of the desk. The contents were of good quality but functional and impersonal: some pens, pencils, stationery, nothing out of the ordinary. A larger drawer containing hanging files appeared to contain only domestic correspondence, with folders bearing mundane labels such as "Utilities", "Maintenance". The impression that Harry and Sir Robert had was that Quinton used his Dolphin Square flat as little more than a hotel room.

Sir Robert picked up the Filofax. 'Shall we take a look?'

Flicking the organiser open at the black plastic divider, Sir Robert found himself looking at a week-to-view calendar, for the earlier part of the week. Putting aside his personal disapproval of diaries that ran Sunday to Saturday, his eye was drawn to the entry for Friday just past.

'Well, well. Look at this.'

Harry stepped towards the desk as Sir Robert turned the Filofax to face him. The entry for Friday read "VB 12pm. Sm Sq".

'It can't be.'

Harry was taken aback; the inference was obvious. "VB". Veronica Blakeridge.

'If she was meeting Quinton after me, why pretend she was giving herself up, and why panic when she saw him?'

'A change of heart, perhaps? But why arrange to meet you so close to the time she was meeting Quinton? Unless she had another appointment that morning – something she couldn't get out of...? No. A hypothesis to explain a hypothesis. Makes no sense. Let's not jump to conclusions.' Taking the Filofax back, Sir Robert turned the page. The entry for Sunday – that very day – read "VB 10 am".

'Well, we have our suspect. It's just a matter of confirming who they are.'

Harry read the entry for himself. 'Well, it fits with the MO not being Tschesche's or Fredericks' – whatever he calls himself.'

Mentally, Harry was trying to create an image of Veronica with a gun, shooting somebody. "Ron", the young lady he had worked with for the last few years. No, he could not picture it. "Veronica", the lady who had confronted him at the National Portrait Gallery? He wasn't so sure. What could possibly have happened to her in the short time since she fled to Greece? Not for the first time, he was troubled by the thought he could have been wrong about her all along.

Sir Robert picked up the envelope, took out the letter inside and unfolded it. 'Vera Beamann.'

There was something about the way Sir Robert spoke the name that triggered an uncertainty in Harry's mind, but before he could say something, Sir Robert passed the letter over. As he read it, Sir Robert gave him a précis.

'VB: Vera Beamann. A journalist, apparently. Wanted to interview Quinton.'

Harry looked his colleague straight in the eye. 'You know her, don't you?'

Sir Robert was hesitant, something Harry had rarely seen.

'Know her? No. I can't possibly.' Sir Robert paused, something clearly troubling him. 'I knew, or rather knew of, a Vera Beamann, but that was thirty years ago. She disappeared.'

Harry did a quick mental calculation.

'When you were in Berlin?' he asked.

'First case I was involved with. She'd been one of those

people useful to both sides. Born in the East, Frankfurt – the other Frankfurt – an der Oder, if I remember. Had moved to Berlin after the war, defected to the West before the Wall was built. No one was really sure where her true loyalties lay, but as I say, useful to both sides. An intermediary. There was no doubt the East Germans knew who she was, but she was still allowed to come and go across the Wall. One day she went across and, well, disappeared.'

'An East German defector, arrested back in the East, why the fuss?'

Harry wondered if he was being naive; surely any defector who went to the East risked arrest?

'The fuss, Harry, wasn't so much *how* she disappeared but *why*. The worry was that someone in the West, one of our people, had leaked something. Maybe she was involved in something bigger, not just an intermediary. I don't know – I was moved off the case. But I digress. It was a surprise seeing the name, but it can't be the same person. If she had been arrested in the East, it's doubtful she would have survived. I don't think there's anything else for us in this office. Let's get this letter and Filofax secured, and forensics can take it back to Scotland Yard. We need to concentrate on Miss Slowik, find out exactly what she was doing at St John's on Friday.'

'If indeed it was her I saw.'

Harry was beginning to doubt himself; it had been a fleeting glimpse only.

'We'll find out tomorrow, Harry. Oxford. Early start. I think we should go sooner rather than later. We can take the train.'

CHAPTER 35

Day fifteen: Monday, morning

'Hamilton?'

The surprise in Slowik's voice confirmed what Harry had already suspected when Sir Robert had suggested taking the train to Oxford. This visit was not on the record.

The house was about ten minutes' walk from the railway station. A corner plot behind St John Street, not quite a leafy lane but very pleasant. More importantly, the corner location gave two escape routes to the front of the house, the walled garden giving access to a side lane connecting to the street behind. Most curious of all was the small two-storey house at the rear of the garden, having no doorway onto either the lane or the street at the rear of the property. In fact, as they had passed that way, Harry noticed a doorway had been bricked up. This was a bunker, one that could accommodate guardians if necessary. Slowik's home was the sort of house that the security services reserved for their most important guests.

'Better come in.' Slowik looked at Harry. 'Mr Nevile, if I recall correctly.'

Harry no longer had any doubts; the lady he had seen outside St John's, Smith Square, had been Slowik. Of course, she had been wearing a wig – her treatment would have led to her losing her hair.

Slowik showed them into the front parlour. 'Some coffee,

I think, before we talk.'

Slowik pointed to a couple of armchairs for Harry and Sir Robert to sit on, then disappeared towards the back of the house. Harry was on alert, but the sound of coffee grinding reassured him. He recalled Sir Robert saying she was one of the people he trusted most.

Several minutes later, Anna Slowik returned with a tray bearing a coffee pot, milk jug and mugs.

'Hope neither of you takes sugar,' she joked. 'Don't have any.'

She set the tray down on the low table in front of the chairs and sat on the sofa opposite Harry and Sir Robert. She took a deep breath, a look of seriousness taking over her face. As she started pouring the coffee, she spoke. Although not looking at Sir Robert, her words were clearly directed at him.

'I wasn't expecting you so soon. You've worked it out, haven't you? Vera Beamann?' She passed a mug of coffee to Sir Robert.

'I wasn't sure,' he said. 'It was strange when Harry here saw you outside St John's a few minutes before Quinton turned up. I saw the letter you sent. At first, I didn't connect you with Vera Beamann, it was only later, back home, that I recalled that you had both been in Frankfurt Oder when Quinton's duties would have taken him there.'

'I think, Hamilton, I need to explain a few things. Your poor friend here looks at a complete loss.' She smiled as she handed a mug of coffee to Harry.

'Yes, Vera and I were friends in Frankfurt, before she moved to Berlin and I was assigned there. Mr Bickley-Morris, Lieutenant Bickley-Morris, I think he was, took a fancy to her, but she would have none of it. He persisted, and in the end, she persuaded a couple of Russian soldiers to use some persuasion of their own. Years later, I discovered the person who had fed lies about her to the Stasi was part of our London operation. It was Foder.' Slowik looked at Harry. 'Foder was Bickley-Morris's codename.'

'Is that why you did it?'

Sir Robert's question triggered Harry's realisation: Slowik had killed Quinton.

'No. It's why I chose the name, though. You know, he didn't recognise it – the name, I mean. Meant nothing to him, discarded, didn't care that his lies had signed her death warrant. He'd had his revenge. That was all that mattered to him.'

'Then why?' Sir Robert was pushing her for the truth.

'Ach, why indeed? Do you know what his last word was? "Don't." He didn't know the meaning of that word in the 1940s. "Don't," I begged him. I was only sixteen, displaced, living on my wits, thinking I was helping build a secure future. "Don't", I begged him, but how could a frail young girl fight off a British officer? One who had pointed a gun at her? It was one of the reasons, a few years later, when the Ministry for State Security was formed, that I joined up. I hated the British, their allies.'

'Tell me what happened yesterday.'

Realising that Slowik was meandering away from the point, and that the anger her memories were triggering was hijacking her thoughts, Sir Robert brought her back to the present.

'He slipped away, and when I came across him again, I couldn't touch him. He was an asset, they said. *Wie dem auch sei*, be that as it may, I never stopped hating him, wanting my revenge.'

She had never thought she would see Bickley-Morris – or Foder as he was known – again, until Sir Robert had shown her that photograph last year. His arrest had felt like a victory. She would have been satisfied with helping to send him to prison; justice, of a sort, would have been done. But it hadn't happened, and she had learned that time was running out for her. She had come up with the idea of posing as a journalist, interested in his story, something his conceit and vanity would not be able to resist.

Their meeting in Smith Square had been to outline her planned interview. She had asked if she could visit his London flat, arguing that an interview, filmed on his own ground, so to speak, would have more impact than one recorded in a soulless studio or a public place. Quinton hadn't recognised her, neither at lunch nor at his flat. It could have been the disguise, but she suspected it was also that she had meant nothing to him; she was no more than a name to him. She had made sure he knew who she was, but by then it was too late; she already had a gun pointing at him. Afterwards, she had thrown the wig – she had more than one – and the gun into the Thames.

'How was he found so quickly?' she asked Sir Robert.

There was a certain irony to that, Sir Robert explained. A neighbour had almost caught her leaving. She had heard the shot, but with classic British indecision, had convinced herself it couldn't have been – more likely a car backfiring. In the end, curiosity had got the better of her, but when she looked in the hallway, nobody else seemed to have been disturbed by the noise. She had seen somebody leaving by the stairway – one of Mr Bickley-Morris' ladies, she had assumed. Quinton often entertained ladies at his flat, apparently. The irony was that it was one of his lady visitors who had found him. There had been no response to his intercom, but by chance, a resident was leaving the building, and she had taken advantage of the opened door. Quinton hadn't answered his flat door, but she had tried the handle, and it wasn't locked.

Harry and Sir Robert sat pondering the implications of what they had just been told. Slowik, however, hadn't finished telling her story.

'There was a child. I had a child. The authorities took him, said they could give him a better future.' She paused, then continued, as if she needed to explain herself. 'I was only seventeen. Germany was still in chaos. Trials were going on, retribution being meted out. The future was still uncertain. Years later, I tried to look for him. By then, I had realised the socialist dream was becoming a nightmare. Thought if I found him, we could escape to the West together, both have a life of our choosing. That's when I found the truth about the institutions where orphans had been sent. Cold, heartless places where indoctrination replaced love. That was if they were lucky – many suffered much worse. The brutal pigs who ran those places, no one controlled them, no one cared. The children in their care weren't people. Farm animals were better looked after than some of those children. They didn't even keep records, not in those days. He was untraceable.'

Slowik stopped, tears beginning to fill her eyes.

'I only ever found out one thing about him. His name. They called him Tobias.'

Epilogue

Eleven months later

'Good of you to come, Harry. Let me get some coffees.'

Harry sat at one of the tables in the churchyard, enjoying the warmth of an Indian summer whilst Sir Robert disappeared through the blue-painted Gothic doors that led across a small courtyard and into the formerly redundant church, since reborn as a café and craft centre. It had been a while since Harry had seen his former senior officer. Sir Robert had spent a couple of months in Germany, partly helping to build the case against Tschesche and partly smoothing the diplomatic waters after Tschesche revealed that Anna Slowik hadn't disappeared but had been in the care of Her Majesty's government. He had also spent some time trying to trace the history of Tobias Tschesche, with very little success, and even less co-operation from Tschesche himself. All he had discovered was that he had been an East German orphan, educated, not that "educated" was a word Sir Robert would have chosen, under Soviet supervision before taking up service with the Ministry for State Security, the Stasi, in Berlin.

On his return to the UK, Sir Robert had formally retired, though he was retained by the security services and was a member of a couple of advisory panels. Harry's own professional attention had been taken by the reorganisation of the Bioweapons Counter-Espionage Unit. Although it had

309

now been absorbed into a wider, more integrated counter-terrorism operation, Harry had been delighted that the Tufton Street office had been retained. Part of Harry suspected that it was still necessary to maintain an anonymous front to the wider operation in the building behind and the floors above, and that no other group could be persuaded to move into the rather spartan and cramped rooms of the first-floor offices.

Sir Robert returned with a tray bearing two coffees and some cake.

'I'm sorry I didn't get much chance to talk to you at the funeral the other day. The turnout was somewhat larger than expected.'

There were aspects of Slowik's funeral that troubled Harry, but for the moment, he kept the conversation light.

'Did I see Hank "The Tank" in the background?'

'Our American friend? Yes, he's quite a senior figure now.' Sir Robert allowed himself a small chuckle. 'I think he still believes that sending in the tanks is the way to deal with most situations, but at least he's realised that the logistics make it a little tricky.'

'Is that story about him and Margaret Thatcher true?'

'Oh, yes. I was at the dinner. He asked her what she thought of the Mossad, but with that dreadful drawl of his, it came out "Mowzaard". The dear lady misheard and replied, "Well, I am quite fond of his 'Jupiter' Symphony".

'But, on to more serious things, Harry. I haven't been able to keep up, but is there any news of Mrs Blakeridge?'

'No, not a trace. She went into that bookshop and vanished. Hasn't accessed her bank account or used her credit card since. It's either a very professional new identity or...' Harry hesitated. 'Or we must fear the worst. I don't know which it is. She may have duped us all, but I could have done much more.'

Harry explained that he felt bad about what had probably happened to her. If he had really listened to her that day in the National Portrait Gallery, he could have persuaded her to let him bring her in. She would still be alive.

'But wasn't it her decision, Harry?' Sir Robert was recalling what Harry had told him about her rather cold and inflexible behaviour that day. 'Whatever happened to her wasn't your fault.'

'No, but I could have been more persuasive, more alert to the danger. I feel guilty about not doing more. Has Tschesche ever said anything? Anything at all about her?'

'No. Says he knows nothing and that we should ask our friend Mr Gifford. "Perhaps she was one of his team" has been his only comment. I'm afraid his activities in London formed no part of his trial in the end. There was more than enough evidence from Berlin to put him away for the rest of his life.'

'Ah. Gifford. I understand he gave us everything in the end.'

Sir Robert nodded. 'Quinton's death, following so close upon Mathis', really shook him. He was prepared to tell all in return for a guarantee of safety. When the Wall came down, there were quite a few people who wanted to protect themselves, and that included keeping the Federal Republic's overseas resources quiet and under control. With the Republic's so-called diplomatic staff gone, they needed a loyal servant to step up to the mark, and Gifford did just that. Kept the organisation together, looked after people like Quinton, though it's clear there was no love lost between

Gifford and Quinton. Quinton was only ever in it for the money.'

'What will happen to him?'

'Gifford? Oh, his trial will be before the end of the year. He'll plead guilty, we'll present the evidence, and he'll be sentenced. After that, he'll be spirited out of the country to serve his term under a new identity in one of our commonwealth establishments.'

'At least justice will be done, even if it's not seen to be done.'

Sir Robert guessed where Harry was leading the conversation and tried to change tack by asking how Huxley was faring.

'He's well. Throwing himself into his work.'

Suspecting there was an unspoken "but", Sir Robert raised his eyebrows and looked at Harry. Taking a sip of his coffee and a mouthful of cake, Harry bought himself some time, wondering how best to reply, if at all. In the end, he confessed that there were times when he was concerned that Huxley was in a form of denial. He seemed to have convinced himself that Veronica had been in danger and, worried that an attack might take place at his home, she had left in order to protect him. The only reason Huxley could think of as to why she went to the bookshop was that she was confused and wanted to confront Reid. She had no idea who Reid was. Probably thought he had been duped, liked her, and wanted to warn him. The bookshop, where she had picked up the dossier, was the only place she knew of in the UK where she might be able to contact Reid. If she'd died at the hands of Tschesche, it was because she was trying to save others.

Sir Robert reminded Harry of something Harry himself

312

had said, "In the less than clear waters of the intelligence services, you don't have the luxury of dotting all the i's and crossing all the t's. You do your best with the parts you can connect."

'Let him believe it, Harry. This is real life. What really happens – it would never make a novel, too many loose ends. We just make the most sense we can of the little we know. And you and I know no better.'

Harry's response was hard-hitting. 'But sometimes we do, and we do nothing about it.'

Sir Robert knew what was troubling Harry; a remark Harry had made at Slowik's funeral had alerted him.

'You mean Anna?'

'Yes.' Harry took a deep breath and looked round, as if to check nobody could overhear them. He knew Sir Robert would not agree with what he was about to say, but he knew his friend would respect his honesty. 'I never knew her, Bob, never had any direct dealings, but that send-off, all those people. It doesn't feel right. Whichever way you look at it, she got away with murder.'

'Harry, they say you should never speak ill of the dead, but the police did look at it. The DPP said a safe conviction was unlikely. This is England, and thank God for that. You can't be convicted on your own confession alone, not without any evidence. And we had none.'

Harry knew that, but he was still uncomfortable.

'Even so, it didn't feel right. Whatever she did in Berlin, you can't ignore what she did to Quinton. Maybe he did have it coming to him, but I'm sorry, justice has not been served. How can you justify what almost amounted to feting her as a heroine? The greater good?'

'Goodness, Harry, flows from mercy, not from justice. Her information did save a lot of lives. Not just British; our allies too. That's why Hank was there. And remember, she was never brought to trial, never found guilty. Under English law, that makes her innocent.'

'Innocent, Bob? But she wasn't, was she? We all know that.'

'There are none of us perfect, Harry.'

ACKNOWLEDGEMENTS

I had not intended to write a trilogy when I started *The Death of a Smoker*. Nor was the plot planned out in advance. I knew the starting point, but from there the storyline took its own direction. As the plot developed I tried to think about how an ordinary person, you or I, might react to the situation that had emerged.

The problem was that I could not think of a suitable way to deal with the dastardly Quinton Bickley-Morris, so I let him slip away. Inevitably that led to a sequel, *Unsavoury Business*, but even then I couldn't bring myself to kill him off. I thought that by putting him in jail, justice had been served.

It was not to be. So my first acknowledgment has to be to all those readers who asked, 'What happened next?' *Imperfectly Innocent* would not have been created without you. Although I kept to the unplanned, dynamic style of plot development, there was one difference to the previous two novels. This time I knew what the ending was, and had to work on what the beginning could be and how I could connect the two.

As I have said before, writing a book is one thing, publishing it is another matter entirely. The book you have just read would not have happened without the people at Cranthorpe Millner. I am beginning to suspect there are manuscript gremlins who start to work the moment an author delivers a manuscript to the publisher. After several pre-submission read throughs, I was convinced the manuscript was perfect, but on a read through a week post-submission I was shocked to find about 50 typos and errors. Spread over 35 or so chapters, it didn't seem a disaster. When I reviewed the editor's first proof, it seemed to me that those gremlins had continued their quest and put about 50 errors and typos on each page. So apologies to Louise Holtby, Andrea Roux and Kirsty Jackson, my editors, for making you work so hard. You did a magnificent job.

I must also give a thank you to Mike Cram. When I was looking for small details to characterise Giles Gifford, details that would also catch him out, a chance remark by Mike reminded me about embroidered shirt cuffs.

Will there be another Tufton Street adventure? I don't know, it is quite possible, but I do have a couple of part written manuscripts involving a completely different set of characters. You can keep in touch with further developments at www.tonyauffret.com, where you will also find links to Facebook, Instagram and Twitter feeds.